JENNY C

Where Dolphins Fly

New Smyrna Journals of
Capt. Douglas Dummett 1806-1873

outskirts
press

DEDICATION

In Memory of Charles Dummett;
1844~1860
New Smyrna Beach, Florida

Dear Charles…you have haunted me my entire life.

Your island gravesite in the shade of great oaks offered a place of retreat and quiet to a young Kansas girl far from home. It became a place of solace to pour my lonesome heart…and I felt you heard.

I thought about your life; how it must have been in wild and beautiful Florida in the time of Seminoles, slavery, and looming Civil War. In my mind you are tall and gently strong like your father with an easy laugh, a doting big brother to your three little sisters… and a loving son possessed of your mother's amazingly green eyes. And I wondered why you died so young.

Constructing a timeline of your family, integrating historical events occurring in America, formed a window into early pioneer life in territorial Florida in the age of Osceola. It is a glimpse of grit and carnage, triumph and loss…perseverance and great love.

I am truly sorry for the angst you suffered and prejudice you faced as a true son of New Smyrna… and hope in your awful death you found the peace you sought.

With love…….

PROLOGUE

1842

"I was nigh on sixteen first time I laid eyes on Captain Douglas Dummett. He was ridin' a tall black stallion that fancy walked like he was steppin' on hot coals. Muscles was fairly bustin' out his buckskins, and his hair…well, it was blowin' light in the sunshine and was the color of lemons in the shade. 'Fore my Massa Woodruff was killed, he served with Dummett in the militia, the 'Moskito Roarers'; sayin' the Captain was a fine man and the best Injun fighter he ever seen. Mammy Sue's tea leaves say the Captain had powerful tragedy in his life and sadness rode his shoulders like a widow's cloak. But all I knowed was when he looked at me…there was summer lightnin' in his eyes!

Best start at the beginnin'…"

ONE

April 5th, 1830

Post to Col. Thomas Dummett; the Plantation Rosetta; County of Volusia, Territory of Florida

Dearest Father,

I am writing to inform you that due to an injury inflicted by an unfortunately fleet Osage warrior, the U.S. Army has seen fit to release me early from my conscription to the Cavalry. Be assured the wound is merely troublesome and will completely heal under Mum's doting care.

The timing is surely destined, as Florida will sorely need the rifles of her sons in the coming Seminole conflicts as Andrew Jackson will soon sign the Indian Removal Act. He intends to move all tribes to reservations in the Oklahoma territory, and our scouts have confirmed Osceola and Micanopy, aided by runaway slaves, have already begun organizing their resistance.

I will be bringing Chieftain on a clipper from Washington, D.C. to the Port of Savannah: then will ride to St. Augustine to gather my beautiful Francesca. Once there, I will arrange passage on Capt. Brock's steamer for the trip to Palatka.

You will be impressed with my Andalusian stallion. With careful selections of quality mares, we will soon be possessed of a strong, handsome line of horses.

On long nights under western stars and lantern light, I rendered crude drawings of my dreams and desires for the manor house of Mont Pleasant. She will not be quite as grand as your Rosetta, but I imagine her with Doric columns, graceful and white in the shade of New Smyrna's oaks. There will be tall windows to catch sea breezes, and from its hillside vantage, views overlooking the river from a wide porch. I am anxious to acquire the seedlings waiting in Savannah; and am confident when grafted with Florida's native oranges; they will produce heavenly sweet nectar. It is my intention that Mont Pleasant will be known for her perfect and divine citrus, if that should fail, I shall ask for your help and expertise with sugar cane. Rum would surely erase all memories of failed fruit!

For the present, my heart is full of longings for home and my darling Francesca, and pray we may be blessed with fat, healthy babies as we build our lives and future.

Give Mum my love. I bring her exquisite western turquoise, and for you...a fine Kentucky rifle!

As ever your loving son,
Douglas

Moonlight glistened on the sweating stallion, his breathing foamed and bubbling, steam blowing from nostrils flaring with every pounding stride. Still he ran; heart over muscle, urged ever faster by insistent moccasins of the rider against his flanks. Sensing they were on the home stretch; the big horse instinctively knew cool water and rest waited ahead. With only intermittent stops, both dripped exhaustion from three hard days ride from Savannah. The Andalusian's smooth up and down rhythm was rocking and hypnotic.

Douglas Dummett was on a mission this bright night. Usually more mindful of overgrown roads rife with tangled roots and marauding Seminoles, he was throwing caution to the winds to reach his young bride waiting for him in St. Augustine. With a Yale education securing his rank as an officer in the U.S. Army Cavalry, he had spent four years escorting settlers and protecting their homesteads in the Missouri Territory's westward expansion. Captain Dummett became an experienced Indian fighter during his enlistment, learning necessary survival skills around campfires from grizzled western scouts. Tales related about famous contemporary frontiersman, Dave Crockett; and exploits of family friend and knife fighter, Jim Bowie, were lessons themselves in waging and surviving hand-to-hand combat. Were it not for his long blonde hair tied tightly back by a leather thong, Dummett could easily have been mistaken for a Cheyenne warrior in fringed buckskins.

He and his bride had been married a year earlier with the decision made for her to remain in safety with her parents until his return. Closing his eyes, he could bring her face into his mind… her scent…and the giddy feeling in his stomach at the thought of her.

She was fire and wind with gold-hooped earrings and red lacquered lips. A raven-haired Spanish beauty like her mother, Francesca Hunter was the only daughter of Jonathon Hunter; a wealthy St. Augustine judge and entrepreneur. She was the most beautiful creature Douglas had ever seen, and from his youth he knew one day he would have her. A child of privilege, she was spoiled and petulant; but Dummett could not see past her teasing eyes and voluptuous figure.

Douglas was the youngest son of Thomas Dummett; a wealthy British Marine officer and large plantation owner. When anti-slavery laws were enacted in Barbados with resultant revolt and carnage, Thomas escaped hanging by hiding in a wine cask to be loaded aboard ship. Sailing his family and slaves to the United States in 1807, they lived between New Haven, Connecticut and St. Augustine, Florida. In 1825, Thomas acquired the abandoned Moultrie property, Rosetta; a sugar cane and indigo plantation in the tropical clime and wilds of the beautiful undeveloped Florida territory, ceded from Spain to the United States in 1821. The two patriarchs, Thomas and Jonathon, became fast friends and business partners in several lucrative ventures.

Their children were joined in marriage in a lavish ceremony on gated palatial grounds of the Hunter estate. Wearing white silk and her grandmother's antique Spanish lace and jewels; Francesca was a vision befitting the royal status of her family's position in the top echelon of St. Augustine society. Douglas was as blue-eyed and blonde as she was dark and brunette. Handsome in his navy blue Army dress uniform, he presented just as regally with neatly trimmed mustache and goatee, brass buckles, medals, and buttons polished to flash, contrasting against white gloves. His silver sword with its engraved grip and brass hilt gleamed against the oiled leather scabbard hanging from his red waist sash. His boots were mirrored black. Two hundred invited guests from the South's elite and wealthiest families were treated to a wedding gala unlike any they had ever seen.

Stretching clipped and green to the riverbank, the rear lawn was transformed to a carpeted wonderland of candlelit walkways, lanterns, and fluttering white draped tables; each massed with fragrant bouquets of jasmine, camellias, and lilies. Mounded bowls of finest tropical delicacies were painstakingly prepared. Steaming crab legs hung in crooked masses over rims of large Dresden platters, carried and expertly balanced overhead by an endless parade of somber faced slaves, clean shaven and immaculate in crisply starched white shirts and hibiscus leis. Each dining table was centered by tall ornate silver candelabras with crystal globes alive with flickering candles. Serving tables teemed with carved melons, kiwis, avocados, and chunked pineapple. Plump strawberries lusciously soaked in rum were drenched in imported chocolate. Mushroom caps stuffed with buttered, roasted scallops were interspersed between tiers of sweet broiled butterflied rock shrimp. Delectable cream puffs shaped into small, long-necked swans were arranged on silver trays in graceful flocks.

Their honeymoon cruise to Spain had to be postponed until Douglas's army conscription was completed, but their marital night was spent in a private riverfront gazebo at the far edge of the lawn. Transformed and curtained for the romantic occasion, the trellised summerhouse was decorated with hurricane lamps, candles, and roped swags of sweetheart roses. A thickly stuffed feather bed had been prepared with silken sheets, an opulent embroidered bedspread, and finest down pillows. Chiffon netting tied from the ceiling billowed in the light breeze, splaying cloudlike over the four-poster. Sparkling in the moonlight, the river lapped and splashed against oak dock pilings extending from the delicate structure. A pair of dolphins, silvered by the night light, rolled gracefully as they fished; blowing in unison as they surfaced and breathed, diving under diamond scattered water.

Douglas remembered how she looked that night; the scent of orange blossoms and vanilla on her skin, how she blushed and caught her breath as he untied her nightgown letting it fall...how she reached for him; melting warm and lush against him. The feel and taste of her....

It is said nights were made for poets and madmen. That night...he was both!

TWO

With darkness morphing to day; blackness of shadowed hammock on the east side of the King's Road dappled as first rays of morning sun speared through dense vegetation. The big stallion frothed as Douglas nosed him into the palm-lined, sand and shell drive of the Hunter's St. Augustine plantation... Bella Rio. Beyond stone columns supporting tall curved iron gates, the manor house rose opulently from manicured lawns, a grand turreted coquina castle of two stories with white verandas gracing the facade. Massive limestone pillars supported the wide upstairs mezzanine. Ornate black wrought iron railings, custom designed and fabricated in Spain, stretched across the front of the house encasing the balcony. White wicker furniture dressed both lower and upper porches, while thorny bougainvillea climbed the rough walls in a festival of blooms exploding in myriad pinks and fiery magentas. Larks and mockingbirds flitted about the railings, competing with their songs.

Toiling at the front of the house, three slaves were making use of the cool of morning; one clipping hedges, one cutting flowers for house bouquets and pulling weeds, and a third standing sentry on veranda steps near the front door. Stern countenance of the older guard changed to a wide, white grin as he recognized the rider.

"MASSA DOUGLAS!!! WE DON KNOW YOU WAS DUE, TODAY!" Big John stepped forward, grabbing the bridle of the wheezing horse.

Big John was one of sixty slaves Thomas Dummett fled with from Barbados after Great Britain passed the Slave Trade Act of 1807. Though his hair was now brushed with white; John was a Mandinka standing almost seven feet. Uncommonly tall, broad shouldered and muscled from years of physical labor in sugar cane fields, he had been selected with another trusted slave, Moses, to serve and safeguard Francesca until Douglas's return from his Army conscription in the Missouri Territory.

Protection for plantations was necessary as it was only nine years since Florida was ceded to the United States from Spain. In violation of treaties made with Indian nations; a steady stream of homesteaders into this wild new territory was causing unrest within native tribes being pushed from their villages, home-lands and hunting grounds. Several tribes mounted uprisings against the encroaching pioneers causing the U.S. government to make the ultimate decision to move warring tribes to west-ern reservations in Oklahoma and Kansas. Georgian Cree, Mikasuki, Appalachee, other lesser tribes, and many run-away slaves who had been driven south by constant European in-flux joined together as Seminoles, settling in north Florida. Now, they were being pushed even further south. Instead, they refused to leave their new lands proving to be formidable, mili-tarily adept fighters. Chiefs originally befriending the settlers trading meat for goods, guns, and ammunition, learned treaties signed in good faith were worthless; their lands divided off into huge land grants and plantations for white settlers. It became evident their only recourse for survival was to fight the usurp-ers. Oak and saw palmetto hammocks provided excellent cover for Seminoles slipping among familiar thick undergrowth like ghosts, led by fearsome warriors such as Osceola, Micanopy, and King Phillip's son… Coacoochee; known to settlers for his brutality as Wildcat.

"Great seeing you, John; but I've got business to tend to!"

Dummett easily swung his right leg over his horse's back, dropping catlike to the ground, wincing slightly as he shook out stiffness in the left, handing the reins to the now stuttering slave.

"But sir…BUT, SIR…"

"LATER, JOHN!!" Douglas slapped the huge slave on his muscled shoulder.

"Take care of Chief and oil the Hawken for me. Seedlings are in the burlap bags, they'll need watered down."

Charging the veranda and grabbing the iron knocker hanging on the massive oak door, he almost lost his balance as Clarice; one of Hunter's house maids suddenly jerked the door open, her eyes wide in shock.

"MISTA DUMMETT!!" "MISTA DUMMETT!!!" "WHAT YOU DOIN' HERE??" "WE NOT 'SPECTIN' YOU YET!!" Yelping as Douglas picked her up, swinging her around; her swirling skirt sent a vase of lilies flying off a marble entry table.

"You're as beautiful as I remember," Douglas laughed as he twirled her…"but you'll have to find your own man…I'm already spoken for!!" Giggling, the young slave girl covered her face in embarrassment, dizzily regaining her footing.

Grabbing a handful of scattered flowers off the floor with one thought in mind, Douglas bounded up the staircase, three steps at a time disregarding pain searing his left leg. Running to Francesca's room at the end of the hall, he jubilantly threw open the door to a scene his mind would replay for the rest of his life.

There, on their marital four poster was his young bride; rocking stark naked on her knees, her long ebony hair draped over her face, full pendulous breasts swinging wildly to the feral stroking of the similarly naked Lt. Mario Otero. Perched beside the bed, the focused officer was hammering like a man possessed; primal noises ripping from his throat as he pounded, slamming into her from behind.

One by one, lilies dropped to the floor.

At first stunned, Douglas could only stare, his brain attempting to process what his eyes were seeing.

Then the screaming started!

"DOUGLAS!!" "DOUGLAS!!!" "MADRE DE DIOS!!" "WHAT ARE YOU DOING HERE???!" Rolling and unceremoniously disengaging from her lover; Francesca grabbed sheets, thrashing with them in a futile attempt to cover herself.

Otero fell over backwards, tripping over black trousers wrapped around his ankles. Scrambling to his feet while yanking up his pants; he scanned frantically, looking for his sword. Unluckily for him, the scabbard lay out of reach across the room on an ottoman where he had dropped his belt. He met Douglas's narrowed gaze whose face had now hardened from shock to anger.

Catlike, the frontiersman leapt towards the inexperienced Spaniard, tossing his Bowie knife from one hand to the other, charging the stunned man in a blitz attack ably learned through years of Indian fighting. Otero again stumbled backwards, losing his balance tripping over his boots. Douglas' fist tangled in the young officer's hair, slipping until he could get a grip on the oily tresses tied back in a tail. Jerking the man's head up to expose his throat; he raised the massive blade in the classic 'killing' arc.

"NO, DOUGLAS!! POR FAVOR!! NO!!!" Francesca sobbed and begged, plaintively holding her hands palms up towards him, pleading for mercy for the young officer.

"DOUGLAS!" Douglas turned to see Francesca's horrified parents standing in the doorway behind him.

Continuing to grip the terrified man's hair, the young husband hesitated for a brief moment. Everyone in the room thought he was going to release the lieutenant, but with a sudden flash of the blade, he swung the knife downward, kicking the Spaniard in the back, rolling him forward with a sickening sound. Douglas straddled over him holding the man's hair, still tied in a ribbon… but he had only taken the tail, not the scalp. Otero yelped; clawing at the back of his head expecting blood; hearing and feeling his hair ripping as it was sliced off.

Douglas spun around facing his wife; derisively throwing her lover's tail onto her lap. With the Bowie knife still threateningly clutched in his hand, he stood hyperventilating.

Stepping forward, Hunter calmly placed his right arm around his son-in-law's shoulders, carefully pushing the knife down with his left.

"Come with me…please. Douglas, come with me."

Hunter gestured wildly towards Otero. "GET OUT OF MY HOUSE…NOW!!!" Turning his fiery attention to his daughter, he fixed her with an angry stare.

"You have shamed our home. YOU HAVE SHAMED YOUR HUSBAND!! You are no longer my daughter!!"

"NO, PAPA…NO!!!" Crumpling forward onto her pillow, Francesca hid her face, her cries and pleas falling on deaf ears.

Hurriedly pulling on his boots, the disgraced lieutenant grabbed the rest of his clothes and plumed hat, bumping Douglas as he rushed out of the bedroom door.

Turning to face his wife, Douglas removed his wedding ring exposing engraving on the inside. It was etched with one word…'FOREVER'.

"FOREVER, FRANCESCA??! FOREVER??! FROM THIS DAY, I DO NOT CLAIM YOU AS MY WIFE!! BURN IN HELL AS THE DEVIL YOU ARE!!"

Storming the bed he raged, throwing the ring at his wife; raising his arm as to strike her. Francesca sat up, hands covering her breasts, ducking her head for the inevitable blow; but he wasn't swinging at her. The target was their silver-framed wedding portrait standing on a small easel on the bedside table; a silent witness to her infidelities. Backhanding the picture, it was sent flying across the room smashing against the wall. The photograph landed face up, lethal shards piercing the smiling, sepia-toned bride and groom. Broken glass scattered across plush Turkish carpet like so many broken vows, broken dreams... broken hearts.

The next few minutes were a teary blur for the young husband. He remembered the stairway, he remembered being in Jonathon's mahogany office, he remembered taking offered brandy ...but he could not recall leaving the bedroom or how he got down a flight of stairs. He was an incoherent man in a nightmare daze, his life and future, all their dreams...done...gone. Francesca's father was trying to be steady and calm in his embarrassment, hoping to prevent Douglas from acting in further violence.

"Son," he started in a quiet voice...

Douglas cut him off. "I'm NOT your son; don't call me that... I'm NOT your son!"

"Alright, Douglas...I am at a loss at what to say to you, other than I am so sorry for the inexcusable actions of our daughter. Her mother and I stand in humiliation...what can we do? What can I do?"

Douglas tilted the glass, taking a long drink of pungent liquor; clenching his eyes at the burning in his throat and the sting of tears. Closing his eyes hurt worse than helping, all he could see was her. Clutching his head as her vision and murderous thoughts churned through his mind, he tried to determine his next move…a course of action. All he really wanted was his life back, his beautiful Francesca…but he knew that couldn't be. For the rest of his life he would remember her face and sensuous body in throes of passion with another man. Taking another slug of brandy, clearing his throat, he turned to face her father.

"I'll take my slaves…Big John and Moses, my horses, and any property I left here. I want nothing of hers…or yours. I never want to see her again. As soon as we load the horses, we'll head for the docks to book passage south on the 'George Washington'. My father is waiting for me to return to Rosetta to help him with the cane and citrus groves."

Words fell out faster than he had intended. Taking a deep breath, he was doing his best to regain his composure.

"I do not mean to offend or be rude to you and your wife, sir…but I cannot stay here."

A beaten man, Douglas walked trance like out of the massive door he had joyfully run through no more than ten minutes earlier. Barely making it off the porch with his stomach lurching, he vomited among the 'Bird of Paradise'. Wiping his mouth on the back of his sleeve, he laughed to himself at the horrible irony of it.

"BIG JOHN!!! MOSES!!" The two slaves, both guilty in the knowledge of the cause of his misery, awkwardly approached their owner with downcast eyes.

"I need you two to saddle all my horses and load up my gear…don't forget the rifles, and pack whatever you brought. We're heading for the river to book passage on the next steamer to Palatka; hopefully, day after tomorrow, we'll be back at Rosetta."

"That GOOD news, Massa Douglas, that REAL good news...
I been missin' my Etta, sir. I been missin' her real bad!" Big John
smiled down at Dummett; then suddenly his face fell.

"But, what about Moses, Massa Douglas?"

"What do you mean? Moses is coming with us."

"Massa Douglas; Moses and Clarice jumped the broom a few
moons ago...Clarice with child! You weren't here to ask...they
was right together and had a powerful, big love. Your daddy always try to keep folks together, sir."

Big John was obviously uncomfortable confronting the issue
by reminding the younger Dummett of his father's policies.

Initially angry, Douglas turned to face Moses who stood staring with frightened but defiant eyes. Straightening with a resigned
sigh, he looked the scared slave in the face..."I'll see what I can
do: but you know Clarice belongs to Mrs. Hunter."

"I be beholden, sir, Clarice is strong and a good worker! She
can help your momma with dos house chores...she got a way
with flowers too, I know your momma loves her flowers!" Moses
was doing his best to sell Clarice's attributes.

"Can she cook?"

"Lordy, Lordy; she got the best fried pies...and chick'n fixin's
and dumplin's!" Moses grinned, rubbing exaggerated circles over
his stomach.

"I'll talk to Mr. Hunter; I'm going to be building a house on
my own land... I'll be needing cooks and house slaves myself."

Jonathon Hunter was obviously watching from the window,
as soon as Douglas stepped back onto the veranda, his father-in-
law met him at the front door.

"I've changed my mind, sir. There is one thing I would like
from you. I'm told that your girl, Clarice, has jumped the broom

with my Moses. Since I won't be taking your daughter to New Smyrna, I would appreciate it if instead, you would give me Clarice. That is of course, if you were serious about giving me anything I wanted?"

Hunter shook his head in assent motioning Douglas to come back inside. "I have her papers in my office; I'll sign her over to you. CLARICE! Gather your clothes…you're leaving with Capt. Dummett; you belong to him, now!"

Flourishing his signature with a white quill, the older man blew the ink dry, handing the ownership paper to Douglas. "I can't say this is the best of trades, sir, but your chivalry will always be appreciated in my home. Please give my best to your father and mother. I hope you and your family will not hold me responsible for the foolishness of my young daughter…and pray that in time, you might be able to forgive her."

Douglas took the ownership parchment transferring Clarice to him, folding and stuffing it into his breast pocket. Taking a step back; snapped his heels together; proffering his hand to the mortified man. Hunter shook his son-in-law's hand; pulling him into a stiff hug, patting his back.

Within a few minutes; Douglas and the three slaves were loaded onto packed horses and heading out the drive. He stroked the still damp neck of his stallion.

"Sorry, Chief, I thought we'd get more of a rest…but guess we'll have to wait for the river cruise."

"Big John, do you know how to get us to the steamboat dock?"

"Yassir, I made plenty of buckboard runs to the river to pick up supplies for Massa Hunter…you just follow Big John…I can already smell dat black water!!"

Douglas was relieved to have someone else in charge, even for a short time. Big John had been with the Dummett family since he was a boy and was as completely trusted as a slave could be. His wife, Etta, was a beloved nanny to the Dummett children both in Barbados and this new world.

"Keep a wary eye out, talk in Savannah was Osceola, Coacoochee, and John Caesar, have burned several homesteads."

He turned, grinning at the obviously worried slaves while lifting his long, blonde hair into the air. "I imagine any Seminole warrior would be happy with this scalp on their belt." He did his best to muster a laugh.

Big John and Moses looked somberly at the golden hair; then at each other with wide, scared eyes. The rest of the ride to the river was made in silence.

Loud and bustling, the Port of St. Augustine reeked of sweat and dung. Cargo wagons were being loaded and bawling livestock led hesitatingly up bouncy ramps onto boats and barges docked on the St. John's River. Groups of wealthy land speculators stood to the side waiting to board, wearing black top hats and expensive northern suits of materials unsuited for Florida heat. Sickeningly sweet tobacco smoke rising from expensive cigars hung low over crowded docks; humidity intensifying the mixture of pungent odors of livestock, mildew, and wood smoke from steam boilers. Even in April, temperatures soared high into the eighties at midday. The northern bejeweled wives were just as uncomfortable as their husbands with unfurling curls, melting rouge, and skin blotching in the blistering sun. Shading themselves as best they could with dainty ruffled parasols, their misery was compounded by tightly laced corsets, lace pantaloons, layers of hoop skirts, and heavy dresses. All in all, they created a miserable, perspiring pastel parade.

While Big John searched for fresh water for the horses, Douglas walked along the dock watching organized chaos, losing himself in the laughter and conversations of bystanders. One group crowded around a Negro with his foot propped up on a stump, singing and flailing a banjo, his grinning partner dancing a shuffle while reaching into the audience with his hat for donations. Balancing easily up the gangplank in his moccasins onto the large, multi-decked paddle wheeler, Douglas found an empty spot along the rail to observe and admire smoothly orchestrated tasks of experienced deckhands. A practiced line of slaves sang a low cadence as they passed crate after crate up the ramps to the lading deck. Performing final checks before untethering the boat from massive pilings, crewmen waited for the Captain to make his last inspection of the checklist before issuing cast off orders and getting under way.

As the first paddle wheeler to navigate tricky waters of the St. John's, the 'George Washington' floated under able piloting of Captain Jacob Brock. Standing three levels high, she shone clean and bright in the sunshine, decks and rails spit polished to high gleam. She was a side-wheeler, both port and starboard wheels sporting feathered paddles. Though wider than stern-wheelers, the two side wheels provided better maneuverability on winding and tricky rivers. Upper sections of the wheels were encased, providing passengers protection from heavy spray.

The St. John's River is the only waterway in the east with current running from south to north. Their trip southward, down to Palatka, was actually upriver and could prove unnerving to less experienced pilots. Much of the trip floated through shifting sandbars and meandering water tunnels of Jurassic trees outlined by creased and muddy banks. Oyster beds menaced from shallows, while long-beaked birds voiced displeasure at the interruption of their fishing. Dummett leaned both elbows on the rail watching the jungle slowly pass in loud silence; mesmerized by hypnotic splashing of wake and air full of heady perfume of Confederate Jasmine and sweet Nicotiana. Floating southward navigating the curving river, the 'George Washington' displaced dark water circling and splashing against cypress knees bayonetting from murky depths. A cardinal pacing the steamer exposed brilliant flashes of sporadic crimson among the leaves. In more densely wooded stretches, chartreuse snakes sunbathed on overhanging branches; some sliding down to slither among pink blooms of water hyacinths; others casually dropping onboard, thudding to the wooden decks to startled screams and curses of passengers…all to the great amusement of the crew. Overhead limbs threatening upper decks and stacks were expertly hacked away by machete wielding deckhands. Long-legged, hairy, black and yellow striped banana spiders watched, dangling warily overhead from huge webs suspended between banks. It was a silent, eerie, yet profoundly beautiful cruise.

THREE

"**S**HOOT HIM!!! SHOOT HIM BEFORE HE GETS INTO THE WHEEL!!!"

Douglas Dummett leaned over the 'George Washington's port rail watching the mounting excitement caused by an approaching fourteen foot alligator, tacking his way gracefully towards the ship. Winding through the wake, the massive black and green armored saurian was nearing the paddle wheel on the port side of the steamer. Captain Jacob Brock ran back to the stern, pointing and barking orders to his crew with firm commands learned from years of floating hazardous waterways. Should a beast this size get tangled in the wooden wheel…it would be disastrous for both. Brock knew well the perils of being adrift in this river, but he also knew their greatest danger lurked in the palmettos. From his vantage in the pilot house on the third level, he had seen shadows moving in the undergrowth along the banks. Experience and the hair on the back of his neck, which never lied, told him they were being watched by invisible eyes.

Two shotgun blasts lifted the gator partially out of the water, throwing him into a frenzied death roll. Roaring, the big bull thrashed, sinking beneath the tannic river in a spray of bloody froth. Suddenly, the seemingly deserted banks came alive as at least forty gators slithered from their palmetto dens, the giant lizards slipping quickly and silently down mud slides on the riverbanks, snapping, grunting, and rolling in a maelstrom of primal feeding frenzy. As soon as they appeared…they were gone, disappearing under the dark water. Passengers on the second level erupted in cheers. Ladies waved lacy handkerchiefs pulled from damp cleavages while men laughed and toasted with splashing steins of beer.

Noisy clouds of egrets launched upwards from treetops by the repercussions floated down like disturbed angels, flapping brilliantly white wings to take their footholds back on the prehistoric limbs.

"NICE SHOOTING!!" Dummett tipped his hat to the young marksman enjoying the raucous celebration with his crewmates. The sailor acknowledged the compliment with an exaggerated bow and a toothless grin.

Douglas opened his gold pocket watch checking the time, catching a brief glance of his wife's face in a small oval photograph mounted in the lid, tucking it quickly back into his buckskin vest. Black eyes and black hair he mused to himself...to match her black heart! His own long, blonde hair was tied with a cord at the nape and laid wet against his neck. After four years at Yale starting at age fourteen, two at West Point, and three years in the military fighting Plains Indians during the settling of the Missouri Territory, he had almost forgotten how unrelenting and sultry the Florida heat could be. Even with river breezes, sweat trickled down his back, pooling at his waistband.

In 1821 after Spain ceded Florida to the U.S., his father, Maj. Thomas Dummett, bought land from two plantations totaling about 4600 acres along the Tomoka River on the east coast of Florida. After two failed seasons, the elder Dummett brought a manager from Barbados who was an expert in sugar cane to help with the contrary crop in Florida. Now that several seasons of fields had produced, he was rebuilding the old sugar mill abandoned on his property from the failed Addison plantation; modernizing production with the addition of the first steam engine in Florida procured from the Cold Springs, New York foundry. Along with sugar cane, cotton, and indigo; citrus groves were planted in anticipation of his son's eventual arrival. Douglas had devised a cold-bud method of grafting sweet orange seedlings with the local, sour oranges; developing a strain between the two bursting with delightful, sweet juice…but with the hardiness of a native plant. His strains would eventually command highest prices in the North becoming known as 'Indian River Citrus'.

The younger Dummett had already staked a claim on a forty-three acre land parcel at New Smyrna. Situated on the barrier island on the east side of the Hillsborough River at Callalisa Creek; he would homestead with plans to build his own plantation. Rich, loamy soil with freshwater for irrigation and channels for egress made the location perfect. An ancient Timucua oyster mound rising high above the river bank near Callalisa Creek would provide a solid foundation for the manor house. With the Atlantic Ocean on the east, the river to the west, and giant oaks providing cool shade…it promised to be the tropical Eden of his dreams. He believed there wasn't a lovelier spot on earth…and it would be named 'Mount Pleasant'.

Douglas winced, thinking about the home he had wanted to build with his wife, and the plans and dreams he thought they both shared.

Now twenty-four and of strong pioneer stock, Douglas was ready to forgo trappings of city refinements his father's wealth had provided in St. Augustine and New Haven. Wild, beautiful Florida beckoned with sultry promises of perpetual growing seasons, alabaster sand beaches, unlimited opportunities, and abundant wild game. Living and studying in the North, he missed the fresh delicacies they enjoyed in the territorial wilderness of

Rosetta; buckets of shrimp, huge lobsters waving delectable claws, sea scallops, stone and blue crab, and a myriad of juicy, colorful fruits and berries. Turkey, deer, and hogs grew fat and plentiful in the palmettos and scrubs, their tracks creating winding trails to sun speckled locations of wild sweet potatoes, butter beans, and black-eyed peas. Monster fish in these waters were legendary to Northerners, but commonplace to Florida's settlers. It was good to be going home. Smiling to himself he thought of words written by an earlier settler, Englishman Andrew Turnbull, who named his failed 1768 colony attempt after his wife's birthplace in Greece…Smyrnea. Describing beauty of the place in his journals, Turnbull wrote… "New Smyrna was a swan among ducks."

Great live oaks and cypress guarded the riverbanks, many with girths of more than eighteen feet. Branches stretched horizontally, gracefully draped in Spanish moss forming a tunnel between opposite banks. Resembling arthritic old crones, trees seemingly waved their gnarled arms covered by tattered, grey shawls. Palms and pines stood erect and tall in the crowded mix, reaching for their share of sun, nodding their fronds and needled heads in breezes cooled by the Atlantic. Herds of white-tailed deer at the water's edge alerted at the approaching steamer, wide-eyed with faces raised in curiosity, turning and scattering, bounding long-legged into cabbage palms and undergrowth in flashes of white. Vines of Confederate Jasmine twisted upwards, climbing and hanging onto trunks and limbs, their yellow flowers like lanterns in the shadows. Head sized blossoms of wild hibiscus exploded in vivid red hues, while azaleas blushed in endless blankets of pinks, whites, and purples. Poisonous oleander and thorny bougainvillea, their pink blooms luring the unwary brought additional fiery colors to the palette backed by leaves and fronds in a thousand shades of green. Wake from the 'George Washington' rolled up onto rutted banks in waves, splashing and dragging mud down into dusky water. Great blue herons wading at water's edge ignored seagulls chattering overhead. Anhinga diving birds drip-dried on branches over the river standing upright, heads back staring at the heavens, their wings wide open and extended as crosses. Known to locals as 'devil birds'; Douglas wondered to himself if they might be an omen of things to come.

He turned, assessing other passengers; sweating, red-faced, and fat with northern money and liquor, blissfully ignorant of imminent danger stalking them from the banks.

Glancing up at the pilot house, he locked eyes with Captain Brock who summoned him with a nod of his head. Climbing the smooth wooden ladder two rungs at a time, Douglas swung himself easily next to the Captain manning the ship's wheel. Brock reached to shake with a meaty but sun-cracked hand, then pulled the long-haired young man into a hearty hug.

"Good to see you again, Douglas!"

"Thank you sir, it's good to be on the way home." He was pleased the Captain had recognized him out of his Army uniform.

"I assume you're headed for Rosetta. It's been awhile since I've seen your parents."

"Yessir, I'm bringing orange seedlings to graft in Father's groves first; then I'll be heading to my land on the island at New Smyrna to break ground on my homestead. That's all I've dreamed about the past few years, naming her Mount Pleasant. I'm looking mightily forward to lying in the grass during the violet hour with a bottle of Father's best rum while the sun drops into the river... and watching the dolphins fly."

Brock nodded, smiling at the visuals. "Bully for you! That's a beautiful beach on that island; whitest, softest sand I've seen anywhere…and I've been most everywhere!"

Douglas nodded in assent. "Agreed! I believe Mother Earth sings her best songs in New Smyrna."

Brock's face suddenly darkened. "Getting to the matter at hand, I'm damned glad to have you aboard. Since you are a military man; I gather you've noticed we're being followed."

Douglas nodded in assent at the older man, noting the worried expression he was doing his best to conceal. His years of western combat had taught him to be proficient in reading faces.

"I'm assuming your crew is well armed?" he asked.

"You can count on it, but some of these hands tend to be corned on Monongahela whiskey by midday, so we can always use another straight shooter on the rail. Not sure if it's Wildcat or not, but his and John Caesar's bands have overrun smaller schooners to steal weapons and ammo and rob passengers. I'm sure you have some knowledge of what they do with white captives. I'm trying to stay mid river, even if that means steering out of the channel a bit, but if we should get stuck on a goldurn sandbar, I'd appreciate having you and your rifle up deck."

Spitting into a brass spittoon sitting under the wheel, Brock's coolness was belied by nervous stroking of his thick mustache and a slick of moisture across his forehead.

"There's a bend a few miles ahead just north of Palatka, there's usually a sandbar on the west side. Depending on how far it has built and shifted out into the river, we might have to swing wide port to avoid running aground…but that will put us right near the east bank. If their intent is to try and board us…that's where it'll be."

"You can count on us, Captain, I'm going to make sure my

horses are secure; then I'll set up on the port rail with two of my slaves. They can both shoot the eyes out of a squirrel!"

"Thanks, Dummett, I'll start running the ladies into their staterooms and find out if any of these fancy men know their butts from a gun barrel. We'll try to keep most of these Yankees from being easy targets!"

Douglas rode the ladders smoothly down to the first level of the steamer where livestock and cargo were loaded. Big John and Moses were deep in discussion, leaning against the rail in the paddock where Chief and the other three horses were stabled. Clarice sat huddled in the straw, chin resting on her knees. Though relieved to be allowed to go with her husband, leaving her siblings had been tearful. At sixteen and pregnant, scared and missing her mother, she was muffling sobs with her long, calico skirt.

"Hush yor blitherin', girl! Massa Douglas be sendin' you back to Augustine lessen you shush!" Moses kissed the distraught girl on top of her head. "Massa Douglas do us a good turn askin' Massa Hunter for you, so buck it up!"

"I ain't never been on no steamin' ship…and how I gonna birth this baby without my mammy?"

"Don't you worry none, Miss Etta be helpin' you wid dat midwifin'! Now, wipe dos tears and no sassin'!"

Moses startled; surprised to see Dummett was standing behind him.

"Looks like we might be having company, I need you boys to arm yourselves. Get four of my Kentucky rifles and my Hawken readied!" "Big John, I want you up top with me. Moses, you line up on the port rail down here by the horses. Clarice, quit that bawling. You need to be extra eyes for Moses, and reload rifles for him."

"Be it 'Wildcat'?" Moses turned a nervous eye to the riverbank.

"Don't know, yet," Douglas answered, "not sure if it's Seminoles just scouting us or if it's Osceola and a war party. They've been trailing us for a while, but now they're moving ahead of us. Captain Brock says a pretty good sandbar has been building up on the big curve off the west side just north of Palatka. We'll have to steer close to the east shore to keep from running aground; so if they mean trouble, that's the most likely place they'll be waiting on us."

The two slaves were quiet, both debating whether or not to speak. Moses broke the silence.

"We been hearin' stories, Massa Douglas, 'bout what Wildcat did to those settlers near Fort Butler. They say he cut de hearts out de menfolk and scalped da babies!!! They killed dose babies so their mommas could watch…then they scalp de women alive a fore they gut 'em!"

"Remember those stories when you take aim…make every shot count."

Douglas's voice and calm demeanor belied the churning in his stomach. He had seen what horrors had been wrought on western settlers, but didn't want his slaves to see his mounting apprehension. Open prairie fighting, as bad as it was, in retrospect was easier than battling an invisible enemy. Pulling the hat brim further down on his forehead to better shade his face, he squinted at the slowly passing maze of ancient trees and thick undergrowth of palmettos and sawgrass along the river; his eyes searching for what he knew was there…but what couldn't be seen.

"Go now; get those rifles oiled up, make sure your horns are full and open the ammo boxes! We need to get on the rails."

Slinging the long Hawken and a knapsack of munitions over his shoulder, Dummett stuffed his moose-skin shooting gloves into his pockets before clambering up the ladder to the top deck.

"HOLY JESUS! I've heard tales about those buffalo guns but never seen one up close! What in the hell caliber is that thing?"

Douglas grinned at Brock's exclamation. "Most are .50 to .53 caliber, but this one's a .60; hand-made with a Kansas black walnut beaver-tail stock with blade sights. I figured if a Hawken was good enough for the likes of plainsman Kit Carson and mountain-man Jim Bridger...it was the rifle I was going to have! My slave, Big John, will take the rail with me. The other will be on the first deck."

Big John set his knapsack on the deck, bracing his rifle atop the brass rail, narrowing his eyes searching the eastern bank. He was oblivious to curious stares of crewmen not used to seeing a giant of a slave standing shoulder to shoulder with white men... sighting a long gun.

"What you think, Massa Douglas? I don see nuthin', but I got me an all overish feelin' of somethin' bad!"

Coacoochee motioned his braves to crouch among thick fountain grasses and saw hammocks on the eastern bank; their tattooed and mud smeared faces and bodies blending into stretching shadows. His warriors knelt as statues, absolutely still, silently frozen in place. The war party was invisible to all on the passing riverboat...invisible to all but one, cacophonous blue heron. Squawking an alarm as he abruptly flapped upward out of the reeds; the tall grey bird virtually pinpointed the war party's position. An immediate barrage of gunfire from upper decks of the boat responded to the frenzied flutter, breaking the attack, scattering braves inland as bullets ripped blindly as crazed hornets through sage and underbrush.

The 'George Washington' made the bend, steering to relative safety of deeper waters midway in the river, temporarily out of reach from unseen dangers lurking on the banks. Capt. Brock blew three celebratory blasts from the steam whistle to cheers of relieved passengers. Douglas remained on the rail with other marksmen keeping wary eyes on the passing scenery. Every slight movement, every leaf blown by lightest of breezes brought nervous rifle sightings to the spot.

This time, the steamboat and its cargo would pass safely; but King Phillip, Micanopy, Osceola, and Coacoochee were experienced strategists. Anger over broken treaties, ruthless advances and raids of Andrew Jackson's army, and the U.S. government's intent of forcing them from their homelands onto reservations in the Oklahoma territory left them no choice but to fight. Joined by sixteen hundred Maroon freedmen and runaway slaves led by John Caesar, the Seminole army was building; aided by harbor, stolen supplies, and recon information provided by plantation slaves. Battles were beginning in earnest with Florida's fledgling settlements and isolated plantations sitting almost defenseless against grisly and efficient wave attacks by increasingly hostile natives. Surreptitious and brutal raids by screaming Seminoles suddenly appearing from the jungle… then just as suddenly silently disappearing into its depths were enough to dissuade survivors. Many settlers left, losing all they had ventured by taking their families and returning back north. Deserted homes and farms were set afire with Seminoles using scorched earth strategies, destroying homesteads and fields to make them unusable for any souls brave enough to return. Winds of war were brewing… and they blew ill for Florida.

FOUR

The Port of Palatka was bustling with men and women of every description and station. Sweat drenched dock hands stacked wooden crates of various sizes and ladings to be loaded aboard arriving steamboats. Though it appeared chaotic, there was a metered rhythm to their stooping, standing, lifting, and carting. Livestock bawled nervously, stomping hooves to the steady pulse of workers while they labored. Chickens and guineas in slatted crates raised their cackles and crows to the cacophony. A putrid stench of animal excrement filled the main street running along the riverfront, gagging passer-byes who covered their noses with grimy handkerchiefs.

While dock men earned livings by the sweat of their brows; ladies of the oldest profession gathered near the base of the gangplank. Smiling and flashing glimpses of ankles and ample bosoms, the women hoped to entice arriving riverboat travelers to 'Sadie's'; a local saloon and house of ill repute. Sadie's was famous for watered whiskey, crooked poker, fat Caribbean cigars, and an upstairs brothel that sought to satisfy any perversion. Tourists and land speculators came flush with cash…and in the Florida heat, they were always thirsty.

Captain Brock signaled the 'George Washington's arrival to the port with three, long blasts of his prized steam whistle. He was most proud of the large brass, and copper whistle he had acquired from the Ansonia Brass factory in New York. Shined and polished daily, it was the gem of the top deck, mirrored and blinding in daily sunshine.

Douglas made a point to take leave of Captain Brock with a standing invitation to 'Rosetta', a firm handshake, and once again extending regards from his father and mother. He then busied with overseeing the unloading of his slaves and horses, their gear, and the burlap bags of sweet orange seedlings.

Leading his stallion down bobbing gangplanks onto the rickety dock, Douglas was confronted by a past prime, extremely buxom, red-haired whore. Grabbing his arm, she coquettishly smiled into his face with a grin of sporadic teeth, rubbing her mostly exposed chest into his. A peacock plume dangled askew from an obviously fake mass of red curls pinned to the top of her head. Perspiration streamed down her face sending rivulets of shocking blue eye-shadow winding through dusty freckles into her cleavage.

"Honey…you pretty boy, you come to Sadie's tonight and ask for 'Big Red'! I promise I'll ride you like a two dollar mule!!"

Douglas laughed, wresting from her slippery grip. "Well Red, that's about the best offer I've had all day!"

Big Red winked a heavily outlined eye, turning and flipping the back of her skirt up over the bustle, revealing bowlegs encased in muddy pantaloons. Sauntering away, she coyly glanced over a hefty shoulder with a toothless smile, curious to see if he was watching the display.

Arrangements were made at the Palatka Livery for stalls for the horses and hay pallets for Big John, Moses, and Clarice to sleep in the barn. Keenly aware of attention Chieftain had garnered, Douglas instructed John and Moses to take turns standing watch during the night. If they left early the next morning, they should make Rosetta, the Dummett plantation at the junction of the Halifax and Tomoka Rivers by evening. It was too dangerous to attempt the trip at night.

Loosening his collar, the bald hotel clerk who was used to men in suits, was visibly taken aback at the sight of a frontiersman in fringed buckskins carrying a long Hawken rifle approaching his counter.

"I'm going to need a room for the night, and I'd appreciate directions to the nearest establishment where a man can get his thirst quenched with some good Kentucky bourbon!"

"Yessir, yessir," the clerk replied, relieved the young man was a customer. "The room is two dollars in advance; Room #4 is last door on the right at the end of the hall. Sadie's Saloon is across the street, three doors down."

Douglas paid the nervous man putting the key in his pocket nodding thanks for directions and climbed the stairs. His room was stifling but luckily was an end corner unit with two windows. Dropping his knapsack on the dresser he opened both to allow a slight cross breeze to blow over the bed. Sitting briefly on the edge of the lumpy mattress for a moment, he assessed the tacky yellow-flowered wallpaper; wondering if the strong odor of urine was exuding from the carpet...or the mysterious stains on the bedspread. Tinkling notes of a distant piano hung in the sultry air, bringing him back to thirsty reality. "Whiskey," he thought to himself... "good Kentucky whiskey"! Standing and stiffly stomping out kinks, he looked into the tall mirror smoothing his hair. "Good as it's going to get," he said out loud to the glass. Grabbing the Hawken, he headed downstairs through the lobby and out onto the muddy street, dodging two oxen carts laden with tilting crates of chickens and squealing pigs.

Approaching the splintering grey board and batten emporium, raucous laughter and off key songs of a drunken soprano led him through the swinging doors. Inside the parlor reeking of beer and cheap perfumes, revelers were wrapped in clutches of assorted prostitutes. Different in ages and ethnicities, all were wearing masks of makeup, cleavage baring corsets, and the same bored smiles numbed by laudanum. Douglas's quick scan of the room registered red velvet gold-trimmed furniture, walls of nude paintings, and about a dozen gaudy women hawking watered whiskey to the riverboat crowd. His intentions were to only have one stiff drink, get a good night's sleep, and an early departure to Rosetta in the morning.

The way to Hell is paved with good intentions.

FIVE

"MASSA DOUGLAS…MASSA DOUGLAS!!" Covering his eyes from the morning light, Dummett tried to bring Big John's blurry face into focus.

"John…JOHN…not so loud, I can hear you! I CAN HEAR YOU!!" The young man rolled to a semi-sitting position, cradling his head. "Oh… my… God; where am I? Am I alive???"

"You in de hotel, Massa Douglas, but I think you ben in dat saloon! From de looks of you and dese bottles, I think dat old demon rum dun bite you hard! You been talkin' real crazy like!"

Pushing hair back from his face, Douglas squinted into unrelenting sunlight streaming through the hotel's dingy lace curtains.

"What are you talking about, what did I say?" Yawning, he rubbed his eyes with dirty fists.

"Didn't make much sense, sir; talkin' bout livestock an such."

"LIVESTOCK??"

"Yassir…I thinks you says you bought a two dollar mule!!"

Moaning, he rolled back onto his side, pulling the faded quilt over his head; then suddenly sat straight up.

"THE HAWKEN…WHERE'S MY HAWKEN!!???"

A cursory check of the room determined the rifle was missing.

"Come on, John, we need to pay a visit to 'Sadie's'!"

Dummett shoved a pistol into his belt next to the tooled leather scabbard securing his Bowie knife and threw his knapsack to John.

Making an imposing pair, the two strode shoulder to shoulder through the swinging doors of the saloon. A rotund bartender stepped from behind the bar, menacing with his bulk; his bushy beard stained with oozing trails of tobacco. Music stopped as the piano player spun on his stool to face them.

"THERE'S NO SLAVES ALLOWED IN HERE!"

Douglas drew his pistol and Indian charged him, jamming it under the man's bulbous red nose before he could react.

"I'm here to get my property; then we'll be gone. My head is splitting, so don't say another word, just point your finger at Big Red's room…or prepare to die on this day!"

Gesturing to the door at the top of the stairs, the barkeep glowered but smartly kept his mouth shut.

Tossing the pistol to Big John, Dummett motioned him to cover those in the bar; then took the stairs three at a time, his moccasins silent on the treads. Big Red, flat on her back with her legs over her head, screamed as her door was kicked off its hinges. The crash interrupted the elderly Parson White's efforts to redeem her soul by his vigorous indoctrination of the missionary position and calls to Jesus! They both froze in place; him balancing obesely naked above her on the pillowed four-poster.

"WHERE'S MY HAWKEN, RED?? Think before you answer, because if I don't like what you say, I'll finish what the good parson started… with this."

In the blink of an eye; the Bowie knife swirled out of the sheath, seemingly with a life of its own. Years of frontier training and efficient killing were evident in Dummett's skillful handling of the large blade. Flourishing it as an extension of his arm, he cut the air with a 'whoosh'; then touched the dagger to Red's throat, running the tip between her sagging breasts and across her belly, all the way down to the quivering clergyman's manhood, now dangling free above her thighs. The good pastor's eyes were tightly clenched, but his lips trembled in silent prayer while maintaining his precarious position on all fours atop the sweaty whore.

"YOUR MONEY POUCH IS IN THE TOP DRAWER, YOU DON'T OWE ME NUTHIN', YOU WAS TOO DRUNK TO DO EITHER OF US ANY GOOD!" She motioned toward the Victorian dresser.

"GOOD GOD, WOMAN. YOU'RE GOOD! I DIDN'T EVEN REALIZE THAT WAS GONE!" Douglas patted his belt and pockets, stuffing his money pouch inside his shirt.

"YOU WERE SO DRUNK…I WAS JUST TAKIN' CARE OF IT FOR YOU! I THINK… MAYBE; YOUR RIFLE MIGHT A… 'ACCIDENTLY'… FELL INTO MY CLOSET!" Red blinked her kohl smeared eyes wildly trying to look innocent to the angry man.

Douglas opened the mirrored armoire, dragging stained, odorous dresses out onto the floor until the big Hawken was revealed standing barrel up in the back of the cabinet, wrapped in a tapestry. Relieved, he kissed the walnut stock and stowed the Bowie.

"Good luck, Parson. Better check your coin purse before you leave, and from where I'm standing, you best prepare a sermon on the 23rd Psalm. It appears you could use some help in the 'rod and staff' department… if you know what I mean!!"

Winking at the two, Douglas smacked the mortified clergyman on his bare butt with his Bible before hustling down the stairs.

Pointing the long buffalo gun in a sweeping arc toward the men in the saloon in silent warning to discourage any followers; he and Big John scrambled backwards through the swinging doors from the infamous 'Sadie's'. Laughing and breathless, the two ran to the livery stable where Moses and Clarice waited at the ready with the horses. Big John spun holding the saddle horn, dancing in circles with one foot in the stirrup before finally swinging his massive bulk up onto the big roan.

Exhausted, he flashed a white grin at Dummett while wiping sweat from his broad brow.

"LAWDY, Massa Douglas, Big John gettin' too OLD for this!!"

"LET'S RIDE!! WE'VE OVERSTAYED OUR WELCOME IN PALATKA!"

Riding hard, the troupe rode eastward, single file over narrow cart path trails towards the rising sun, getting a much later start than they had hoped. Once reaching the King's Road they made the southerly turn with the knowledge it was not much further where safety, good food, cold rum, and welcoming arms of their families waited at Rosetta Plantation.

SIX

The eight hour ride to Rosetta over barely cleared, rutted, and muddy jungle roads full of tangled roots was exhausting but uneventful, with all breathing a sigh of relief when they reached the lane twisting between shrouded oaks to relative safety of the plantation. Baying hounds rushed to greet the travelers, jumping alongside their exhausted horses with a ruckus of howls and shrill barking. Rosetta rose from the distant loaming, candlelight and lanterns illuminating every portal and column. The low, rich baritone cadence of an African song emitting from slave quarters situated behind the big house filled the night silence. Seven or eight field hands communed together around a cook fire as they alternated with each other, their voices joined in rhythmic repetition, cranking the spit bearing a heavy boar impaled and tied to the bar. Juices and fats dripped crackling in the blaze, sending savory aroma into the heavy evening air, assaulting their senses and reminding the weary travelers it had been hours since they had eaten. The more delicious the smell; the louder the stomach...

Rosetta now boasted over four-thousand six hundred acres; originally a two-thousand acre plantation settled by John Moultrie in 1770, it was then abandoned after the British ceded Florida back to Spain in 1783. Part of the property was granted in 1804 to Patrick Dean and John Bunch, Dean's uncle; along with other acquired portions of the failed Turnbull colony property. They worked to reclaim the lands from encroaching jungle and relentless heat, but Dean was killed in 1818 by a Seminole boy he had raised, with his Aunt Cecily Bunch then inheriting his portion. In 1825, the Bunch's sold the plantation and its slaves to Thomas Dummett; moving what was left of their family back north to Charleston. Dummett was also then able to acquire a portion of another plantation bordering Rosetta... Carrickfergus; named after the Irish birthplace of John Addison, a former owner.

Thomas put all his energy to carving a sugar cane, cotton, and indigo plantation out of the Florida wilderness. Abandoned fields cleared by former owners were over grown by nature's relentless march, resisting efforts to clear palmetto scrub and vines deeply rooted in the fertile soil. The balmy climate was much the same as his earlier lands in Barbados, and he was intent on building a modern, steam-powered sugar mill to process his cane to distill dark, full-bodied, perfect rum. He brought his best, strongest, and most knowledgeable slaves from the Caribbean to ensure his success.

Though Rosetta wasn't a formal home, it was a grand coquina and oak structure with deep, wide porches. Situated in the shade of numerous ancient and long-armed angel oaks to take advantage of their protection from the sun, the house was constructed in the manner of sub-tropical structures with wide eaves and tall, shuttered windows. Foundations and rotund porch columns were carefully cut limestone mortared with lime, pulverized shell, and sand, while fragrant cedar shakes were hand-split into shingles for the roof. Floors were pegged oak hewn and milled on the plantation. Cabinetry was mahogany brought from Barbados. Over countless hours, they had been sanded and lovingly waxed to brilliance.

Mary Dummett, Thomas' wife; prided herself on her pristine gardens and fragrant pink floribunda roses. She pruned; fussing and weeding in the gardens among her specially selected slaves, encouraging their labors with her constant credo…"We might live in the wilderness, but we don't need to live like savages!"

Though spending countless hours in the sun, she was always mindful of such, protecting her fair skin with long clothing and floppy-brimmed straw hats or bonnets tied securely under her chin with wide cotton sashes. A beautiful, patrician woman who maintained her white and unblemished skin until she died, she was the perfect partner for Thomas; a regal Scottish lady of gentrified background and education, a loving indulgent mother to their children, an accomplished equestrian, a trusted and passionate wife and a fearless frontierswoman. Now, in her sixties, Mary was starting to show infirmities of age and increasing forgetfulness. Fearing she might be harmed in her wanderings, Thomas planned on moving her to their home in St. Augustine when their son took over operations of Rosetta. He loved her dearly, even more than when they were young, and doted on her whenever he could.

Thomas and Mary rushed outside to the hounds' announcement of their son's arrival, not having seen him in over a year since his wedding in St. Augustine. Several slaves ran from their quarters to greet the travelers and tend the horses, now frothy from the arduous trip. No sooner did Big John slide off his horse that he was assailed by his wife, Etta, as she jumped throwing her ample body into his arms. He swung her in a bear hug, her long skirts flying as she cried, kissing his face.

Douglas hugged his mother, reaching for his father and pulling him into the embrace.

"Your wound…how is your wound?" Mary Dummett pulled back from her son to look down at his leg. "We've been so worried, but you look healthy!"

"I'm fine, Mum; Father's rum will erase any memory of pain!"

He smiled into his mother's anxious face; "and I'm sure Granny Moon's potions will remove any remaining poison in the wound."

Thomas Dummett slowly approached Chieftain, talking quietly as he took the bridle, stroking the big stallion's velvety nose. He smiled knowingly at his son. "You've done well, Douglas, he's a fine, fine handsome specimen!"

Douglas nodded in agreement, proud at his father's obvious pleasure and approval.

"Rosetta and Mount Pleasant will be known throughout the land for their beautiful and strong Andalusians. We'll breed Chieftain to Florida's best mares and our herd will be prized not only for their form, but for their strength, stamina, and speed!! Moses, get a couple of those boys to help wipe these horses down and secure them in the barn with fresh feed and water."

"Mount Pleasant?" The elder Dummett turned quizzically to his son.

Douglas turned at his father's question. "Yes, Father, I have decided to build my plantation on my tract along the Hillsborough River on the island at the settlement of New Smyrna. Many sleepless nights on the western prairies I mulled over names for the home I would build on that shell mound hill at the entrance to Callalisa Creek; and Mount Pleasant it is!"

Mary smiled at her son's revelation. "It's perfect...Mount Pleasant will be beautiful!" As she scanned around the faces, she realized Francesca was not with the party.

"Francesca??" she asked.

"Mum...Father...Francesca is not coming. I do not wish to ruin my homecoming with explanations, but our marriage is over. I have spoken with her father and will seek a divorce once I get settled."

Mary made eye contact with her husband who shrugged and shook his head.

"RUM! This weary traveler has long thirsted for that sweet fire on my lips since I left Missouri territory!" Douglas effectively changed the subject.

Throwing his arm around his son's shoulders, Thomas led him toward the house.

"Sure enough, son, I've got a new blend that we just opened in anticipation of an occasion like this, and Etta just made a pot of deer stew…still steaming on the stove."

"Where are my trouble-making sisters?" Douglas suddenly realized the girls were missing.

"With unrest of the Seminoles, we thought it best at this time they remain near the fort in St. Augustine for their safety and formal schooling. All three are living under the care of our housekeeper and tutors at the Governor's House. Anna has taken responsibility as eldest for Elizabeth and little Sara Jane; they are good girls and I pray they will not test their older sister's good heart and mettle. We visit as often as we can, but travel is increasingly dangerous on this frontier. Of course you know Mortimer decided to return to New Haven where he is establishing his law practice."

The night was a celebration of memories, stories, and excitement for the future for the reunited family.

"Wow, Father, you have outdone yourself! What we would have given for a taste of this combustible on the western front." Douglas smiled, blowing an exaggerated kiss into the air.

"Demands for this elixir increase every day, with rewards far exceeding my expectations! It has allowed us to purchase the majority of the Addison Plantation…'Carrickfergus', which has several hundred more acres cleared for cane, and his sixty-seven slaves. Addison first tried to plant cotton but soon realized sugar cane would be much more profitable. He added on to an abandoned stone mission and extended his sugar mill to 135' before he died, and we are putting it to good use! We'll talk later of family matters we need to discuss about the mill, but for now, we celebrate your homecoming!"

"I wrote I was bringing presents!" Douglas strode to the entryway where his belongings were stacked, picking up a burlap wrapped item he proudly presented to his father.

"For you, Father…a fine Kentucky rifle…feel the weight and balance!"

Gingerly pulling the long gun from the material, the older man turned the gleaming rifle in his hands, running his fingers along the smoothness of the stock feeling the intricacy of the carving; then pulled it to his shoulder, sighting along the length of the barrel.

"She's a beauty, son, it's the finest workmanship I've ever seen. She's perfectly balanced!"

Douglas stood back smiling, proudly watching his father admire the prized gun.

"And Mum, for you, the most beautiful azure stone of the West…turquoise; set in Hopi silver. The Indians believe they are pieces of heaven brought to earth by sky-people. I think it's the very color of the blue-springs; and of course…New Smyrna's ocean at high noon!"

Mary gasped at the beautiful necklace as her son fastened it around her neck.

"Oh, Douglas, it's exquisite! I've never seen a stone of this beautiful color. Thank you, my darling, thank you!"

"ETTA! WHERE'S ETTA!"

The rotund slave gingerly stepped into the room from the kitchen, tucking wisps of grey hair behind her ear. "Here I is, Massa Douglas."

"Surely you didn't think I had forgotten you, did you, Ma Etta?" the young man teased. "I have something for the best cook in the world!" Opening another small pouch, he withdrew a pair of silver earrings of a chandelier style, hung with small pearls.

"MY GOOD LAWD, Massa Douglas, you mean fo' Etta to have dese beautiful things??"

"I do! You don't know how much I missed you those years in the Army, Etta, or how many dreams I had of your chicken dumplings and sweet potato pie! They were what sustained me when we had to eat hard tack and cold beans. I want you to have something that brings you pleasure, just as those memories did for me."

Douglas hugged the older woman while she dabbed tears with her apron.

"Thank you, Massa Douglas. I ne'er had nuthin' purty as dese bobs!"

"Now, Mum, I have waited this long time to hear your beautiful voice in Scottish song."

Mary smiled at her son's request, gracefully seating herself at her treasured piano. Scottish lilts danced from the keys while her husband and son sipped their drinks, fully enjoying the impromptu concert. Thomas's eyes glistened as he proudly watched his wife, her lilting soprano filling the room while her delicate fingers brought the instrument to life. She had entertained their children in Barbados, Connecticut, and St. Augustine, balancing babies at the keyboard in her lap as she played and sang. Those had been happy days; but plague, dysentery, and diphtheria were rampant, unforgiving and untreatable. Now, of eleven babies, six were dead; each death exacting a horrible and lasting toll on their parents. Mary's smile; though beatific, was shadowed by sadness, while Thomas was stoic and better at hiding his emotions; often fortified by rum.

"We'll save more for another night, as I have a wonderful idea for a surprise!" She carefully lowered the cover over the keys, lovingly closing the frayed music book.

Mary wanted to know more about Douglas's wounded leg, her concerns not allayed by the sight of his swollen and festering limb, bound by a now messy, seeping bandage.

"It's usually not quite this bad, Mother. It's just because I've been riding for so many hours. It'll calm down after I rest."

Mary was not convinced and after dinner, while the men were smoking cigars on the porch, she hurried to the slave quarters to have Granny Moon fix a drawing poultice. Granny Moon resided as custodian of ancient herbal recipes for natural tinctures and native medicines from Africa. As the daughter and granddaughter of generations of revered shamans and as resident midwife, her effective painkillers, talismans and cures were legendary within the African communities.

But as Douglas suspected, they were not as effective painkillers as Thomas Dummett's full-bodied and aged rum! As dusk turned to dark and the men's laughter became louder, Mary excused herself to allow father and son to talk privately. Eventually, after more stories of Missouri pioneers and Osage skirmishes, Thomas leaned back in his rocker, drew a deep draw on his cigar, blowing a slow stream of smoke rings before he spoke.

"I'm hesitant to ask this, but why isn't Francesca with you, son?" The question hung heavily in the air between them.

Douglas, with now bleary eyes, turned towards his father. "I'm not ready to talk about her yet, but I sure would appreciate if you could send a bed warmer to my room, because I could really use the feel of a woman tonight."

Thomas nodded in understanding and slowly stood. "I'll send Chloe up. She's not the prettiest, but she knows how to pleasure a man; just make sure she leaves before your mother gets up in the morning. She won't take kindly to nigras being bedded under her roof."

Douglas staggered drunkenly up the stairs to his room, the pounding in his head challenging the incessant pain of his leg. Awkwardly pulling the buckskin shirt over his head, he fell heavily backwards onto the welcoming comfort of an overstuffed mattress. The quilt was familiar, and he knew guiltily that it was loving handiwork of his mother. As the room swirled, he drifted in and out of consciousness; slowly becoming aware of a young woman now standing beside the bed. Crawling between the sheets and straddling atop him; she expertly worked at untying leather lacings of his pants with delicate fingers. He couldn't make out her facial features in the darkness, but moonlight revealed a smile of straight, white teeth, a white eyelet shift, and shiny black hair…long black hair.

The young man startled out of his reverie. "FRANCESCA?? FRANCESCA?!!"

Before the girl could answer or react, he lashed out angrily; punching her full in the face breaking her nose, blood spray spattering across the pristine linens. Douglas slid off the bed dragging the stunned girl sideways and onto her knees, flipping her onto her belly. Yanking her backwards toward him, he threw the nightgown over her head exposing her bare buttocks.

"IS THIS THE WAY YOU LIKE IT, BITCH?? IS THIS THE WAY??!!"

Panicked and sobbing from the unexpected and brutal attack, Chloe tried crawling away from him, but jerking her back he furiously thrust into her as she screamed in pain. His rampage was exacerbated by her cries and flailing that only further enraged him. Choking her... hitting... punching...every bit of hurt and anger in his being flailed down on the helpless slave.

Thomas, Big John, and Etta came running at the screams, flinging open the door. It was all the two men could do to drag Douglas off the struggling girl. As they wrestled with him, Etta gathered the bloody, crumpled form on the bed, wrapping the hysterical girl in a blanket; helping her out of the room. Mary stood in the doorway, horrified at the violence, both hands over her mouth as her son collapsed, spent and exhausted against the wall. Thomas motioned for Big John and Mary to leave. Sliding down to the floor, he pulled his sobbing son against his chest.

"I caught her, Father; I caught her with a man...my Francesca! My beautiful...Francesca!!!"

"Hush, boy. Hush. We'll talk tomorrow."

Deep in the dark, African night songs echoed through ancient trees from the slave quarters; throbbing with rhythmic words of an American hymn of sadness, resignation...and the pulse of grief. Low voices sang in slow cadence and perfect harmony.

"Steal away... steal away... steal away to Jesus.
Steal away, steal away home...I ain't got long... to stay here."

Thomas continued rocking his distraught son until the younger man fell into the fitful sleep of lost and tormented souls.

SEVEN

The next few days were mostly lost on the younger Dummett, acquiescing to his mother's cajoling and accepting African poultices and tinctures administered to his leg wound by Granny Moon. Her famous concoctions in this new territory were much sought and bartered for by other settlers trying to survive wilderness illnesses and injuries without care of doctors and 'modern' medicine. Smooth black stones, cold from soaking in icy spring water, were placed on and along his leg; soothing and cooling the feverish swelling aggravated by his long ride. He hated to admit, but it was nice to be fussed over and tended after so many years of being self-sufficient on the Plains. Leaning back on plush pillows, he closed his eyes, luxuriating in his mother's silken soft linens. Congo Bob's youngest son, ten year old Kojo, tasked with fanning Douglas with a large palmetto frond, stood beside the bed, rhythmically waving light breezes over his face and body and shooing a persistent mosquito. Blessed sleep claimed him as he drifted between frontier perils and restless dreams of Francesca's face, finally able to escape the curse of pain and hyper-alertness… trusting his safety to his loving and watchful family…he slept.

A week after his arrival at Rosetta, dogs once again signaled an unexpected arrival. Francesca led a wagon loaded with covered boxes and furniture being driven by one of six slaves, the rest perched atop the lading. Three fillies and two cows tied to the rear of the wagon were in addition to the team of four wagon horses, and the tall elegant mare the young Mrs. Dummett rode.

Douglas strode onto the porch to confront her as she dismounted, approaching the steps flanked by barking hounds. Francesca knelt in the dust in front of her stoic husband, her arms outstretched.

"I know you are angry with me, and you are right to be; but I'm here as your wife, asking …begging for your forgiveness… forgiveness for a most shameful mistake of a foolish girl. I love you, and once you loved me. Please, I pray you can you find it in your heart to forgive me…and take me back as your wife? I promise to spend the rest of my life showing you how much I love you. Please, Douglas. I beseech you. I love you!"

Francesca grasped Douglas's legs, pulling her anguished face against his knees, waiting for a reply.

After an interminably long breathless silence, Douglas could only muster, "What is this wagon…these slaves, and this livestock??"

Standing to answer him, Francesca wiped her eyes.

"This is my dowry. If you send me away, I shall have nowhere to go. My father has sent me to you, in hopes that you are a better husband, than I a wife. If you cannot accept me as a wife, it is my sincerest hope that you will at least let me be your partner, to live with you in whatever relationship you deem. Your dream as you wrote…is Mount Pleasant, and it is also mine. I bring slaves to help build it, livestock to start with, household goods to furnish it…and gold to fund it. I can be a good wife, Douglas, if you will only give me another chance and let me try."

Douglas looked at the wagon, then back at his young wife, her words and his own emotions swirling in his head. Rocking back and forth, looking at the ground; he brought his eyes to connect with hers.

"I don't know if I will ever love you again...if I ever can love you, again. I can make no promises." Douglas turned to the mystified face of his mother, standing behind him in the doorway.

"Mum, would you show Francesca to the guest room next to mine? She is probably in need of a water basin and towels before dinner. I'll get this wagon stowed under cover in the barn and get her valise. Big John, show these boys where to tend to the animals and where to bed down...and have Clarice get them some tea and goat meat."

Douglas climbed onto the buckboard, chucked the reins heading for the barn, leaving Francesca standing alone in front of the house. Mary stepped down off the porch, opening her arms to her contrite daughter-in-law.

"You've had a long journey, dear. Let's go inside, I'll show you to your room and get you some cool lemonade. You're probably ready to get this road dust washed off."

With the charm and manners of a cultured, well-bred woman, Mary Dummett led Francesca up the stairs to the guest room as directed by her son. Leaving the young woman to settle in, Mary returned down to the great room where Thomas was leaning on the fireplace, throwing down a shot of rum.

"It is not up to us to question!" cautioning her husband, she put her finger to her lips. "I'll take one of those, please."

EIGHT

Journal entry; 3 May, 1830

I do not know if Francesca and I will weather this dark and windy storm. My head spins in one direction; my heart pulls in another. She was my Love, my whole being. If only there was a wise sage on a mountain to guide me. Father says only I can make that decision. I don't know. I just don't know...

> *'She gave to me, a rose;*
> *and vows on breezes borne.*
> *The wind dispersed her promises*
> *...my blood is on the thorn.'*

Enduring a week avoiding the obvious, Douglas finished a bottle of merlot with dinner; then poured a tumbler of rum before joining Francesca on the porch. Mary and Thomas wisely remained inside to give the young couple privacy to talk. The evening was sultry while the Tomoka River sat flat and dark in the breezeless heat. Struck by Francesca's beauty, his heart ached, her obvious sadness with his rejection playing darkly across her face. He wanted to hold her, to kiss her...but the memory of her betrayal burned in his brain, holding him back. In silence, they rocked in high-backed wicker porch chairs listening as a distant nightingale called for his mate. Neither could breach the void between them. Francesca finally stood, smiling with sad eyes, and dejectedly turned slowly, entering the house in silent resignation. Douglas watched her leave, his heart lurching as lantern light from inside illuminated her soft and flawless skin. He took another deep swallow of rum, swirling the smooth libation in his mouth, savoring the distinctly sweet, woody flavor, waiting for its magic to soothe the throbbing in his leg, and hoping it would quiet the aching in his heart.

Mary came out onto the porch sitting next to Douglas in the rocker Francesca had just deserted. Mother and son rocked slowly, their senses filling with scents of jasmine and Mary's roses as the river drifted by, reflecting moonbeams on its mirrored face. Strobes of moonlight through slowly waving palms danced at the slightest breeze. Mary cleared her throat, wanting to impart motherly wisdom to her obviously hurting son, but unsure of exactly what to say…or how to say it. With a silent prayer for the right words, she jumped into difficult waters of a long held and personal secret.

"Douglas, many years ago, your father and I came very close to ending our marriage. After enduring the deaths of our first three children, we pulled apart, not because we didn't love one another, but because to look at the other… brought renewed grief. I could not look at him without seeing the faces of our precious babes, and it was too painful to bear. I cried until there were no more tears, and I dried up inside, closed my heart to everything I loved…including your father. I could not understand how he could smile, or laugh, or proceed with life when I thought I would surely die of the loss. He stood stoic, strong, and seemingly uncaring. As I withdrew and my rejection wore on… he sought solace with another woman."

Mary took a deep breath; turning to look directly into Douglas's shocked eyes as she continued, tears welling in hers.

"And I...I sought relief in the arms of another man; a man with a new and unfamiliar face who could smile at me without mirroring the same pain I was feeling. It was a time in my life that I shall forever regret, and am profoundly, profoundly sorry of. When Thomas finally came to me with the confession of his indiscretion, his sincerity and tears at causing me even more grief were so great, we held each other and cried. We had not before done that together. I realized then what I had forgotten. He was my one true love forever, and that I would spend the rest of my life loving only him, being the best and most faithful wife I could be. I have suspected that he knew, but I never told your father about the other man, and I beseech you to keep my confidence. This secret I carry will torment me beyond death, and I am sorry to burden you with it, but Douglas, it breaks my heart to see you struggling with your feelings. I know Francesca has hurt you deeply; and that she acted foolishly, and I am so, so sorry about that. But, I implore you to consider her youth and obvious regret in her transgression. Love can be very hard, my son, even the most perfect love in the most perfect circumstance, so I share with you, this truth. Your broken heart will heal, though it will protect itself by preserving one part that will remain only unto you, so you can never be hurt so completely, again. This, my dear Douglas, that battered piece of your mended heart, is the price we pay for betrayal."

Mary kissed her son's cheek, smoothed her hair, and dabbed her eyes with a white cotton handkerchief pulled from her bosom.

"Please, do not make this decision with your head. In this instance, in this crucial time...listen to your heart. Never settle just for someone with whom you can live...choose the one you cannot live without."

Douglas stood as his mother arose to walk to the door. Suddenly turning and stepping back to him, she threw her arms around his neck, hugging him close.

"One last snippet of advice I took from my old and wizened Aunt Kate: if you choose to take Francesca back, you can never, ever serve her indiscretion to her for breakfast, or your hearts will never mend. Decide to love her and move on from here…or don't, and send her away. I love you, sweetheart!" Leaning back smiling up at her son, Mary took his anguished face into her hands; then turning…she went back inside.

Douglas remained outside until mosquitoes finally ran him in. Without smudge pots burning, the tiny beasts were merciless. The only night relief to be found was in the comfort of a bed shrouded in fine netting. Throwing back another shot of liquor to help him sleep and rubbing the persistent ache in his leg, he limped up the stairs. Passing to his room, the glow of candlelight still flickering from under Francesca's door caught his attention. Stepping into his bed chamber long enough to retrieve a small pouch from his dresser, he turned debating with himself before returning to the guest room. The door sat ajar in the jamb, taunting in its welcome, enticing in what he knew was on the other side. Standing in the hall arguing with himself; myriad feelings and his mother's words of advice jumbled in his head until he caught the light scent of orange blossoms from the room. Closing his eyes, he breathed deeply, allowing his brain to absorb the sweet nectarous aroma; then slowly pushed the heavy door inward. Francesca sat at the ornate dressing table across the small room, that was made more cramped by the antique walnut bed that had belonged to his grandparents; now a valued heirloom of his mother's dowry.

After Mary's marriage to Thomas, a British Marine Officer; the newlyweds moved the treasured bed to Barbados from England. Carpenters were hired to disassemble it years later for transport to the territory of Florida in the new world of America. It remained stored while they lived in St. Augustine; then moved for a while to Connecticut before they purchased Rosetta. Here, the revered bed was carefully reconstructed and topped with a plush mattress over filled with cotton and down over a bottom pad filled with moss. Aged and fragile, the bed was placed in the guest room so not to bear constant usage. It was an elegant and irreplaceable piece, bringing great pride to Mary who polished it faithfully.

Francesca was sitting with her back to Douglas, carefully brushing her hair by a single candle while looking into the dressing table's mirror. Startled when she saw him in the doorway behind her, she continued making eye contact with him in the glass. Catching her breath and hesitating slightly, she resumed brushing. Douglas awkwardly stepped into the room, closing the door behind him. With their eyes still locked, he walked around the footboard till he stood behind his wife, taking the brush from her hand. Slowly, he ran the bristles of the pearl handled implement through her long hair, becoming giddy at the silky touch of it. Closing her eyes as he stroked, enjoying the sensations of her husband gently brushing her thick, lustrous hair rippling in ebony waves down her back. Neither knew how to break the killing silence; until Douglas finally spoke to her in the familiar voice she remembered…soft, without anger, without heartbreaking hurt.

"I brought you gifts from the West. For months I would turn them in my hands, admiring and imagining how beautiful they would be on you. There were times my dreams were so real I woke, feeling you standing beside my cot. When you weren't there, I found comfort in knowing soon, you would be wearing these against your skin; and that never again would we be apart."

Reaching into the soft doeskin pouch, Douglas withdrew a heavy silver necklace lavishly set with a large turquoise stone surrounded by smaller ones of coral and lapis. Designs engraved into the silver were foreign, depicting birds and bison, while other stones ranging in colors of green and azure accented the beautifully worked and silver beaded chain. Lifting her hair while he fastened the necklace at her nape, the center stone shone against her ivory skin, resting at the start of her cleavage. Long matching silver drop earrings, hanging with turquoise, completed the set. Dropping her hair, she appeared as a princess of Cheyenne royalty. Tentatively touching and stroking the aqua gem, she marveled at the smoothness and veined beauty of the stone. With her color flushing in response to racing of her heart, her cheeks burned red as a warm tingling sensation spread deep in her belly. As her breathing labored, her chest heaved causing the turquoise to lift and fall in her décolletage. Still facing the mirror, Francesca wordlessly responded to his gift, slowly opening and letting her dressing gown slide from her shoulders to the velvet bench where she sat, exposing herself to the waist. Candlelight revealed unmistakable arousal of erect nipples; dark against the paleness of her skin. Time was lost to him as Douglas stared at her reflection, admiring her agonizing beauty. Finally, with no further invitation necessary, Douglas reached around her, cupping and squeezing her breasts in his hands, kissing her neck until she spun into his arms.

Falling onto the bed, Douglas was surprised at how easily and painlessly he was able to pull off his buckskins without feeling the usual ache in his leg. Thrashing with his shirt, Francesca helped pull it over his head; her robe already puddled on the floor. In one quick movement he rolled her onto her back, her lush body glistening nakedly in the heat. Raising herself up onto her elbows; her smile and lips rose to meet his, her legs opening in antici-pation…and welcome. Once again, he found himself driven to madness by desire for her and her passionate response to him as they rolled and chased; touching and teasing; slow strokes pound-ing into violent thrusts on the fragile feather mattress. Feeling the familiar welling in his loins; Douglas was unprepared for the sudden explosion of pure wanton lust.

Just as a primal howl ripped from his throat; the aged slats gave, antique walnut legs splayed outward, the ancient bed crack-ing and moaning before dropping the lovers unceremoniously to the floor in a splintering crash. Both headboard and footboard folded inward over the top of the couple, burying them in a pile of walnut rubble and a misty fog of fluttering down. The may-hem brought Thomas, Mary, and two house slaves running to the room. Panicked, they threw open the door where Mary's lantern exposed a sight no daughter-in-law would ever want her in-laws to see.

Momentarily stunned at the raunchy vision of nudity, carnage, and clouds of feathers floating before them; the elder Dummetts stood awkwardly taking in the scene of destruction, relieved by Douglas and Francesca's chagrined laughter that there were no in-juries. Sheepishly, their son peered out from under the headboard with a meek and obvious explanation…

"Uh…the bed broke!"

With the hilarity of the situation causing the young couple to howl in embarrassed but boisterously uncontrolled laughter, Mary stood speechless and wide-eyed, her lips quivering; staring in shock at the obliteration of her parent's wedding bed. Wordlessly; Thomas pulled her backwards out of the room, hustling the grinning slaves out and closing the door behind them.

Freeing the moss-stuffed under mattress from among the wreckage and spreading it on the floor, Douglas hugged Francesca to him on the makeshift pallet, her hands covering her mortified face.

"Well, Mrs. Dummett, if you can quit laughing, we are going to have to try that again… until we get it right!! Let's just pray this time the floor holds!!"

Laughter rang through the old house, reverberating from the small upstairs room, only to be matched by the hilarity in the slave quarters at the repeated and exaggerated telling of the event.

Once again, Douglas felt the truth of the saying that night was made for madmen and poets; and on this night, this very special night…it would also prove to be magically made for fatherhood.

NINE

"We need to talk, son."

Douglas could tell by the worry shadowing his father's face, the topic was of great importance. Choking back tears as he spoke, Thomas's words fell in a torrent of pent up heartache.

"It's your mother; she hasn't been well. My beautiful Mary is being beset by dementia. For most times she is fine, but other times... she struggles to remember what was recently familiar. I see fear on her lovely face I have never seen before, and it breaks my heart I am helpless to stop its cruel ravage."

"Sit down, Father. Tell me what I can do."

The two men sat next to each other at the table, Thomas leaning forward covering his son's hand with his.

"This is my plan: though not immediately, my intent is to take your mother to the city comfort of our home in St. Augustine. We are both bearing infirmities of the loss of youth, and would have more ease in our old age with nearby benefit of trained doctors. My hope was to have you become familiar with the mill to take over operations here at Rosetta in my stead, as in time, she will be yours. I have drawn up papers for that end; and also to leave the town home in St. Augustine to your sisters. I would additionally count on you to ensure they receive equitable sustenance from the income of Rosetta after my death."

Thomas paused, arthritic hands shaking, nervous in the following silence as he searched his son's face. Douglas's brow furrowed as he pondered his father's words, rocking as he thought. Finally he spoke; taking his father's gnarled hands in his.

"Certainly, Father, I will manage Rosetta with the love you have shown, and your dream will be mine. However, please understand I also intend to pursue building Mount Pleasant on my parcel in New Smyrna. It will be manageable with the able help of your overseer and Big John. I will share time, effort, and concern between both."

Forcing a smile, Thomas shook his head in assent. "You don't know how relieved that makes me, son. I was afraid with your excitement over plans for Mount Pleasant; you would not be willing to assume responsibility or burden of two plantations."

"When that time comes, your only thoughts are to be about Mum. From when you choose, from that day forth, any worry about Rosetta will be carried by me; so make what plans you need for her eventual care."

Douglas hugged his father who was now wiping tears of relief with the back of his hand.

"I will tell your mother when the time is right, but for now, let's not worry her and continue as before. There is much for you to learn."

The next few weeks were lost in a flurry of mill preparations. After the death of Thomas's old friend and fellow planter and rum maker, Rezin Bowie, his sons, Rezin and Jim, decided to sell Bowie's 1800 acre sugar cane plantation 'Arcadia' near Thibodeaux, Louisiana. Younger son Jim was anticipating resettling in Texas. Rezin Sr. was the first planter to buy and use steam powered equipment in Louisiana from the Cold Springs foundry in New York to process his sugar cane as Thomas Dummett was the first in Florida. A deal by Bowie's sons had been struck for

Thomas to buy the elder Rezin's equipment to enlarge Dummett's processing ability at 'Rosetta'. Two Bowie sons, Jim and Rezin Jr., along with several slaves were to deliver the equipment verily by steamboat then wagons. Foundations needed to be excavated and laid up with stone while additional chimneys would be built prior to the new equipment's installation. A contingent of slaves set to digging and stone bracing a third well to supply fresh water on site for boiling the cane. Rosetta buzzed with activity related to the construction, the labors consuming father and son during relentlessly hot days. Evenings were spent pouring over plans and dimensions for the younger Dummett's Mount Pleasant. Now Francesca was joining in the planning excitement for the New Smyrna plantation.

"WAAAA-GONS COMING IN!!!!"

Excitement spread throughout Rosetta with the much anticipated arrival of brothers Jim and Rezin Bowie. Each drove one of two overladen buckboards, straining under weight of the steam engine and other processing equipment. Four muscular slaves were brought along for unloading and additional rifle protection during the long and hazardous journey from Rapides Parrish, Louisiana. The travelers were hot and exhausted after the grueling trek.

Thomas and a pack of screeching hounds were the first to greet the sons of his old friend.

"WELCOME TO FLORIDA, BOYS!! WHAT TOOK YOU SO LONG?!!"

Rough-hewn and tobacco stained, Jim Bowie was a mountain of a man. Jumping down from the wagon exaggeratedly rubbing his backside, he grabbed Thomas; hugging and swinging the older man so vigorously they almost fell.

Legends of Jim's prowess as a frontiersman and knife fighter were not exaggerated. The menacing Bowie knife made famous by his exploits hung ready under his left arm, secured by a leather cross-draw scabbard over his shoulder. A holstered pistol hung from his belt.

"Look at you boys! That Louisiana Cajun food must be agreeing with you!!"

Rezin Bowie, just as rawboned as his younger brother, was actually taller but with a more restrained personality. He shook the elder Dummett's hand, embracing and also lifting him off the ground to the amusement of the gathering crowd and concern of barking dogs.

"Your arrival couldn't have come at a better time; Douglas just came home a few weeks ago, and we all could use some laughter and some of those big Louisiana lies!!"

"Douglas wrote he was getting out early because of that damned Injun shooting his leg. I was hoping to get to see him, brought him a present for him and his missus."

Jim Bowie missed the flinch his comment caused Thomas.

"Big John, take these wagons to the barn, get 'em unhitched and teams watered and fed…and show these boys where they can wash up and spread their rolls. I'll have Etta bring dinner from the house for them. They can rest up tonight. We'll unload tomorrow!"

"Come on, you two! Mary and Douglas are inside, and we're going to show you what REAL rum tastes like, not that fake Louisiana sugar water you're used to! Your daddy never could figure out my secret recipes!!"

Laughing, the three men crossed Rosetta's front porch where Mary excitedly rushed them, embracing the two with spirited hugs.

"Lordy! Lordy!! You boys are a welcome sight. We don't get much company out here; this is going to be a celebration for sure! Congo Bob went crabbing and shrimping last night…it must have been in the stars for you to arrive today! How is your mother, is she well?"

"Mary, Mary!! Let these boys get into the house!!" Thomas kissed his wife while laughing at her excitement.

"Clarice, show our guests where they can wash up!! I'll break the seal on a bottle of our best rum. I think they need a little fortification from their journey…and they look a might thirsty to me!!"

Pulling a magnum from the sideboard, Thomas poured a healthy amount of deep mahogany liquor into pewter steins.

"OH, MY GOD! LOOK WHAT RUMMIES THE DOGS DRAGGED IN!!" Limping gingerly down the stairs, Douglas grinned at the sight of their old friends who were thirstily downing the rum.

"You must rate for Father to break open the 'SPECIAL' rum. He didn't do that when I got home!!"

Douglas wrapped Jim Bowie with an enthusiastic embrace, pounding on his shoulder. "GOOD GAWD, man…I didn't think you could get any uglier. I was WRONG!!!!"

"I heard you slowed down to let some crippled Injun catch you and scratch your leg. Some people will do anything to get out of the Army early!! If you promise to keep this excellent nectar flowing; I'll show you what a REAL man's scars look like…if you're not too lily-livered, that is!!"

When the merriment abated, Jim and Rezin followed Clarice upstairs, returning shortly minus road grime and wearing clean shirts. The Dummett family was already seated at the massive farm table where Thomas was refilling steins with more dark, sweet libation. Both Bowie brothers leaned and kissed Francesca on the cheek as they passed her chair.

"You are almost the prettiest thing I've ever seen," Jim exclaimed. "I have to say 'almost', because one of the reasons I'm selling out in Louisiana and moving to Texas is because of a young Mexican beauty I'm taking for my wife!"

"Congratulations and CHEERS," Mary raised her glass causing the others to lift theirs in a joint toast. "What is the lucky lady's name?"

Jim Bowie smiled widely, showing a gap of a missing tooth. "Thank you, I didn't expect to find another woman willing to tolerate me after Cecelia's death. I'm not real sure how lucky SHE is, but her name is Ursula De Veramendi, and she's purtier than a spotted filly. I'm done with scouting Cheyenne and wrestling grizzlies! I'd just like to live out my time on a small horse ranch, maybe raise some cotton, and stay put with a sweet tempered wife and have a passel of babies! Might do a little silver mine hunting on the side!" Bowie rocked his chair onto the back legs, emptying his stein in one breath.

"WOO-HOO!! KICK A BULL AND SLAP HIS MOMMA!! That's some SMOOTH DRINKIN'!!"Bowie snorted, wiping his shirtsleeve across his mouth. "I'm so hungry; my big ones are eatin' my little ones!!"

Thomas choked, spewing liquor from his nose as everyone laughed at his response. Etta and Clarice scurried about, carting mounds of roasted hog, shrimp, and fried blue crabs, butter beans, and sweet potato pie garnished with pecans to the long table. Blue skies of afternoon turned to violet as laughter and family stories bounced off the walls.

"Ma Etta, that was some damn fine grub!"

Mary stood, tapping her glass with a spoon, ringing for the attention of the room.

"I have a present for Douglas, and I think this is the perfect time to give it to him. "BIG JOHN!"

Grinning, Big John came proudly from the kitchen with Douglas's gleaming cello.

"I jus' got back from St. Augustine with dis big fiddle where its been packed up waitin' for you to come home. Your Mama wanted you to have it real bad, knowin' how you used to love playin' it. Me and Etta shore miss listnin' to you and your Mama makin' dat purty music!"

"Oh, good Lord, I haven't played that cello in at least five years! Mum; thank you! Thank you for keeping it all this time." Douglas got up to run his hands over the burled maple face, stroking a tentative nail across the strings.

"I have had the bow professionally restrung and rosined for you," Mary hugged her son, greatly pleased with her surprise.

"Please, won't you try it, it won't take long to regain your skill, and how lovely it would be to hear this beautiful instrument played in this savage wilderness?"

"Come on, Douglas, play for us, you're among friends!" Bowie grinned at him. "I don't think I've ever seen a fiddle that big!"

"Alright, you asked for it, Jim! Never let it be said that I, in any way, hindered your cultural education in the arts! Prepare to have your first lesson in the …'big fiddle'! Mum, the only piece I might be able to remember is Bach's 'Ave Maria'. Will you accompany me?"

"I would be delighted!" Pulling sheet music from the piano bench; Mary opened the cover over the ivory keys, striking notes for Douglas to tune his strings. "Wait, this old woman needs her spectacles."

Douglas turned to his audience, bowing with an exaggerated flourish.

"Since this performance is unrehearsed, there will be no charge; however, bring your money pouches in the future. I will expect compensation in gold for my concerts."

"Sit down and play before I get Etta to bring us tomatoes!" Jim was enjoying his friend's obvious nervousness.

Finally seated at the keyboard, Mary began playing the intricate intro while Douglas scooted his chair beside the piano, pulling the cello in front of him. Slowly drawing the bow across horsehair strings, the instrument came to life, thrilling the appreciative audience with the melancholy sadness of the violoncello's song. Vibrating into the breeze, rich tones rose and fell, wafting through open windows, the elegant composition as plaintively beautiful as played in any cathedral. Surprised at muscle memory still remaining from years of youthful chamber practice, Douglas closed his eyes letting the music fill him and the house to bursting. Leaning and rocking as he drew the bow back and forth, his hair falling across his face, the young man lost himself in the joy of his first love. The 'Ave Maria' ebbed and flowed until the last notes dwindled from the room, carried up and away into the night. Slave children stood outside their quarters under twinkling stars; stopping their games to listen quietly in wonder at this beautifully foreign and unexpected music. Bach had been brought to Florida's wilderness…and it was magical.

Bowie was first to break the stunned silence.

"Well I'll be goldurned if that weren't the beatingest thing I ever heard! Who knew a big fiddle could sound like that??!"

Laughter finished breaking the spell Bowie's comment had started.

Douglas kissed the soft silver hair on his mother's head, smiling into her face. "Thank you for reminding me how much I missed music." He was touched by the sudden tears in her eyes.

Francesca got up to hug him. "I had forgotten how beautifully you played. I loved it, it was wonderful!"

Giving his wife a cursory peck on the cheek, he winked and laughed. "Let's see how you feel about it in twenty years!"

"Now, I'm ready for more rum and Louisiana lies! What's the next move for the infamous Bowie brothers?"

Standing the cello against the craggy fireplace, he smoothed his hair, retying the leather thong holding it back. Dragging his chair back to the table where his father was refilling their mugs, he stretched his fingers, amazed and pleased his calloused hands were still so responsive on the strings.

"I'm applying for land grants in Texas since we've sold out Father's sugar mill and land which gave me some cash to invest. Mother's going to stay in Louisiana with Rezin and his family; I've always had the wanderlust and Texas has big skies that are callin' to me, and Ursula's father is interested in a partnership to build a cotton mill in the province of Coahuila y Tejas. I figure that once we get set up there, I'll commence to search for one of those lost silver mines...especially the one the Tejanos and Bexarenos talk most about; the Los Almagres mine in San Saba country. That is if I don't lose my scalp to those thievin' Comanches holed up in that part of the God forsakin', cactus ridden desert! Worst part is; I'll be expected to drink that Mescalero whiskey!! They say if you don't get enough wood cut, you can burn that stuff to heat your adobe!"

Laughing at his own joke, Jim motioned towards Clarice with his mug. It was promptly filled from the half empty decanter on the side table.

"Aren't you worried about the Mexican government?" Douglas leaned forward, concern showing on his questioning face. "I've heard talk that Santa Ana, the commandant of their military, is planning an insurgence into Texas territory to take it for Mexico. He's 'laying the table' by buying vessels in the Caribbean to build his navy; I read most recently, two in Jamaica that he's arming as war ships. When those are ready, it's believed his pure intent is to run patrols in Texas waters to blockade our ports to cut off all imports and exports through the gulf! If his efforts transpire, it's going to mean all-out war between the U.S. and Mexico!"

Bowie nodded at his friend. "It seems the U.S. has to fight for every inch we progress as a nation, and with every country that crosses our path! Andrew Jackson has the Maroons and native tribes so riled up and blood lusted; you're more than likely going to be fighting the Seminoles, again! Spain offered freedom to any runaway slaves in Florida to gain their allegiance to help fight the British. Now that Florida has been ceded to the U.S., General Jackson is using the weight of the federal government and Army soldiers as bounty hunters to round up all blacks and return them to their owners. That freed slave, John Caesar, has himself a Cree wife and family. He's smart and a damned good military leader... trained by the Spanish dragoons! Seminoles aren't takin' kindly to the white man breaking more treaties and settlers moving further into Florida. As for the Maroons; we've heard there's over a thousand, maybe up to sixteen hundred blacks hiding out in colonies in the central regions, nearly in your back yard...and they're making the Injuns their slaves! Me; well I'd rather be aiming my rifle at some gold-braided general wearing a red uniform, sittin' atop a horse; than tryin' to sight in on a ghost in the palmettos that I can't even see!"

Douglas shook his head in assent. "Well, old buddy, there is that! Micanopy, King Phillip, and Osceola have been amassing members from other tribes affected by their relocation. They're mostly Cree from Georgia that were pushed into northern Florida; and remnants from the Redlegs from Alabama, and of course the Maroons. Now Jackson wants to break their treaty and move them all to the Oklahoma territory. He's not real sympathetic with the Indians since the massacre at Fort Scott on the Appalachicola in '17. In fact, he's been a real bastard with them. Father has been trading peacefully with Seminoles for meat for years, but if they get pushed much further...they'll draw a line in the sand and fight to the death. King Phillip's son, Coacoochee, is a rising warrior in the Seminole nation. He's an excellent tactician; and pure savage. Settlers call him 'Wildcat' because of the way he stalks and attacks without warning...and he enjoys killing without regard to whether his victim is a man, woman, or child. They say he scalps babies alive, just so the mothers can watch and hear them scream...then he scalps the mothers. I've even heard stories that he cuts babies out of their mother's bellies while the women are still alive! "

"My thoughts are the government is touting this Indian relocation business as a cover to deal with another equally great threat facing all of us in the South," Thomas weighed in. "More and more slaves are running from their owners in other states to Maroon enclaves growing by the day in Florida. They indenture to the natives who allow them to keep part of the food they grow and livestock they steal and contribute the rest to the tribe. They're breeding with Cree and Muskogee and consider themselves and their families free, like they were under the Spanish. Though I don't agree with many of his Army's methods; Jackson is trying to return the slaves who are lost property to their rightful owners. John Caesar, along with being a runaway, is quite the statesman; and according to what I hear from other owners...he's riling plantation slaves all up and down the east coast for them to join the Maroons. Without slaves; there will be no one to work the fields! The South will die on the vine."

"Gentlemen, please, we are all aware we must live under constant threat. Certainly there is kinder conversation for this good evening." Mary raised both hands in a plea to change the topic.

"Before I forget, there's something I'd like to give Douglas and Francesca as a late wedding gift. Here's hoping you can use them sooner than later!"

Bowie handed Francesca a small leather bag secured by a drawstring. Reaching into it, she withdrew a pair of child's soft, fringed doeskin moccasins; intricately and colorfully beaded across the tops.

"I know it's early, but they're for the near future generations of Dummetts."

Surprised by sudden tears brimming her eyes; Francesca clutched the booties to her chest, touched at the rough frontiersman's thoughtfulness. "Thank you, Jim and Rezin...they're darling, absolutely darling."

"Thomas, would you have Daniel come in and play for us while you men enjoy your cigars?" Mary stood, causing all the men to rise from their chairs. "No, please gentlemen, don't get up. I fear the rum is telling me it's time for this old lady to adjourn, but I will enjoy Daniel's music from my room."

Francesca stood with her. "It has been a most enjoyable evening, sirs, but I too hear the nightingales and feel the need to lie down."

With good night hugs around, the women took leave to their bed chambers leaving the men to their steins, cigars, and Louisiana lies.

TEN

"ETTA, IS THAT FRIED PIE I SMELL???"
"Yassir, I be bringin' it now!"

"Gentlemen, should you ever wonder what goes good with rum and cigars; the answer is Etta's fried apple tarts!" Thomas was obviously pleased Ma Etta had surprised their guests with one of her specialties.

A platter of steaming, fried apple tarts was set in the center of the table; the lightly browned pastries dripping in a caramel butter sauce of brown sugar, cinnamon, and a touch of rum.

Well on their way to being drunk, the four friends disregarded offered plates and utensils, instead picking up the small pies with their hands, eating the delicacies like starving men.

"WHAT MADNESS IS THIS?? THESE ARE SURELY AMBROSIA FROM THE GODS!! MA ETTA…WILL YOU MARRY ME?" Jim's exclamation caused laughter around as they all toweled buttery caramel from their faces and hands.

A greying, slightly built slave entered the main room with a waxed and gleaming twelve-string guitar. Carefully setting the case by the fireplace and lifting the lavishly embroidered strap over his head…his eyes fluttered as he began to play. With fingers flying over the strings, the room alternated from Caribbean rhythms of flamenco, Scottish lilts, to slow throbbing runs of African lullabies; all approved and quietly discussed by night birds roosting in the eaves.

Obviously astonished, Bowie stood; enthusiastically clapping.

"I don't rightly remember ever hearing no darkie finger-pick a guitar like that!"

"He was my gift to Mary. His former owners, the Morgans, brought him down from Philadelphia where he was their house boy. They hired a music teacher to tutor their children in the guitar at their home; but Daniel was the only one who showed any knack or talent for the instrument. He picked it up by watching the man play and paying attention to his instructions. When they homesteaded down here, Mr. Morgan took ill and died. His widow sold everything to take her children back to family in the north, so at the sale; I bought Daniel and the guitar. He's not much of a field hand, they gelded him so he could be a house slave; and I don't want him ruining his hands. He doesn't talk much because of the hairlip; but he has been one of the best purchases I could have made for Mary. Music brings a semblance of civility this wilderness lacks and she misses; and it brings a smile to her beautiful face. Sometimes, we even light the candles some evenings and dance like we were newlyweds! He was a good buy, money well spent…"

Missing the sadness in the older man's voice, Bowie took a long swig of rum, savoring the sweet heat in his throat as it slowly washed down.

"Well, this Dummett family is the most all fired musical bunch I know, that's for sure. I'm thinking we're lucky you weren't requiring tickets at the door!" Rezin Bowie finally weighed in, usually content to sit back letting his more gregarious brother lead the conversation.

"BURNS… SO…GOOD!" Jim grinned at his host, slapping the table with a scarred hand missing part of a finger. "Good grub, good friends, and good drink! This is a surely damn fine night!! Well, Douglas, I see you're still carryin' the knife I gave you before you left for the Army." Bowie pulled his own blade from its scabbard, admiring the weight and exaggeratedly felt the sharpness of the hone.

Douglas laid his large, curved handled knife beside Bowie's on the family table. The blades were of the same size, but Douglas's had a more ornately engraved, curved handle above the cross piece.

"This blade cut through buffalo hide, tree branches for kindling, processed some of the finest deer jerky in the west, shaved my face, and on more occasions than I'd like to remember…it saved my scalp! I thank you for this gift, Jim. It has been the most valuable present I've ever received."

Bowie picked up Dummett's knife, admiring and slowly turning it in his large hands, now dwarfed by the blade.

"I'd like to take credit for these bad boys, but I only had the idea for dimensions. My brother here, forged them to my drawings so as to be big and thick enough to fight a grizzly or an Injun, but agile and balanced enough to throw at a rattlesnake. Can't tell you how many men have asked to buy mine from me…but when you've got a good, strong knife, you don't let it go…'cause it can make the difference between life or a very painful death!"

Rezin nodded his head in assent, beaming with pride at his brother's adulations.

"Since yours was a gift, after it was forged I had the handle silvered and engraved to 'pretty it up'. I'm grateful it has served you well and have to admit…this blade is definitely a huckleberry above a persimmon!"

Bowie raised his cup to Douglas who returned the salute, laughing in agreement.

"What's this I hear about you being such a slow horseman that some half-blind, crippled Osage was able to shoot you in the leg? Is that really true…or were you just corned?"

Douglas grinned at his friend's sarcasm, stood and undid his breeches, lowering them to show Bowie the ragged and still festering wound on his left thigh. "Yep, I'm thanking my stars he was shooting on the run and didn't get his rifle aimed higher! The Dummett family name might have ended right there! You were the one in the infamous 'Sandbar Fight'! I heard tall tales discussed about that one around the campfire from incoming soldiers. Seems New York newspapers were particularly fond of your exploits. I understand the more sensational the headline, the more papers that are sold; and from the way it was told, there's not one reason in the world you should be alive! In fact, some supposed that you are really just the ghost of Jim Bowie! How about you enlighten your friends with the truth of the matter…I acquiesce the floor!"

Retying his pants, Douglas bowed deeply with an exaggerated flourish toward Jim, saying…"Let the story-telling begin!!"

Bowie shook his head and laughed. Pushing out his chair and standing, he slipped the shoulder harness over his head unfastening and dropping his gun belt to the floor; then pulled up his shirt to reveal several ugly scars. One long, jagged wound, just off center of his chest was puffy, red, and particularly nasty. Gingerly running his thumb down the length of the scar, Bowie proceeded to explain.

"Sorry Douglas, but this night you're not the biggest toad in this puddle! This is my souvenir from the duel at the sandbar, but first things first, gentleman. The 'Sandbar Fight' happened mostly as a result of this earlier bullet hole on my left side," pointing to another scar, "and this missing tooth!" Bowie pulled his lower lip down, revealing a dark gap where a tooth should have been.

"If you've got plenty of combustibles, I've got plenty of story tellin'; but I best start at the beginning."

Refilling the men's cups, Thomas lit fat cigars for each; then settling down, rocked his chair onto its back legs in anticipation of Bowie's story. Jim took a long draw of the cigar, eyes closed, savoring the flavor and scent of the tobacco, blowing a quick series of smoke rings toward the ceiling. Leaning forward onto the table; Bowie smiled at the waiting faces and started with his tale.

"It was December 14, in 1826. I had just arrived back in Louisiana from a business trip, and Rezin and some other friends picked me up at the Alexandria wharf. On the trip to town they told me that damned Sheriff Norris Wright was telling lies about my land dealings and slandering my character. We found the son of a bitch with a bunch of his cohorts, playing cards in the lobby of Bailey's Hotel. I just intended to talk to him, but the mistake I made was leaving my pistols in my bag in the wagon. I still had my traveling suit on and only had a damned clasp knife in my vest. I confronted Wright calling him a liar; THEN THE BASTARD PULLED OUT HIS PISTOL AND POINTED IT AT ME!!"

Obviously incensed by the memory and well on his way to being drunk, the frontiersman accentuated a slug of rum by banging the mug decisively onto the table.

"The only thing I could pick up to defend myself with was a GOL-DURN CHAIR! Held it up in front of me like a lion-tamer in a circus to try and deflect his bullet. We stood there in a Mexican stand-off...him with a gun pointin' at me... me with a CHAIR pointin' at him! I decided since he was hesitating, I'd go on the offense; raised the chair up over my head and charged the chicken shit...AND THEN THE SON OF A BITCH SHOT ME!! Took the ball in my side, knocked me whopper jawed and made me drop that damned chair; I was mostly dumfungled but had enough speed to get to him and body slammed him before he could get off another shot. We fought and pummeled each other to bloody hell; rolling around the hotel lobby like a couple of wild hogs with people jumping out of our way or gettin' knocked over!"

"I finally got that fopdoodle on his back, me on top, and I pulled out that USELESS goldarn clasp knife trying to open it with my teeth. Almost had it open and locked when his and my buddies started draggin' me off him 'cause they knew my pure intent was to KILL the bastard! My friends were pullin' me backwards and his friends were pulling him out from under me, Wright swung on me one last time and I caught his fist and a finger with my teeth. Damn near bit it off. He screamed like a little girl, yanking his hand back; but he weren't fast enuff and went home with my front tooth stuck deep in the bone of his thumb! He and his friends thought he had killed me for sure and ran like sissies when they saw my blood trail, but the blood weren't so much from the gunshot...IT WAS FROM MY DAMN TOOTH!!"

Bowie scanned his stunned audience with a diabolical laugh. "Alright, gentlemen...guess what the goldarn moral of this story is?"

Douglas glanced over at his father sitting in stunned disbelief. He shrugged, shaking his head.

"We give up!! What's the goldarn moral?"

Bowie grinned wide with an incomplete lower row of teeth. "NEVER TAKE A CHAIR TO A DAMN GUNFIGHT!!!"

Thomas lurched forward choking; spitting and spewing rum spraying from his mouth and nose.

"GOOD GOD, JIM!! You're damned near going to make me choke to death!! If you think this rum burns going down your throat…you should feel the burn coming out through your nose!!!"

"Sorry guys, but I got to piss like a cow on a flat rock!" After laughter and table slapping subsided, the group went outside to answer nature's call off the side of the porch.

"Alright, Jim," Thomas chided, "I know you're a badass, and you go bear hunting with a stick, but if you pee on Miss Mary's roses, the devil himself won't be able to protect you!"

Bowie gave a 'thumbs up' and moved down the porch.

"Lordy, Jim, you about had me busting a gut!" Douglas rubbed both eyes with the heels of his palms. "I can't remember when I've laughed so hard! But I heard you killed that Sheriff?"

"Let's sit back down, heave one last drink and I'll tell you the rest of the story."

With everyone seated back at the gathering table, Bowie continued ….

"It seems the townfolk didn't take too kindly to any man, even a Sheriff… shootin' a man armed with a chair! Whole incident served to bring him down in the eyes and popularity of his constituents and voters. His dislike for me…and my animosity for him…just grew to a bodacious hatred. I learned a hard lesson because of that fight. No matter how I might be dressed, or where I might be goin', even if I don't have my pistols on me; I'll always have my 'Louisiana Sticker' in a scabbard on my waist or under my arm. I'll never again miss a necessary kill because of seconds wasted trying to open a damned clasp knife with my goldurn teeth! If there's a next time…thanks to my brother, here…I'll be ready!"

To add emphasis to his statement, Jim slammed his namesake knife onto the table, the blade flashing in the lantern light.

After the near brush with death, and recuperating from that fight in the Bailey Hotel, Jim Bowie was true to his word. Spending weeks in bed recovering from his gunshot wound, he used the time fashioning and tooling a leather scabbard to measurements of a huge knife he envisioned and described to his older brother. While visiting him, Rezin made a drawing of a large dagger to Jim's specifications. Knowing his brother's propensity for hand to hand fighting, Rezin had his blacksmith fire up the forge at his Louisiana plantation, Avoyelles, and used an old file for the iron stock, hammering out a strong, burly knife forged to Jim's design and measurements. The blade was wide by a bit over nine inches long…thick and heavy with a curved tip. A keen edge was honed on one side with a grinder; then a crosspiece added, separating the handle from the blade to keep the user's hand from sliding down the razor edge. Simple, heavy and completely utilitarian, the knife was a frightening weapon to behold. Rezin proudly gifted his brother this massive frontier dagger, later to become known as the famous 'Bowie Knife'. Jim Bowie was never again without the storied blade secured to his belt, swearing to his brothers the promise he would "wear it as long as he lived." And he did.

"Tell 'em about the 'Sandbar Fight'," Rezin urged.

Refreshed and relieved, the four men made themselves comfortable, savoring freshly filled mugs, and noisily sucking on juicy peach slices Clarice had just set in the center of the table.

"Okay, Jim. Finish the story on how you killed that Sheriff

Wright while I'm still sober enough to appreciate it!" Douglas's comment caused laughter around.

"Well, as directly as I can, old Wright and I weren't even supposed to fight on that particular day, September 19, 1827. I remember it well. Two other idiots were dueling on the river sandbar just outside of Natchez…on the Mississippi side. It had turned into quite a spectacle with, they say, a boodle of about two-hundred drunken fools out to witness some bloodshed. We were seconds for them; me for Cecelia's pa, Montfort Wells; and Wright for Thomas Maddox… but it was high noon, hotter than Hell, and neither Wells nor Maddox could hit the broad side of a barn! After two times of each of them firing and missing each other, they decided to shake hands and call their differences settled!"

"Maddox, Wright, and their friends started walking off the sandbar… with Wells and our friends walking behind, when the first group reached the trees one of the bastards named Crain swung around with a gun and commenced firing at me! I drew my pistol and shot a hole in his cravat…and holy hell broke loose!! Crain pulled another pistol, shot at me but hit Dr. Cuny in the thigh, severing an artery! I missed with my second pistol, but thanks to Rezin here, I had my trusty knife!! I ran after that running son-of-a bitch with full intent to row him up Salt Crick and yelled, 'CRAIN, YOU HAVE SHOT AT ME; AND I WILL KILL YOU IF I CAN!!!' The bastard pulled foot but then turned around and threw his empty pistol at me, caught me in the side of the head, knocked me to my knees! 'Bout that time, all those scoundrels, Wright included, turned and charged me. I didn't have a gun now, both being empty, and saw Wright raise his. I yelled at him…"SHOOT, AND BE DAMNED!!!!"

Bowie stood, angry at the recollection, slamming his mug

causing rum to splash over the side. Yanking his shirt open, he exposed his scar covered torso and started jabbing at specific welts and angry red lesions with a crooked finger.

"Wright's bullet hit me full in the breast going clear through my lung. The asshole turned to run but I lunged at him, almost had him when the two bastard Blanchard brothers shot me twice more. The bullet in my leg took me down. That's when the two cowards, Wright and one of the Blanchards came at me with their swords. I was on my back and pretty well hacked, they were thrustin' and cuttin'; I was thrashing best I could, cut Wright pretty good twice, but he stabbed me clear through. Bent his sword on my breastbone, then the blade slipped down through these two ribs pinning me to the ground. They thought they had killed me 'cause I was layin' real still playin' 'possum. Wright stood over me with a big, stupid smile, put his foot on my chest to pull out his sword, but then made the fatal mistake of leaning down over me. I smiled up into his ugly mug and said, "Now, Major, YOU DIE!!" With everything I had left in me, I swung my knife up, cut through his heart strings, and gutted him like the dirty swine he was!! He looked down at me with wide black eyes. He knew I had killed him. He crumpled and fell on top of me, his fat ass so heavy I couldn't move!! That damned Blanchard kept stabbing me till Wells shot him. I cut him pretty good though, too!"

"They convened a damned Grand Jury in Natchez with that pansy prosecutor wanting to indict me for murdering the Sheriff, but there were enough witnesses who saw I was defendin' myself and purely justified in cuttin' that bastard's heart out."

"You wanted to know the story of the Sandbar Duel. That was it. Took me damn near a year to get back on my feet again, and here I am…still kickin'; not as high as I used to, spittin' blood now and again; but still kickin' and ready to dance with the Devil!"

Douglas, Thomas, and Rezin sat stunned and speechless; the descriptive horror of the fight and gravity of Jim's wounds affecting them all.

Douglas raised his decanter leading the others in a toast.

"Here's to you, old friend…I always thought your bear and gator wrestling scars were the worst I had ever seen. Apparently the devil doesn't want you, or from what I've heard…HE COULDN'T STAND THE COMPETITION!!"

"ALMIGHTY GAWD!" Thomas stood up, scraping the chair backwards on the floor. "Don't know about the rest of you, but that fight exhausted the hell out of me!! I'm going to join my Mary upstairs."

After hugs around, the men adjourned to their beds. Along with horrific scars and nightmares; Jim Bowie would suffer with bouts of consumption and lung problems from injuries he sustained in the 'Sandbar Duel' for the rest of his life.

Journal entry; 12 June 1830

It is unfathomable what our friend, Jim Bowie, has suffered. Newspaper reports and campfire retellings of the 'Sandbar Duel', though gruesome themselves, did not do justice to the barbarism and true bloody mayhem of the fight. I have read various accounts of him as a frontiersman, referring to him as a 'Tiger' in battle. I have no words to describe what we just heard. We are fortunate to not have lost him…I cannot believe he still lives.

Jim and Rezin extended their stay, riding with Douglas to his homestead parcel in New Smyrna. He was anxious to show their friends the beauty of the island, the excellent situation between the ocean and river, and the building spot he had chosen for Mount Pleasant's house and slave quarters. They had seen his plans and drawings at Rosetta and were now able to visualize his descriptions of the plantation's layout, sharing in his excitement. Before leaving New Smyrna, Bowie extended invitations to Douglas and Francesca to come west to visit him and the beautiful Senorita Veramendi after their marriage in Texas.

ELEVEN

Mount Pleasant slowly rose from Douglas's dreams, materializing on the shady riverbank from tightly grained oak, long leaf pine, and native limestone. He kept true to plans he envisioned those long Army nights under starry, western skies. Pages of drawings, scratched designs and ever changing measurements fueled his determination to build a fitting plantation home for Mount Pleasant. It would be a house for generations of Dummetts; providing protection, shelter, and welcome for all their friends and family.

Walls were raised atop a hand cut and chipped limestone foundation, the stone blocks carefully laid and aligned, shimmed, and mortared with a wet coquina paste of ground shells and sand. Shipped from Savannah, tall double hung windows facing the Hillsborough River to the west were framed in along with the front porch. The eastern back wall was designed with opposing, equally tall windows providing continuous cross ventilation of the rooms from the ocean and river breezes. The gathering room with a hand hewn oak plank floor took most of the first floor, front to back. At the north end was Douglas's office wing and staircase to the upstairs bedrooms, while the preparation kitchen was housed in the south wing. Wide roof eaves extended outside the south wing to provide cover for the 'summer kitchen' patio where the majority of cooking would be done to keep heat out of the house. A large stone oven was constructed outside, along with a circular stone fire pit for spit cooking. Drinking water was carried by buckets and barrels from a cold walled spring about forty feet from the house, while the springhouse provided cool storage for perishables that weren't canned. A smokehouse beyond the summer kitchen enabled meats to be smoked and cured, along with a large copper vat used to boil seawater down to salt.

Francesca's six dowry slaves proved invaluable during construction. They, along with Thomas and Mary's gift of Big John and Etta, Moses and Clarice, and four other slaves, provided needed muscle to get the house, barn, corrals, and row of single room slave cabins built behind the main house. Big John led a group to a stand of cedars where they felled, cut, and trimmed logs into two foot sections, slicing them into shingles. Valuable construction skills were gleaned and learned by younger men under Big John's tutelage, enabling them to build solid, mostly weather tight quarters for their families, currently sheltering in elevated palmetto chickees.

As soon as Mt. Pleasant's main house was enclosed and under roof, Douglas started marking saw palms and underbrush, laying out a grove, carefully digging, transplanting, and grafting starts he had initially planted at Rosetta. Slowly, wilderness yielded to their labors, relinquishing its hold on the virgin land. Seedlings thrived in fertile soil, growing tall and strong in warm, temperate climate and plentiful rain. Fish; planted in between rows for additional fertilizer, augmented root systems along with regular buckets of nutrient rich water drawn from the river.

Just as Mt. Pleasant grew from the ground up, Francesca was also blossoming; full, round, and heavy in her pregnancy. Big John was sent to Rosetta to bring Granny Moon to perform as doula for the imminent birth.

In the cool of night of February 10, at high tide under a bright full moon, Adeline Maria came kicking and screaming into the world.

Journal entry; 10 February 1831

My heart will surely burst with joy I feel at the birth of our first darling daughter, Adeline Maria Hunter Dummett. Granny Moon says a child born under the full moon will surely prosper and prove a great value to our community. We rejoice at these beloved blessings, that Adeline is healthy and perfect in all ways, and that Francesca is hale and happy. If I should die on the morrow, it will be as the happiest of men.

The fledgling settlement of New Smyrna struggled and grew as more families homesteaded the newly opened territory, carving homes and farms from reluctant wilderness. Each brought new and different sets of skills and talents to further the community's growth. Verdant land, waters, and forests, yielded food for sustenance and crops for commerce. Meat was plentiful with wild hog, turkeys, bear, squirrel, and deer; while the river, ocean, and Moskito Lagoon provided sources of abundant supplies of fish, shrimp and crab, delectable lobster, oysters, clams, conch and mussels. Florida provided her bounty unselfishly with generous harvests, endless sunshine, shady cool forests, and mystical springs bubbling cold, clear water from deep limestone aquifers. Morning skies cooked and boiled until thunder announced the inevitable bursting of clouds, bringing afternoon showers offering brief respite from the day's heat. Threats were also plentiful in paradise with pioneers living in consort with descendants of ancient dragons filling the waterways, poisonous serpents, spiders, and buzzing hordes of disease bearing mosquitoes. Panthers, black bears, wolves, and Seminoles were constant threats to life and livestock. Lightning plunged unannounced from blue skies, catching victims in fields and yards; while hurricanes' deadly winds and drenching rains destroyed homes, crops, and families! Paradise exacted a cruel price from those willing to chance their scalps to stay, suffer, and work for the rewards.

TWELVE

Our beautiful Adeline grows and thrives with round, rosy cheeks and fat legs and fingers. She is a beauty such as her mother, but with the fair English complexion of my lineage. She awakens happy, her flaxen curls in mad disarray…and I am smitten by her giggles and grasping hands. To look into her eyes is to see an old and wise soul looking back at me. She is surely a gift of the Angels. I wax poetic!

'ANGELS LET HER STAY'

'Adeline Maria came from Heaven, on a blessed February day.
Keeping her cherubic dimples…she lost her wings along the way.
She cuddled into our family's arms where she is safe and warm;
Entering our lives like sunshine…but taking our hearts by storm.
Addie laughs and talks with Angels, though we can't see them, there.
They guard and watch her sleeping…casting moonbeams in her hair.
We thought we knew what joy was, until that precious day
When Love took the form of a baby…and the Angels let Adeline stay.'

Hounds, Max and Molly, signaled the arrival of Thomas and Mary's carriage. Douglas ran out to help his mother step down; extending a hand to his father and motioning for Moses to tend the horses.

"This is a welcome surprise, we didn't expect you today!"

"Well, Grandmother has a gift for her first granddaughter that couldn't bear waiting another day!" Thomas affectionately blew a kiss at his wife who waved him off with a flourish of her handkerchief.

"Douglas, we brought an old friend of yours I think Adeline will love as much as you did. I have kept him safely in my room all these years, and I cannot imagine her growing up without having him to cuddle and share her secrets with!"

Douglas turned quizzically to his father who shrugged, feigning ignorance.

Mary carefully unwound a small dark form wrapped in a pillowcase. It was a stuffed toy bear made of softest mink pelt. His embroidered smile was slightly offset in his face, and he had obviously been well loved. One button eye was missing, but his expression was still wise and friendly.

"FOREVERMORE! IT'S 'ONE-EYED BROWNIE'!! MUM...I can't believe you kept him all this time!"

"I knew... just knew that someday you would have a child to love Brownie as much as you did. I debated whether or not to fix him and sew on another button, but this is the way you loved him, and if he had both eyes, he wouldn't be 'One-Eyed Brownie' anymore."

"Oh Mum; thank you...thank you! Addie will love him. I can't believe this! He's going right into the crib with her! Let's show Francesca, I think she's feeding Addie, now." Climbing the stairs, Douglas hugged his mother with one arm, 'One-Eyed Brownie' with the other.

"I'll wait down here, Douglas. I have news when you come back down." Douglas could tell by his father's face the news was not good. Returning to the main room, Thomas had already poured two glasses of rum. Handing one to his son, he sat in one of the overstuffed chairs by the fireplace.

"What news do you have?"

Taking a long drink, the old man leaned forward towards his son, his words spilling out in a hushed voice.

"I wanted to warn you to be alert and mindful of Negroes having meetings. About six weeks ago in August in Southhampton County, Virginia, there was a slave uprising led by a minister named Nat Turner whose mistress had taught him to read the Bible. His owner thought he was just preaching the good word to the Negroes, but his pure intent was to rile them up. When that eclipse happened last month, Turner took it as a sign from God for them to take their freedom, so he and his murderous band of about seventy slaves slaughtered every white man, woman, and child they could find. Those black bastards hacked them to death in their beds with machetes, hoes and scythes; then stole their rifles and pistols. That heartless Turner knew he had missed killing his master's little son and even hunted for him, but the boy ducked down and hid in the fireplace till the cowards gave up and left. They killed sixty whites before the militia could get the rebellion under control, but thankfully it didn't last long and most of those slaves involved were shot or hung…altogether about two-hundred were killed if they were thought to be sympathetic. Several of their heads were cut off by the militia and stuck on gate and fence posts as warning along roadways to any others trying to escape."

Thomas stopped talking in deference to the women who had just come down the stairs.

Douglas nodded to his father. "I'll be mindful."

Under directions and careful guidance of Francesca, aided by her mother-in-law; Mount Pleasant arose as a beautiful and tastefully decorated home. Sumptuous furniture pieces from Francesca's dowry, along with those culled and donated from Rosetta and the 'Governor's House' in St. Augustine, contributed a richness of patina to the interior while four large Doric columns lent graceful elegance to the facade in this new wilderness intrusion. Viewed from the water, Mount Pleasant shone dull white in the island shadows of the encompassing oaks.

Facing the small but growing settlement of New Smyrna across the river, the wide hewn front porch displayed masses of richly colored hibiscus planted in a collection of large, clay pots; their heavy blossoms staked at attention. Climbing trellises at both ends of the porch held purple star columbine punctuated by intruding morning glories of bright blue. Spreading masses of baby-pink floribunda roses flanked the stairs, their scent perfuming the porch. All had been carefully transplanted from Mary's beloved Rosetta garden. Night-blooming jasmine thrived at bases of several yard trees, lending their small yellow flowers to subtle fragrance of white nicotiana. Huge bougainvillea's wound high into an angel oak shading the south yard, delicate horizontal branches extending as arms, dripping with silver moss that danced in the slightest breeze.

The young couple finally was able to retrieve another valued wedding gift stored for them at Rosetta. A plush, fringed Persian carpet was unbound and rolled out in front of the fireplace; deep reds and golds of the large, thick rug added a royal lushness of privilege to the room. Heavy, dark green velvet drapes, crystal hurricane lanterns, and silver candlesticks brought a quiet, romantic ambience. From oak planks and cedar shakes, native stone and whitewash; Douglas's prairie dreams of Mount Pleasant became a solid and splendid reality.

Adeline was the apple of her father's eye. With first halting steps taken barefooted on the Persian rug, she and 'Brownie' were off and running. Douglas and Francesca laughed at her antics dragging the little bear while she danced through the rooms on short, fat toes, her swinging shift revealing white ruffled pantaloons of eyelet lace. Addie beguiled her grandparents, Thomas and Mary, with squeals and enthusiastic hugs of pure delight when they arrived to visit, and they were as smitten and doting as her parents.

Douglas enjoyed taking his young daughter to the mainland in his cat boat, the 'Flying Fish', proudly showing her off, bragging on her talents at the trading post that served as a general store. Perching her on the rough-sawn counter, he allowed her to select two prizes; one for her and always one for 'Brownie'. The store's blown glass apothecary jar held colorful hard candies and taffy, exchanged for entertaining those present with a song. She was a consummate charmer already recognizing the feminine value of using her smile, big blue eyes, and lush eyelashes to melt her audience.

1832 brought the addition of a much needed physician, Dr. Gerard Bousquet, his wife Connie and young daughters; and a Canadian carpenter, Donald Armstrong and his wife Rachel; a singer and vivacious teacher. The fledgling settlement grew to fourteen families scattered along the Hillsborough River and ten miles inland.

Businessmen Henry Cruger and William DePeyster bought six-hundred acres of the original Turnbull Grant in 1830. Situated along the western edge of New Smyrna by a constantly running, spring-fed creek; the property was ideal for the establishment of a sugar cane plantation. Obtaining a $10,000 loan they began buying steam equipment, also from the West Point Foundry in Cold Springs, New York to build a processing mill. Newlyweds John and Jane Sheldon were hired as managers, proving to be valuable assets to the fledgling mill. The tall arched stone and coquina mission on the property, abandoned by Spanish Friars when Florida was turned over to the English was cleared of vines, animals, and flora that had taken over the structure. Slowly the jungle gave up its grasp as the large old mission was repaired and altered for the purpose of housing the steam engine and sugar processing machinery. John Sheldon was already a renowned Indian fighter, his reputation secured by years of employment by the U.S. government as a military scout. Providing an excellent marital partner for her frontiersman husband, Jane was the quint-essential pioneer wife; a brave and storied riflewoman and hunter in her own right. As an isolated plantation, the Cruger-DePeyster mill was constantly besieged by Seminoles and freed slaves from Maroon colonies stealing supplies and livestock from their barns and corn houses. Plantation slaves, sympathetic to the Freedmen's cause; provided intelligence, aiding and covering thefts. However, vital information from Jane's Negro maid-servant who reported seeing a painted war party of Seminoles would eventually save the lives of all whites on the plantation.

Thomas Stamp, his wife, and eight children came from South Carolina to homestead one-hundred acres of Ambrose Hull's abandoned Mount Olive plantation, regionally famous for its heavily bearing olive trees and flavorful oils. Initially planting cotton, they eventually changed to planting more lucrative ribbon sugar cane.

Bachelor Bartholomew Pons became mail rider, while Douglas was made captain of the local militia; the 'Moskito Roarers'. Tasked with providing protection against raiding Seminoles or any roaming miscreants, the 'Roarers' consisted of farmers and shopkeepers of varying skills and experience. Without a town Marshall or Sheriff; Dummett's militia of townsmen provided the early law enforcement for the small settlement. Within the year he would also be elected Justice of the Peace. An Irish blacksmith, Seamus O'Conner, set up shop on Canal Street, providing needed farrier and some veterinary services. Circuit Parson Tom Alcorn and his wife, Lucy, arrived in 1833; ministering non-denominational baptisms, christenings, funerals, and redemption to lost or doubting souls. Goods and services were bartered freely, trading with neighbor helping neighbor. Survival was guaranteed only by cooperation, constant compromise, and back-breaking, blistering work.

New arrivals to New Smyrna were welcomed and assisted with house and barn construction by other community members. Sundays were days of rest and church services, even for slaves celebrating their own gatherings with shared deer or wild hog. Judiciously turned by experienced hands, juices dripped and popped in banked fires, casting delicious aromas as meats roasted on open spits. Whatever berries were in season were foraged, picked, and prepared for luscious pies and boiled for jellies; providing prideful competition and hard fought status among slave women who jealously guarded their special recipes, handed down from mothers and grandmothers.

Each Sabbath Day, whites assembled their families in the gathering room of the trading post for Bible readings, and to feel lifting power of Parson Alcorn's fiery, baritone sermons preaching from a large worn, gilt-edged Bible; particularly valuable due to colorful illustrations of old masters. Faces of bearded apostles, saints, and buxom Rubenesque angels graced the sacred book, their eyes reaching plaintively from delicate pages, their hands and wings lifting upward. Some promised Heaven and salvation, others depicted the damnation of Hell. Voices were raised in praise to familiar hymns sung from Rachel Armstrong's tattered green Methodist hymnals, led by her strong mezzo-soprano voice. Occasionally some members brought their guitars and fiddles to further orchestrate music generated by Armstrong's small but highly prized pump organ; enthusiastically pumped and played by the talented and bouncing Rachel. On rare and special evenings to a most appreciative audience, Douglas brought his gleaming cello to accompany her beautiful voice in concerts under the stars. In those escapes into joyful noise, the wilderness became less savage, less lonely… less forbidding.

Periodically two Seminoles; trusted and introduced to the town by Thomas Dummett; provided meat by trading wild game and colorfully dyed woven goods for various supplies, ammunition, or food stuffs cultivated and grown by the settlers. It was an uneasy partnership with sporadic news reports of grisly Seminole attacks against secluded families, stranded and helpless by their isolation.

Tensions were increasingly growing higher, with more and more incursions into the open territory by settlers violating standing treaties made between indigenous people and the U.S. government. Seminoles were being pushed again off their lands, losing homes and crops to settlers anxious to take advantage of homesteading this strange and beautiful land. They came, encouraged by stories of soil so rich a twig stuck in the ground would offer shade the following year; that every cast of nets brought bountiful fish and shellfish; and that any man willing to work could forge his own, private paradise. Florida was a demanding mistress, alternating between heaven and hell, and those who could not bear her adversity and demands were forced to leave... or perish.

Journal entry, July 23, 1833

Today we received a missive of great sadness from our dear friend, Jim Bowie. His beloved wife Ursula, his young son, and infant daughter succumbed to the cholera epidemic while visiting her parents in Mexico. Words elude me. I sorely fear he will resume the recklessness of his unfettered youth without grounding of loving family. My poor Jim, he will not be able to display these newest scars with drunken stories of heroic tales... though sadly, they are surely the deepest and most grievous wounds of all.

THIRTEEN

August 1833

Douglas rolled over in bed, his soaked nightshirt clinging and twisted from the heat. Francesca was gone from the bed so he scooted to her side where the sheets were cooler and dry. Adjusting his eyes to the dark, he could see her silhouette across the room in the moonlight holding Adeline at the window. Fussing, the toddler was hot and miserable, refusing even to be distracted by 'One-eyed Brownie'. Francesca mopped her face, head, and arms with a cool wet rag to no avail.

"Our poor little girl can't sleep in this brutish heat, I'm sorry we wakened you, Clarice has been trying to soothe her crying. I had hoped to catch river breezes from the window to comfort her…but there are none."

Stretching, Douglas sat up peeling his wet nightshirt over his head, dropping it to the floor. Sitting naked at the edge of the bed, he rubbed his eyes before standing and pulling on his breeches.

"I have an idea, wife. I know where there is always coolness on this island, and it will be especially beautiful under this full moon!"

Walking out into the hall, he exclaimed, "If we can't sleep, we might well avail ourselves of the bounty God provides us!"

"CLARICE!! Have Moses bring Chieftain and Blaze around front, just with bridles and reins, no saddles."

"Yassir, I'll wake him."

Francesca looked quizzically at her husband, but smiled at his boyish enthusiasm.

"Douglas; it's two o'clock in the morning! We're going riding?? Where?"

"To the beach my dearest; we'll take advantage of the ice cold relief of the always invigorating Atlantic!! Listen to how the surf is crashing, I'm sure the winds will be cool and refreshing."

"I think you are a bit mad," Francesca smiled coyly, "but I will try anything to get this pitiful child to sleep! Just give me a moment to dress."

"Here is all you need." Douglas pulled a filmy robe from the bedpost, draping it over her nude body with a wink, kissing her cheek.

"We shall be like Adam and Eve…the only humans in the garden…or at the beach!"

"You are incorrigible, husband, but on this miserable night I am willing to embark on a search for Eden's fig leaves… if you promise they will be cool!"

Blushing with the sheer night dress billowing around her, Francesca picked up Addie and chased her husband down the stairs to the drive where Moses was waiting with the horses, carefully averting his eyes, doing his best to not stare at her translucent form.

Douglas took Adeline from her mother, lifting the restless child atop Chieftain's broad back. Grabbing a handful of mane, he vaulted up lightly behind her. Moses interlaced his fingers making a step up for Francesca as she mounted Blaze. The brilliant moon lit the winding pathway of sugar sand through the trees to the beach, when after the short twisting ride, jungled overgrowth suddenly opened to reveal dunes bristling with stands of undulating sea oats, beyond which was a wide expanse of crystalline beach sparkling in the moonlight. Turning their horses northward toward the inlet, they brought them to an easy gallop in the compacted sand frothing at the water's edge. Breakers rolled and rose; their dark faces revealing startling green and blue fluorescence from millions of tiny bioluminescent sea creatures lifted in the surf, shining through and reflected by the huge moon until the waves curved, breaking in waterfalls of brilliant splash. Emerging from tiny holes in the sand, thousands of sand crabs skittered and ran, running sideways from the encroaching tide making the beach itself appear to be alive and moving.

Adeline laughed; now fully awake and relishing refreshing wind and sea spray on her face. Even the horses seemed to enjoy the cool splashing as they kicked through the waves, hooves throwing clods of wet sand as they ran.

After her initial elation, Adeline finally began succumbing to the gentle rocking of Chieftain's gait, her head lolling sideways, comfortable and safe against her father's bare chest. Douglas motioned to Francesca who rode up beside to smile at their sleeping child, blonde hair draped over her face. Slowing to a walk, the couple rode side by side in silence, each marveling at the natural beauty surrounding them; an ocean covered by moon diamonds, pearlescent sugar white dunes stretching endlessly ahead, topped by a huge dome of starry sky above.

Smoothing damp curls from Addie's rosy-cheeked face, Douglas tucked errant ringlets behind his daughter's ears, gently kissed the top of her head.

"This, my beautiful wife, is the stuff of dreams that poets write about."

Reining the big stallion into powdery dunes, Douglas slid

deftly off his back, carefully lifting the sleeping child down against his shoulder. Dragging the blanket off the horse, he spread it out for Adeline who briefly smiled as she hugged One-eyed Brownie. Immediately rolling onto her tummy, she sank comfortably into pillows of soft sand, lulled fast asleep by the rhythmic surf.

Francesca led Blaze beside Chieftain, knotting reins loosely around a palmetto scrub; then with a wink and sly smile over her shoulder, issued an unspoken invitation to her husband. Dropping her robe, she ran naked across the sand, squealing into the cold waves.

Tripping as he chased, Douglas hopped in circles from one foot to the other trying to strip off his leggings without falling, finally casting them into the air as he chased her, now freely nude, high-stepping and splashing into the frigid water.

Catching her, she spun laughing, slippery and wet into his kiss, and on that sultry, starry night... the heavens shone just for them.

FOURTEEN

May 12, 1834

It was one of those perfect days.

Adeline was thrilled to finally be big enough to wear the moccasins brought by Jim Bowie. At just over three years, she was a beauty like her mother, but with her father's delicate coloring. Throwing herself into Douglas's hug, she pointed at the colorfully beaded and intricately sewn mocs exclaiming:

"LOOK, PAPA, PRETTY SHOES…PRETTY SHOES!!"

Scooping the toddler up into his arms, Douglas squeezed her toes in the soft moccasins.

"Are you sure you're a big enough girl to wear these? A friend of Papa's made them especially for my favorite girl!"

"YES, Papa…MINE!" she declared, giggling and wriggling to free herself from his grip.

"I DANCE, PAPA!! I DANCE!!"

Leaning her head against his shoulder, Francesca took Douglas's hand as they watched their daughter spin and twirl, her wild curls exploding in the sunshine forming a bouncing, blonde cloud floating around her head. She ran leaping, waving her arms and pointing her toes in the soft moccasins in exaggerated balletic movements.

"Come on, silly girl, Big John and Ma Etta are waiting in the wagon! Etta fried chicken for our picnic…and I'm pretty sure, by the delicious smells coming from the kitchen, that she made your favorite cookies!"

Big John grinned broadly standing beside the yoke, checking the harness, extremely proud to be included in this family outing.

"I do believe, Miss Adeline, dat there just might be a sweet 'tater pie in dat basket, too."

Francesca chased Adeline, clapping and squealing to the wagon with Douglas following behind, smiling at their antics. Helping his wife up to her seat, he handed Adeline up, then vaulted into the carriage pulling his daughter to his lap.

"ETTA MADE PIE, PAPA!! PIE!! Addie stood, pushing her forehead against her father's looking into his eyes with the announcement, ensuring he had heard the good news.

"WAIT, PAPA!! BROWNIE??" Adeline's expression changed as she looked at her father, her blue eyes wide with concern at forgetting her bear.

"Brownie can stay home today; I think he's ready for a nice, long nap because his eye was looking pretty tired. You can tell him all about our picnic when we get back, besides; I think he'd be too hot in the sun in that fur coat."

Considering her father's words and finally nodding in agreement, she settled in for the bumpy ride to the lagoon.

"Don't tarry, John, we need to get moving to get some breeze stirred up, and I'm not sure if I can wait to get into that basket. That chicken smells mighty good, Etta, and might I say you look especially pretty today!"

The grandmotherly slave turned from her seat next to her husband, waving her apron shushing the young man. She had chosen to wear her silver and pearl earrings on this sunny day and was enjoying showing them off.

"No suh, Massa Douglas, dat chicken is special fo dis picnic. If'n you look real careful, you might find a jar of Etta's special onions and cukes in vinegar and sugared up, just the way you like 'em, but Etta smack any fingers in dat basket fo we get to dat lake!"

Etta's admonishment caused everyone to laugh. Adeline took her daddy's face in her chubby hands…

"Mama Etta's gonna spank you, Papa!" she mocked seriously.

Douglas hugged her tightly.

"You protect Papa, okay?!"

Adeline nodded assent, pursing her lips and pointing a fat finger in warning at Etta.

Leaning back, Douglas looked up at flashes of blue sky through the canopy of oaks, the rocking of the carriage and clopping of hooves almost lulling him to sleep. He smiled to himself at how lucky he was, how blessed they were, how God was good. Raucous squalls of two buzzards fighting over a hapless armadillo startled him back into consciousness.

Big John steered the wagon down a gradual incline leading to the oasis. As the pathway tracks made a break to the right, the lake came into view. The secluded pool wasn't really a lake, but a small idyllic lagoon. Formed by a freshwater spring, it connected with a narrow creek off the river with a shady knoll leading down to a small, sugar white beach of talcum soft sand. Crystal clear, the water sparkled in dappled sunshine, a beautiful aqua-green for about twenty feet; then gradated to cobalt blue as its depths veiled and masked in deepening darkness. Lily pads and water hyacinths lined the shores, supporting hundreds of pink and white lilies. Mosquito hawks droned overhead chasing flies; their translucent wings buzzing and sparkling turquoise and violet in the light, while large blossoms of bright red hibiscus played hide and seek in the surrounding forest. Bougainvillea climbed high into the oaks and palms, blanketing trunks and tree tops in blooms of fiery magenta.

Every shade of imaginable green surrounded them, from evergreen firs to light chartreuse of golden dieffenbachia, to emerald grasses. It was their secret garden, a magical Eden of beauty where water, sky, and earth harmonized in perfect wonder.

Great White Egrets pecking bugs along the lagoon's edge noisily discussed the wagon's unexpected intrusion, strutting proudly in their finery and gossiping like nervous brides. Adeline waved her arms, laughing and running into the flock causing the crowned birds to lift their skirts and run, folding stick-thin legs underneath them as they stretched their lovely wings, reaching and pulling into the air. Cackling, up they went; pure white grace against the bluest sky until disappearing beyond the trees.

Adeline gleefully clapped her hands at the freedom of being able to run in the soft grass; then returned, running to the rope swing Douglas had fashioned for her a few months earlier. A thick, knotted rope securely hung the swing from a horizontal oak limb, the seat carefully carved and sanded smooth in the wood shed by her doting grandfather.

"HELP ME, MAMA!"

Francesca lifted Addie into the swing as the child squealed in delight.

"PUSH ME, MAMA!! PUSH ME! HIGHER, HIGHER MAMA!!"

Etta busied herself spreading quilts under a tree near the edge of the beach for their picnic; then set about opening baskets and preparing the feast. Big John was wiping down the horses while Douglas watched Francesca pushing Adeline, her hair flying as she lifted, swinging higher and higher.

"LOOK AT ME, PAPA!!! I FLY!!"

"ENOUGH, ADDIE, YOU'RE WEARING ME OUT!! LET'S DANCE!"

Francesca slowed the swing enough to pull the laughing girl off, setting her on the ground.

"Ring around the rosies...pocket full of posies...ashes, ashes...we all fall DOWN!!"

Mother and daughter spun dancing and laughing until Francesca dropped dizzily into a heap, Adeline falling giggling on top of her.

"You ladies best cool down afore eatin' Etta's food!" Etta admonished. "You keep spinnin' like two fools; you'll both be gettin' bellyaches!!"

Shaking his head and smiling at their antics from the picnic quilt, Douglas sat with his back against the tree, relishing coolness of shade and the slight breeze. A mockingbird trilled in joyful serenade, hidden in a massive philodendron to the young man's right. Folding another blanket, Douglas plumped it behind his head, closing his eyes and leaning back, comfortably content.

Francesca was now lying in the grass while Adeline was standing just beyond her in the sand, facing towards the lagoon. Bending over to pick up a shell; she turned to proudly wave it at her father.

"LOOK, PAPA... I FIND PRETTY SHELL!!"

Using his hand to shield against the sun, Douglas opened one eye, smiling at his daughter.

No one saw the danger stalking her.

He was an enormous armored gator, almost fourteen feet long; his killing skills inherited and honed from prehistoric dragons that were cunning and efficient hunters. Nosing silently into the sheltered lagoon from the river, the monster lizard dove smoothly, barely rippling the surface of the placid water scanning for otters or juicy turtles. This small bay had always proved to be fertile hunting ground, rife with fish and inattentive cormorants busily diving for fish of their own. Occasionally, he had surprised unwary deer grazing on lush greenery at the water's edge. Surfacing only hooded eyes through the lily pads and reeds, he honed in without blinking; assessing his prey through reptilian yellow orbs, now narrowed to slits. Silently he glided forward, until without warning his huge strong claws and thickly muscled legs and tail thrust him rocketing out of the depths onto the beach.

Douglas stared, initially in shock, sitting frozen in disbelief, unwilling to process the unfolding horror. For a moment, unable to move or react, he watched the alligator in slow motion as it lunged, massive jaws open, snapping shut on Adeline; shaking and dragging her backwards like a rag doll toward the water. In a blur of seconds, she was gone. Francesca was the first to scream.

Still not believing what he had seen, but with adrenaline spiking his heart, Douglas leapt up racing across the sand into the lagoon. Drawing the silver dagger from the sheath on his belt, he jumped, high kicking as he tried to run through the water towards the gator. Spinning, the beast began the death roll just as the young father caught him, frantically stabbing at the thrashing monster; crying and briefly grabbing hold of Adeline's foot until she was forcibly jerked from his grasp and taken under again. Crazed and stabbing like a madman, one shallow blow connected piercing one of the saurian's eyes, the orb deflating in a gelatinous burst. When the beast rolled back upright, with a maniacal scream and all his strength, Douglas thrust the knife with both hands; impaling and burying the blade to the curved hilt into the alligator's bony skull.

By this time, Big John had come splashing into the lagoon, joining the fray next to Douglas, but seeing the futility of fighting further, began wrestling and struggling with the young man to keep him from also being pulled under and drowned. Forcing Douglas to release his grip on Adeline's lifeless body, the slave dragged him fighting and screaming back towards shore. Disappearing with the toddler, the gator retreated backwards into deep, muddy swirls; the silver handle of the big Bowie knife cutting a swath in the bloodied froth of widening red water, disappearing with the beast as it sank into the shadowy depths.

"PLEASE, MASSA DOUGLAS... SHE GONE!! DAT SWEET BABY; GONE!!!"

Big John drug and wrested the sobbing father onto the beach where Francesca was being restrained by Etta, struggling to keep Francesca's face turned away from witnessing the horror of her daughter's death. Realizing her husband didn't have Adeline, she fell to the ground in catatonic shock, rocking back and forth in the fetal position. Hands covering her eyes, her mouth gaped in silent sobs.

Falling to his knees on the beach, an unrecognizable sound ripped from the depths of his soul... as an animal's primal cry of grief that only a parent who has lost a child can understand. Reaching to the heavens, Douglas beseeched God, imploring for his daughter's life while offering his own for hers; but this prayer would not be answered... and the cruel skies were silent.

Time stopped, his own cries reverberating mercilessly in his ears. This couldn't be happening, couldn't be real. Finally realizing he was clutching something; Douglas opened his fist revealing one small beaded moccasin. Lifting it skyward...he wailed.

FIFTEEN

Weeks passed in an interminable blur for the Dummetts. Francesca languished, lost in a black pit of inconsolable hell, alternating between anger and madness. The couple, instead of seeking solace in each other, drew increasingly apart in their grief. Calling for Adeline, for months Francesca was found wandering the riverbanks at night; not eating, sleeping, or bathing. At times for her own safety, she had to be held in restraints. She blamed Douglas, he blamed himself; rum became the only respite from the hold of unrelenting sadness.

Douglas gave an outwardly stalwart appearance, but on long nights alone at his desk with his journal, 'One-eyed Brownie' was pulled from the depths of a drawer, his soft fur muffling the young father's sobs.

Though still legally wed…the marriage fell apart.

Journal entry: 10 September 1834

I shall surely die of grief for my darling Adeline. My heart aches with pain that takes my breath. Her horrible death has also taken Francesca from me, as we are but shells of our former selves and can offer no comfort to the other. I wish a merciful God had taken me rather than our sweet, sweet little daughter, but He has forsaken us, and I curse his name. We are truly lost and cannot find our way.

On the last day of May, a memorial service was held for Adeline along the river's edge at Mount Pleasant. Parson Alcorn recited the 23rd Psalm after which Mrs. Armstrong, at Mary Dummett's request; sang Bach's 'Ave Maria'. Providing small pink rosebuds to mourners; blossoms were tossed one by one into the slowly moving water. Douglas originally planned to have a marble statue of a child angel sculpted in Savannah, but after a Great Snowy Egret landed on the grass during the service, he consulted with the artist deciding to have the bird sculpted instead. To be mounted on a podium, the monument would eventually stand in the front yard facing the river. Depicting a toddler, the statuary had the girl child grasping legs of a large egret; wide white marble wings angelically outstretched in flight, lifting her towards Heaven.

As sad day turned to sad night, Mount Pleasant's slaves gathered around dying embers in the quarters fire pit; clustering around Etta standing stoically with Big John's arm around her shoulders, her cheeks wet and shiny with tears. Reaching out to have others join hands forming a growing circle, she began slowly swaying, humming an old slave lullaby accompanied by Daniel's guitar. Rocking in synchronized rhythm; Etta's rich, honeyed contralto melted into the mournful song; her voice pure, liquid grief.

Hush-a-bye, don't you cry...go to sleepy little baby.
When you wake, you shall have...all the pretty little horses.
Blacks and Bays...Dapples and Greys
...all the pretty little horses.
Way down yonder in the meadow...lies my poor little lambie.
Bees and butterflies peckin' out her eyes,
poor little thing is cryin' ... Mammy.
Blacks and Bays...Dapples and Greys

...all the pretty little horses.
Hush-a-bye, don't you cry...go to sleepy little baby.
When you wake, you shall have...all the pretty little horses.

Over the next months and years after Adeline's death, the grieving family hung posters in store windows, taverns and hostelries, placing notices in numerous periodicals up and down the east coast. A reward of two-hundred dollars gold was offered to any hunter bringing the head of the alligator impaled with Douglas's Bowie knife to the bereft father. Sightings were reported from Jacksonville to Merritt Island, but the beast was wary and proved elusive.

Life continued for Douglas and Francesca; but it was forever changed and would never be good for them again.

Mary Dummett's dementia was reaching a point she was requiring constant care in St. Augustine. Knowing his infirmities of age prevented him from ever returning to the management of Rosetta, Thomas worried about his son's decline into grief with grueling responsibilities of two plantations overwhelming him further. The decision was made to sell all the Carrickfergus property and most of Rosetta and her field slaves to brothers Kenneth and Duncan Macrae. Intending to build a sugar mill utilizing the old Addison blockhouse; the brothers had cash and were anxious to start. Douglas would be free to follow his own dreams of Mount Pleasant, now with working capital to expand his citrus groves on additional acreage he was purchasing at Merritt Island.

SIXTEEN

Journal entry; October 4, 1835

Today I received a missive from Jim sounding much like his old self. He was quite elated to inform me I am now outranked as Captain with the 'Moskito Roarers' militiamen by his much gloried promotion to Colonel of the Texas Volunteers. He is excited to be serving under Generals Sherman and Fannin in their quest against Santa Ana in Texas, and urges me to join him in the expedition. Their objective will be to enforce the correct boundaries set forth in the Adams-Onis Treaty ceding Florida, Texas, and other southern lands from Spain to the U.S. In preparation for the arrival of General Fannin and his regular soldiers, Texians from the Republic of Texas are being sent in advance with a small Army contingent to secure a Spanish mission for use as a fort near San Antonio. The mission is small and described as not easily defended, but the location near Mexico is strategic. Until then, Lt. Col. William Travis will be commanding the Army troops, while Jim will command the volunteer militia of Texian patriots.

I posted my regrets, telling him of increased turmoil with Seminoles and Maroons here at home. Florida will need her sons to defend her territory from those marauders. Were it not for these building hostilities and raids against our homes and fields, I would be sorely tempted to join Jim in Texas at that place called the Alamo.

Florida's small settlements were growing as pioneers came to claim their piece of Eden; chopping tropical undergrowth, clearing fields of limestone boulders, logs, and roots, tilling the dark soil to scratch a better living for their families. Virgin land provided abundant exportable crops of sugar cane, cotton, indigo, and masses of table crops. Corn houses were stocked for personal consumption with extra used for barter or sale. Wealth was established by the number of slaves owned. Without them, there could be no expansion for the new territory.

The influx of white settlers being granted blocks of acreage infringed on historic lands, homes, and ample waters promised the Native Americans by treaties; pushing the tribes further south into Florida. A large colony of Maroons estimated at sixteen-hundred runaway slaves and Freedmen, slaves given their freedom by the Spanish in return for help fighting the British; thrived in the interior of Florida. With Florida ceded by Spain to the United States in 1821, the Maroons believed their contracts with Spain would be honored and they would remain free, but plantation owners sent bounty hunters and slave chasers after them, increasingly demanding assistance from the government in the form of military intervention to regain their property from the reservation. The Maroon leader was a runaway slave named John Caesar; a tall persuasive orator and military leader skilled in Indian wiles and methods of battle.

Prior to the Adams-Onis Treaty ceding Florida from Spain to the United States in 1821; the United States Army was called upon both to protect settlers moving onto Indian lands, and to also invade Maroon colonies. Capturing runaway slaves and returning them to their owners became an ugly sideline, essentially turning Army soldiers into taxpayer paid bounty hunters. Major

General Andrew Jackson was deployed as commanding officer to carry out the government's unsavory mission.

Leading an Army expedition in 1814, Jackson fought Creek Indians in the Battle of Horseshoe Bend (in present day Alabama near the Georgia border). Badly defeated, chiefs were then co-erced into a treaty forcing them to surrender tribal lands of more than twenty million acres to the United States government. Those lands comprised almost one half of present day Alabama and a fifth of Georgia. Native Americans were then forced south into Florida. With free rein and little oversight throughout the next decade, Jackson led continued brutal military incursions against the Indians, indiscriminately killing men, women, and children... violating nine of eleven treaties.

Maroons in Florida and tribes of the Creek nation; Cree, Cherokee, Chickasaw, Choctaw, even Florida's southern glades Indians, the Micasuki; had come to realize they could not fight Jackson and the U.S. Army individually. Merging together was their only means of survival. As tribes married among themselves, they also intermarried with runaways from plantations and freed slaves; eventually forming and consolidating into one tribe...the Seminole. Famous Seminole leaders included Osceola, Micanopy, King Phillip and his son, the fearsome Coacoochee; the dreaded warrior settlers called 'Wildcat'.

Two years after the United States officially purchased Florida from Spain in 1821; the Treaty of Moultrie Creek established a large Seminole reservation in central Florida. Andrew Jackson, disregarding and breaking numerous treaties made with the Indians, was instrumental in relocating thousands of indigenous people from their homes. The U.S. government cast a blind eye to his brutal methods; his raids often annihilating all inhabitants of native villages; slaughtering the elderly, women, and children. A majority of Seminoles had been moved onto the reservation by 1827.

Colonel Duncan L. Clinch was assigned to construct Fort King near current day Ocala where Indian matters were administered and handled by agent Wiley Thompson. Five years passed in relative peace until issues of settler violations of the treaty, Indians leaving the reservation to hunt, and Seminoles offering sanctuary to escaped slaves reached the boiling point.

Becoming president in 1829; Andrew Jackson's goal was to remove all southeastern Indians to reservations in Kansas and Oklahoma by urging Congress to adopt the Removal Act of 1830.

The government's answer to the growing unrest was to pass the act which called for relocating all Native Americans in the east to reservations in the west. Calling Seminole chiefs to a meeting in 1832, the Treaty of Payne's Landing was signed. It stated that after inspecting the western lands, if a council of chiefs agreed; the tribes would relocate. Returning to Florida after the inspections, the chiefs claimed they had been forced to sign the document of agreement. Despite their protests, the US Senate ratified the treaty giving Seminoles three years to vacate their lands and move west to reservations established in Oklahoma.

Indian Agent, Wiley Thompson, assigned to Fort King, relayed troubling reports to his superiors of Seminoles amassing weapons. Chiefs were also angrily stating they were going to disregard the treaty. Colonel Clinch alerted Washington that force might be necessary to compel the relocation with Thompson instructed to stop the sale of guns and ammunition to the Indians. His compliance with that order would cost him his scalp at the hands of Osceola.

Finally realizing treaties were useless and the United States government intended to take all their lands, forcing them to prairie reservations with those resisting being imprisoned or slaughtered; Seminoles began organizing and escalating their rebellion joined by cavalries of Maroons led by John Caesar. Attacks orchestrated by Chiefs Micanopy and King Philip, and led by warriors Osceola and Coacoochee began occurring in earnest with grisly massacres at isolated homesteads and settlements. By late December 1835; differences between Native tribes and the U.S. government in the struggling territory of Florida were beyond resolution.

The Second Seminole War exploded, ripping through Florida from 1835-1842. All settlements and plantations for over two-hundred miles along the eastern coast of Florida were looted and reduced to smoking ruins; homes, fields, and mills destroyed. All commerce was obliterated…nothing was spared except slave quarters and corn houses. Whites who couldn't escape were subjected to unspeakable tortures and massacred; many scalped alive. Most plantation slaves chose freedom by joining the Seminoles or Maroons. It was a long, costly, bloody war lasting seven violent years…with mayhem and atrocities committed by both sides. Though history reports the Second Seminole War as an Indian war, it was also the largest slave revolt in America.

SEVENTEEN

Christmas evening, December 25, 1835

"Gerard, something's got Belle all in a tither!" Constance Bousquet set her youngest daughter, Karen, onto the floor with her sisters; Stephanie and Denise. She stood up from the big nursing rocker pulling homespun curtains aside, peering into the gathering dusk. Playing with their new dolls, the girls rolled giggling on the soft oval rag rug in front of the fireplace where colorfully striped stockings hung from the mantle. Draping a shawl around her shoulders and head, the young mother stepped out onto the back porch. Coolness of the breeze took her breath, as this December had been surprisingly cold. Smoothing hair back from her face and tucking errant wisps under her scarf, she scanned the woods at the rear of their home. Belle, their large bay mare was running in circles, snorting and pawing the dirt in the small corral, wide eyed at danger she sensed. Her ears stood erect, pointing towards the thick palmetto hammock to the west. Talking quietly to calm the horse, Constance opened the gate slowly approaching the excited animal, taking her bridle and petting the velvety nose.

"What is it, pretty girl? I don't see anything...is it that black bear again?"

Carrying a rifle, Gerard Bousquet joined his very pregnant wife in the paddock.

"I don't like it, Gerry. It's blowing an ill wind. I can't see it... but I can feel it. Did you hear shots?"

"I'll put her in the barn, maybe that'll settle her."

Casting a nervous eye quickly about the property, Gerard took the bridle without answering, leading Belle to her stall in the relative safety of the barn. She calmed, but he could tell by her stomping and flared nostrils she was still alerting on some unseen threat that was frightening her.

Waiting on her husband in the yard, Constance searched his face for the alarm she knew he felt…but was trying to hide from her. Large with their fourth child due in mid-February, her distended belly was growing more uncomfortable each day. They had already agreed that if this pregnancy bore a son, they were going to name him after her father; Robert Spellman. He had come with their family to settle in Florida from the Ohio territory, and had just died the day before Thanksgiving, leaving a terrible void in their lives. A boy child would help alleviate the grief of her father's loss…Rob Bousquet…she liked the sound of the name, having a secret dream he would follow his father's path into medicine.

Situated on the mainland side along the river; the Bousquet homestead sat about a quarter mile south of Tom Stamps' house built atop the old fort foundation. A small room in the front of their home served as Dr. Bousquet's examination room and office. Harshness of pioneer life often necessitated the space be used for surgeries and emergency treatments until the fledgling community could build a designated infirmary. Trained by her husband, Constance was a competent nurse.

Approaching his shivering wife, Gerard put his arm around her shoulders, pulling her close to him as they headed for the house. Just reaching the back porch, sounds of horse's hooves pounding the roadway at speed broke the silence of the evening.

"Get in the house and bar the doors, I'll go around front to see who it is!"

Connie hustled through the main room to the front window to see the horseman was Bartholomew Pons; New Smyrna's mail rider and their bachelor neighbor whose cabin was just about a mile northwest of their home. She could see that Bartholomew was pointing and obviously agitated. Whirling his steaming Appaloosa back northward, its hooves threw clods of sand as he disappeared into the fog. Throwing the front door open to her husband who was running toward the house through the gathering gloom, she could see he was panicked!

"Wildcat and about a hundred warriors and John Caesar leading about fifty Maroons are burning plantations on their way to New Smyrna! They've just hit the Stamp's place. John Caesar tried to lure Tom out to the barn with the pretense of selling horses, but he was just trying to get him outside without his rifle. Tom didn't fall for it and ran back into the house. They were able to drive the raiding party back long enough to get the family out. The savages have already set fire to the Cruger-DePeyster Mill, but a slave of Jane Sheldon's warned them so they got out. The bastards have slaughtered four families that Pons knows of, and they're coming this way!! Get coats on the girls, I'll get the horses and open the barn so the other livestock can get away into the woods! Pons is on his way to ring the church bell and alert the rest of the town!"

"What are we going to do, Gerry? WHERE WILL WE GO?"

"We're going to load the girls onto the boat and go across river to Captain Dummett's. When he hears the bell; he and his men will provide rifle fire to cover us while we're rowing across. We'll lead the horses to swim behind us. That's the plan the militia has

made. Once we're gathered there, we'll go together to the inlet
where the schooners are moored to sail to Bulow's plantation! I've
got to saddle the horses while you get the girls ready! Hurry wife,
grab only essentials! We've got to go NOW!!"

Fastening his gun belt with the holstered pistol over his coat,
Gerard grabbed the shotgun and rifle from the rack over the mantle, tossing handfuls of balls and shot into a handled tapestry bag.
Running to the barn, he threw open the paddock and chicken
house doors waving his arms, shooing the reluctant animals cackling into the yard and bordering underbrush. Recalcitrant, the
two cows were next and stood confused, refusing to take off until
slapped on their rumps. Bawling displeasure, they sidled into the
woods now filling with choking haze. Horses Belle and Bandit
were quickly saddled, bridled and led to the front of the house;
nervously prancing at the smell of rapidly building smoke.

Constance fought rising terror in her throat, not wanting to
scare the children. Pulling coats and scarves from the rack, she
forced a smile at their quizzical faces while doling the garments.

"Why is Papa running with his guns?" Eldest daughter,
Stephanie, knew something was wrong.

"Hustle, girls, we're going on a Christmas journey!!" Constance
smiled with a brave face at their young daughters who weren't
sure if they should be excited or scared at the frantic actions of
their obviously upset parents…and the sudden flurry of activity of
undeniable urgency.

"Why, Momma?" Dede whined. "It's cold outside? We want
to play dolls!"

"Button your coats and wrap your headscarves. We'll take
your dolls; you girls put that hardtack into my case…and grab
your blankets. I need to bundle Karen! Hustle! HUSTLE!!"

"COME ON GIRLS! WE'RE GOING ON AN ADVENTURE, A BOAT RIDE TO MOUNT PLEASANT; CAPTAIN DUMMETT'S HOUSE OUT ON THE ISLAND!!"

Taking the two older girls by their hands, Gerard ran with them through the front yard and across the roadway to a bobbing rowboat tied to a piling along the river. Constance handed Karen to Dede so she could use both hands to climb aboard. Frightened faced parents were running toward the boats, dragging crying children while anxiously scanning the darkness behind them; now suddenly filled with distant rifle fire and hideous screams.

"CONNIE!! I FORGOT MY BAG...CAN YOU FETCH IT FROM THE OFFICE?!"

Constance clumsily turned holding her belly to run back to the house to retrieve the medical case, horrified at the rapidly reddening sky and rising smoke from the west and north, knowing Wildcat was burning their neighbor's homes.

"Please God," she prayed to herself as she ran, "Please let our friends get away, and please watch over our family!"

Putting his hand on eight year old Stephanie's shoulder, Dr. Bousquet smiled reassuringly into her scared face.

"Honey, I need you to be a brave girl for me tonight and ride Belle across the river. I have to row the boat because your mother can't. She's too close to term and I fear the exertion would be too much strain on the baby. Don't worry about leading Bandit. He'll swim across following Belle, and we need both horses on the island. All you need to do is ride Belle across; she won't swim without being ridden."

Stephanie looked earnestly at her father. "I can do it, Daddy; Belle minds me real good!"

"Good girl!" Giving her a quick kiss on the head, he boosted her up onto the saddle. "Wrap up and hold on tight. GO, HONEY, HEAD FOR CAPTAIN DUMMETT'S; DON'T LOOK BACK NO MATTER WHAT YOU HEAR... AND DON'T STOP FOR ANYTHING!!!"

Seeming to sense the urgency, the gentle bay waded into the current spurred by quick kicks to her haunches. Bandit went in without prodding; catching up to Belle, swimming beside her towards the island lantern light on the eastern bank of the river.

Grabbing her husband's medical bag, Connie lumbered as quickly as she could back down to the boat where the girls waited with terrified eyes. Holding her ungainly belly with one hand, she could feel the baby's frantic kicking, her fear and excitement transferring and being felt by the child. Gerard helped her into the small craft, shoving them off towards Mt. Pleasant on the opposite bank. As he rowed, flames became visible behind them, and now...they could see the horror pursuing them.

Those who escaped their homes were running for the river dragging crying children, chased by yipping Seminole warriors suddenly materializing out of the dark on foot, wielding rifles, pistols, and knives. Maroons on horseback swinging hatchets and war clubs galloped through groups of panicked families, circling and killing with sickening precision, taking full advantage of their element of surprise. It was a frightening, chaotic scene of children's cries and carnage with Seminoles raising bloody scalps overhead with triumphant yells.

With Gerry rowing, Connie threw a blanket over Karen and Dede; turning and swinging the big Springfield rifle aft, balancing it onto the stern. Taking and holding a deep breath as her father had taught her as a young girl hunting in Ohio, she blew out slowly, sighting atop the barrel, squeezing the trigger at painted braves chasing them into the river. The first ball struck one of the warriors in the chest, the blast lifting and blowing him backwards, his arms outstretched as he submerged. Without time to reload as another Seminole lunged after their boat; Connie jabbed at him with the barrel of the long gun, jamming him in the eye. Instinctively grabbing his bloody face and losing his grip on the port gunwale, he slipped flailing under the freezing water with a blood-curdling scream. Gerry was struggling with the unwieldly boat, trying to row into deeper water with a warrior hanging onto the starboard side effectively acting as a drag anchor. Seeing their predicament, Bartholomew Pons urged his Appaloosa to swim towards them, firing a close range shot from horseback virtually taking off the Seminole's head; sending blood spattering over Constance and the girls. Now, shots came from ahead of them striking the fourth pursuing their boat…it was Dummett and others providing cover fire from the island.

"HURRY, HURRY!" Big John and Tom Stamps waded out to grab the bow, hauling the Bousquet family onto the bank. John Mathews reached for Belle's and Bandit's bridles; lifting Stephanie off the mare.

"COME ON! We've got a wagon hooked up for women and children. MEN…reload and grab a horse!!"

A series of explosions suddenly rocked the mainland shore sending plumes of flames and sparks high into nearby trees.

"OH, MY GOD!! It's Judge Dunham's place; the fire must have gotten into his black powder!! Douglas and Tom Stamps shielded their eyes, searching the shoreline for any sign of Mary and David Dunham. Their elegant, two-story frame house was the largest in New Smyrna, almost directly across the river from

Mount Pleasant; six tall columns had stretched across the white-washed façade. Now the complete north end of the structure was destroyed and lay in smoking rubble. Only two columns remained standing, the others cast across the yard like mammoth bleached bones. In the firelight the men could make out a horde of about one hundred Negroes and Seminoles swarming the remaining portion of the burning manor house. Shots could be heard coming from inside…then the screaming sickeningly stopped.

"LET'S GET A HEAD COUNT!" Dummett made a quick assessment of their numbers as they handed children onto the wagon to their mothers. Tom Stamps, his wife and eight children; John and Brandi Mathews and their twin sons, Dylan and Conner, and daughter Makenna; Don and Rachel Armstrong; Bartholomew Pons; Connie and Gerry Bousquet and their three daughters, Stephanie, Karen, and Denise; John and Jane Sheldon; and Douglas and Francesca completed the group totaling twenty-seven. Thirteen adults and fourteen children survived to this juncture.

"Reverend Alcorn… and Lucy?" Dummett frantically turned to John Mathews who shook his head in wordless answer.

"DOC, can you handle the wagon?" Matthews held reins of the nervous team that was excitedly stomping, twisting against their harnesses in fear.

The doctor was stopped by the raised hand of Jane Sheldon, an unlit cigar clenched tightly between her teeth and a holstered pistol hanging at her hip.

"I'll drive the damned team, you men handle the rifles!"

A gritty pioneer woman, Jane Sheldon climbed onto the buckboard seat, unwinding and expertly snapping the reins sending the wide-eyed horses lurching forward, swinging the wagon almost full circle to straighten onto the plantation lane heading north to the inlet trail. Mothers huddled low in the back, bouncing with their frightened children wrapped in blankets, pulling them close; turning their faces away from the sight of the firestorm.

"BIG JOHN, YOU AND MA ETTA COME WITH US!!"

"Naw sir, Massa Douglas; won't be room in dos boats! We'll be fine, here. Dos 'noles don't mean us no harm; and maybe we can save somethin' of Mount Pleasant!"

"Alright, John, be safe. If you can; hide the livestock in the south woods corral, especially the Andalusian mares until I get back with the soldiers! I'll turn Chief loose at the inlet; if the Seminoles don't catch him, he'll find his way back to his mares!"

Douglas turned Chieftain to chase the small group northward; all knowing they were fleeing for their lives, dreading consequences for their families should they be caught. Already, Coacoochee and his warriors were reaching the island using boats dragged from hiding places by mainland slaves, pulling themselves up the slippery river bank to continue the pursuit. Their night had been mostly successful with the burning of New Smyrna and slaughter of unsuspecting families; comfortable in front of their fireplaces.

The Seminole and Maroon attacks were well planned and executed, utterly destroying every plantation and settlement along two-hundred miles of eastern Florida south of St. Augustine, killing every white man, woman, or child they could find; sparing only the slaves. Amongst ashes and rubble of homes and fields; slave quarters and corn houses with their larder were the only structures left standing.

Winding through thick forest, the four-mile trail to the inlet was dark and hazardous with holes, roots, and low branches threatening the racing riders and overloaded axles of the wagon. Jane Sheldon's whip cracked over the team not allowing the horses to slow, the buckboard slinging around curves on two wooden wheels, bouncing airborne off hilly drops, threatening to roll or break apart.

Arriving at the inlet, quickly stowing saddles and bridles in underbrush, the escapees scattered the horses into oak thickets; hurriedly shoving small boats hidden in the dunes to the water, loading and launching their families into their only means of escape...the treacherous inlet. Douglas stroked Chief's muzzle as he slipped off his bridle.

"Your girls are waiting for you, buddy...you'll find them in the woods with Big John, so go hide till I get back...NOW GO!!"

Bousquet's horses, Belle and Bandit, ran closely behind; sensing imminent danger with their urgent and hurried release. The small herd that effectively saved their owners lives by getting them to the inlet escape route ahead of the Indians, disappeared quickly into the forest; dense foliage and deep sand muffling the pounding of hooves.

Disregarding wounds and throbbing muscles, settlers rowed through waves to the sailboat anchored in deep water inside the inlet. Working in unison handing children up to waiting arms of mothers and fathers, everyone was loaded aboard the small schooner. Connie Bousquet, her cumbersome belly slowing her progress; was heaved and pulled unceremoniously onboard, landing heavily on the deck.

Warning the light-keeper of the impending attack, he and his wife abandoned their hut at the base of the original wooden lighthouse on the south side of the inlet, fleeing with New Smyrna's survivors sailing up the Halifax River to Bulowville. Red skies flanking western banks bore silent witness to fires destroying their homes and life works. Passing out of sight beyond the land mass north of the white-capped inlet, they watched the familiar beacon atop the tower go dark. Sailing in silence and safe for the short term, they gathered in prayer giving thanks for fair winds and a merciful tide. All were grateful to be alive at this moment in time, but worried and unsure of what awaited ahead...what danger lay around the next bend.

By the time Coacoochee's band made it to the inlet by foot, billowing sails of their quarry were just visible making the turn northward from the inlet into the Halifax River with a fortunate breeze coming out of the southwest. With this group of settlers out of reach for now, the Seminoles turned their attentions to the lighthouse, looting it of food supplies, silver candlesticks, and copper pots brought from England by the light-keeper's wife. Before torching the tall, long-needle pine and Live Oak structure; Coacoochee climbed rough sawn rungs to the top of the lighthouse removing reflective lens mirrors used for signal lamps forming the warning beacon. He would later use those reflectors to fashion a headpiece and breastplate to wear in battle, presenting a horrifying image with his mirrored armament flashing in the sun or moon light as he rode; painted in ghoulish black and white war paint. Believing the magic glass gave him great and godly powers of protection, Wildcat rode fearlessly bareback atop a muscular, light grey stallion; a black mask painted around its' eyes, blood red handprints outlined on his flanks, and charcoal lightning bolts drawn down his haunches. As a warrior, his ferocity was unmatched in battle. Swinging his knobby cypress war club over his head, he led his screaming warriors charging enemies without mercy. Brutality and gruesome killing skills made him a very real and frightening legend, and just as the settlers... he was fighting for his home.

EIGHTEEN

Dawn rose ablaze on the east horizon, lending some comfort of light for the exhausted New Smyrna refugees crammed in the sail boat. Relieved they wouldn't be navigating narrow passages from the Tomoka River up Bulow Creek to Bulow's plantation in the dark of night, they were thankful for the arrival of sunrise…and the added ability to sight in on any surprise attacks. Mangrove thickets passed slowly; silently dense with pines, cypress, and cedars jungled along both banks of the waterway. All watched with nervous eyes for any sudden movements or excited birds flapping alarm, while huge gators slid down muddy slides from both sides of the river; noiselessly slipping into murky water in expanding ripples adding to tension on the boat. Any splash, any disturbance might signal another attack.

Tacking into the wind making the turn from the Halifax onto the Tomoka River, Douglas could smell smoke from the direction of Rosetta, but couldn't see flames. Lowering his head in silent prayer, he thanked God his parents had left earlier to the safety of their home in St. Augustine near the fort and didn't have to flee in the night…or worse. Maybe, just maybe Rosetta was still standing, safe and dark in the trees, his mother's pink roses still blooming by the porch.

The journey up the winding creek to John Bulow's plantation was the most stressful of the trip. Depths were shallow and Douglas was concerned about their overloaded sailboat's draft in these unfamiliar waters, dreading each scraping sound of sandbars and gouging of oyster beds. Overhanging branches grabbed the masts and threatened their sails. With the narrowness of the canal; any warriors hiding in the palmettos with advantage of high ground or high limbs would have clear and short shots down into the boat from the steep banks. Some places were narrow enough a determined warrior could run and leap; throwing himself aboard. "Like shooting monkeys in a barrel," he thought to himself.

With the transfer of Florida from Spain to the U.S. in 1821; settlers emigrating south were buying or homesteading large blocks of land now opening in this new territory. Charles Bulow came from Charleston, South Carolina, acquiring six-thousand acres to establish a sugar cane plantation in the wilds of Florida a few miles north of what is now; Ormond Beach. Bringing three-hundred slaves, he was able to get twenty five hundred acres cleared and planted; then started building a large sugar mill to process the cane. He died three years after the purchase, leaving the unfinished plantation to his seventeen year old son, John Joachim Bulow who was attending school in Paris. After completion of his studies, the flamboyant young man returned to build the largest and most lucrative sugar mill in Florida. Bulow Plantation grew into a small settlement of its own, eventually becoming known as Bulowville. The same age and both sons of planters; Douglas and John Joachim had been friends since they were boys.

Finally, Bulowville's docks came into view. Further around the bend, the large, white-washed house with porches across the first and second stories stood ghostly and unblemished.

John Audubon had been a guest of Bulowville in 1832 during his tour to draw and paint the strange, southern birds of this wilderness territory. He had praised Bulow's plantation in accolades as he wrote of Florida and this jungled and beautiful place in his books and magazines, using the plantation for a base as he searched for previously undocumented water fowl in these uncharted backwaters. With Bulow's parties reflecting plenty, alcohol, and decadence experienced at the French court while living in Paris; John Joachim enjoyed putting his wealth on display for Audubon. He commissioned a small barge to be outfitted with a striped canopy tenting over plush cushions for him and his guests for river excursions. Rowed by four pairs of eight shirtless slaves pulling long oars, they rowed in unison to cadences called by an overseer. With a princely fortune at his disposal, John Joachim did his best to emulate drawings from books of ornate barges used by Egyptian Queen Cleopatra. Docking the boats at rickety piers, John Bulow and several slaves helped the bedraggled settlers tie up and disembark the women and children. Broadly smiling at Douglas, the young man offered a hearty hand shake.

"Good to see you again, Dummett, though not under these circumstances. I'm assuming since you all are here, that New Smyrna was attacked too??!"

Douglas nodded. "From what we could see from the island, it looked as if the whole settlement was on fire. I'm not sure if anyone else got away land side, but those who could get across the river, did; then we fled to the inlet boats with Wildcat on our heels! I'm just proud our militias had foresight to put this plan in place, and we're grateful to you for opening your home. Thank God it still stands!"

"Come on in and join the others, get some food and water. I have rum for the men! About forty poor souls have arrived from all over the Halifax region telling the same story. We're fortifying the stockade as a bastion…musket balls won't penetrate the log walls as long as we can deflect torches or flaming arrows. Those bastards are intent on killing every white man in Florida. From what they've related, every place along the King's Road south of us and past Cape Canaveral is going to be destroyed and they're working their way north. Haven't hit us yet, probably because I have a good trading agreement with King Philip, plus my stockade is well armed. He knows it'll take more than a raiding party to breach us. But, when they have the numbers, they'll come. Their scouts surely know by now that we're staging here. "

Douglas jumped off the dock, turning to help Francesca, wincing in pain when he twisted his knee. "DAMN!! DAMNED LEG!!" Bulow gave his hand to Francesca, helping her off the dock.

"Did you get wounded back there?" John's face showed genuine concern.

"Not by the Seminole, this is an Osage ball I still carry in my leg. It's usually not too bothersome, except when I push my luck running from Wildcat and jumping off docks!" Douglas forced a sardonic grin.

Bulow slapped him on the back, laughing at Dummett's forced attempt at humor.

"Come on, old friend, I have the cure in the house. Let's relieve some of that pain; then we need to make a plan on how to outsmart Wildcat, and hopefully come out of this mess alive!"

NINETEEN

December 28, 1835; Dade Massacre

With news of increasing Seminole attacks concentrated against settlements and isolated plantations in the center and along the east coast of Florida, a military decision was made to move additional soldiers from the west coast outpost of Fort Brooke (near Tampa) to reinforce the more centralized location of Fort King (Ocala). The distance between forts for the foot soldiers was one-hundred miles.

One-hundred eighteen troops of two U.S. companies comprised from the 2nd and 3rd Artillery, and 4th Infantry Regiments under Major Francis Langhorne Dade, departed from Fort Brooke to march to Fort King. They were guided by mulatto slave Louis Pachelo who also acted as interpreter. Their mission was to resupply and reinforce Fort King. Dade expected Seminole attacks at river crossings or in areas of dense jungle where bands of Indians could easily hide, making defense difficult. Unbeknownst to Major Dade, King Philip's scouts were stalking the Army's movements, delaying their assault even past the most advantageous battle positions because they were waiting for Osceola. Once the soldiers crossed the upper Withlacoochee River and reached clearer terrain of pine-barrens where visibility between trees was better, Dade thought they were safer from attack. Making the decision to recall his flanking scouts to enable the column to move faster proved to be a fatal mistake.

Dade's troops, dressed in sky-blue wool uniforms, had been marching through winter jungle shadows for five days in uneasy quiet, but under surreptitious eyes of Seminole scouts. Since Osceola still hadn't arrived, King Phillip and Micanopy made the decision not to wait longer and to attack the Army troops before they reached Fort King. Utilizing a guerilla battle plan, warriors prostrated flat on the ground, covering themselves with fronds and pine needles making them invisible to the passing troops. Just south of the present day town of Bushnell, about twenty-five miles south of the fort, all one-hundred ten government soldiers and eight officers marched smartly in a double column, blindly into the ambush.

The first shot, fired by Chief Micanopy; killed Major Dade who was on horseback. Command then passed to Captain George W. Gardiner, but most soldiers struggling to pull flint-locks from under long winter coats were shot in the initial volley. With the sudden element of surprise and familiarity of terrain, the Seminole attack was fast and murderous.

An eyewitness report by Seminole leader Halpatter Tustenuggee; known to whites as 'Alligator', reads as follows:

"We had been preparing for this more than a year…Just as the day was breaking, we moved out of the swamp into the pine-barren. I counted, by direction of Jumper, one hundred and eighty warriors. Upon approaching the road, each man chose his position on the west side…about nine o'clock in the morning the command approached… So soon as all the soldiers were opposite…Jumper gave the whoop. Micanopy fired the first rifle, the signal agreed upon, when every Indian arose and fired, which laid upon the ground, dead, more than half the white men. The cannon was discharged several times, but

the men who loaded it were shot down as soon as the smoke cleared away...As we were returning to the swamp supposing all were dead, an Indian came up and said the white men were building a fort of logs. Jumper and myself, with ten warriors, returned. As we approached, we saw six men behind two logs placed one above another, with the cannon a short distance off... We soon came near, as the balls went over us. They had guns, but no powder. We looked in the boxes afterwards and found they were empty."

According to survivor, Private Ransom Clarke's statement; the Indians left at about sunset after robbing and stripping the bodies. Later, a group of "about forty or fifty Negroes rode in on horseback", butchering the remaining wounded they found.

Three U.S. soldiers were reportedly the only survivors of the attack. Private Edward Decourcey who had been covered by a pile of dead bodies; Ransom Clarke, who because of his injuries; appeared "dead enough" with five wounds and massive bleeding from his head; and Private Joseph Sprague, also badly wounded. They were each able to crawl away and hide in underbrush or feign death to escape the scalping and final mutilations by the Maroons.

Mulatto guide Pachelo was reportedly taken hostage by the Seminole; though it was suspected he was actually a spy who led the troops to their demise.

Not knowing if Fort King had fallen, the three gravely wounded soldiers attempted to maneuver back to Fort Brooke, but were spotted and chased by a warrior horseman. Splitting up to avoid all three being captured; Decourcey was chased down and mortally wounded, with reports he survived long enough to make it back to the fort before dying of his injuries. Ransom Clarke's is the only written eyewitness report of an Army survivor of the massacre. Joe Sprague made it back to the fort and continued his military service, but since he was illiterate; he did not make a report of the battle.

STATEMENT OF RANSOM CLARKE
(19 years old)

"It was 8 o'clock. Suddenly I heard a rifle shot in the direction of the advance guard, and this was immediately followed by a musket shot from that quarter. Captain Fraser had rode by me a moment before in that direction. I never saw him afterwards. I had not time to think of the meaning of these shots, before a volley, as if from a thousand rifles, was poured in upon us from the front, and all along our left flank. I looked around me, and it seemed as if I was the only one left standing in the right wing. Neither could I, until several other vollies had been fired at us, see an enemy and when I did, I could only see their heads and arms peering out from the long grass, far and near, and from behind pine trees. The ground seemed to me to be an open pine barren, no hammock near that I could see. On our right, and a little to our rear, was a large pond of water some distance off. All around us were heavy pine trees, very open, particularly towards the left and abounding with long high grass. The first fire of the Indians was the most destructive, seemingly killing or disabling one half our men."

"We promptly threw ourselves behind trees, and opened a sharp fire of musketry. I for one, never fired without seeing my man, that is, his head and shoulders—the Indians chiefly fired lying or squatting in the grass. Lieutenant Bassinger fired five or six rounds of canister from the cannon. This appeared to frighten the Indians, and they

retreated over a little hill to our left, one half or three quarters of a mile off, after firing not more than 12 or 15 rounds. We immediately then began to fell trees, and erect a little triangular breastwork. Some of us went forward to gather cartridge boxes from the dead, and to assist the wounded. I had seen Major Dade fall to the ground by the first volley, and his horse dashed into the midst of the enemy. Whilst gathering the cartridges I saw Lieutenant Mudge sitting with his back reclining against a tree—his head fallen, and evidently dying. I spoke to him, but he did not answer. The interpreter, Louis, it is said, fell by the first fire. (We have since learned that this fellow shammed death—that his life was afterwards spared through the intercession of the Chief Jumper, and that being an educated negro, he read all the dispatches and letters that were found about the dead to the victors.)"

"We had barely raised our breastwork knee high, when we again saw the Indians advancing in great numbers over the hill to our left. They came on boldly till within a long musket shot, when they spread themselves from tree to tree to surround us. We immediately extended as Light Infantry, covering ourselves by the trees, and opening a brisk fire from cannon and musketry. The former I don't think could have done much mischief, the Indians were so scattered."

"Captain Gardner, Lieutenant Bassinger, and Dr. Gatlin, were the only officers left unhurt by the volley which killed Major Dade. Lieutenant Henderson had his left arm broken, but he continued to load his musket and fire it, resting on the stump, until he was finally shot down towards the close of the second attack, and during the day he kept up his spirits and cheered the men. Lieutenant Keyes had both his arms broken in the first attack; they were bound up and slung in a handkerchief, and he sat for the remainder of the day until he was killed, reclining against the breastwork—his head often reposing upon it—regardless of everything that was passing around him."

"Our men were by degrees all cut down. We had maintained a steady fight from 8 until 2p.m. or thereabouts, and allowing three quarters of an hour interval between the first and second attack, had been pretty busily engaged for more than 5 hours. Lieutenant B. was the only officer left alive and severely wounded. He told me as the Indians approached to lay down and feign myself dead. I looked through the logs and saw the savages approaching in great numbers. A heavy made Indian of middle stature, painted down to the waist (corresponding in description to Micanopy) seemed to be chief. He made them a speech frequently pointing to the breastwork. At length, they charged into the work; there was none to offer resistance, and they did not seem to suspect the wounded being alive—offering no indignity, but stepping about carefully, quietly stripping off our accoutrements and carrying away our arms. They then retired in a body in the direction from whence they came."

"Immediately upon their retreat, forty or fifty negroes on horseback galloped up and alighted, tied their beasts, and commenced with horrid shouts and yells the butchery of the wounded, together with an indiscriminate plunder, stripping the bodies of the dead of clothing, watches, and money, and splitting open the heads of all who showed the least sign of life, with their axes and knives, and accompanying their bloody work with obscene and taunting derisions, and with frequent cries of "what have you got to sell?"

"Lieutenant B. hearing the negroes butchering the wounded, at length sprang up and asked them to spare his life. They met him with the blows of their axes, and their fiendish laughter. Having been wounded in five different places myself, I was pretty well covered with blood, and two scratches that I had received on my head gave to me the appearance of having been shot through the brain, for the negroes, after catching me up by my heels, threw me down saying "d—n him,

he's dead enough!" They then stripped me of my clothes, shoes, and hat, and left me. After stripping all the dead in this manner, they trundled off the cannon in the direction the Indians had gone, and went away. I saw them first shoot down the oxen in their gear, and burn the wagon."

"One of the soldiers who escaped, says they threw the cannon into the pond, and burned its carriage also. Shortly after the negroes went away, one Wilson, of Captain G's company, crept from under some of the dead bodies, and hardly seemed to be hurt at all. He asked me to go back to the Fort, and I was going to follow him, when, as he jumped over the breastwork, an Indian sprang from behind a tree and shot him down. I then lay quiet until 9 o'clock that night, when Decourcy the only living soul beside myself, and I started upon our journey. We knew it was nearest to go to Fort King, but we did not know the way, and we had seen enemies retreat in that direction. As I came out I saw Dr. G. lying stripped among the dead. The last I saw of him whilst living, was kneeling behind the breastwork, with two double barrel guns by him, and he said, "Well, I have got four barrels for them!" Captain G. after being severely wounded, cried out, "I can give you no more orders, my lads, do your best!" I last saw a negro spurn his body, saying with an oath, "that's one of their officers." (G. was dressed in soldier clothes)."

"My comrade and myself got along quite well until the next day, when we met an Indian on horseback, and with rifle coming up the road. Our only chance was to separate—we did so. I took the right, and he took the left of the road. The Indian pursued him. Shortly afterwards I heard a rifle shot, and a little after, another. I concealed myself among some scrub and saw palmetto, and after awhile saw the Indian pass, looking for me. Suddenly, however, he put spurs to his horse and went off at a gallop towards the road."

"I made something of a circuit before I struck the beaten track again. That night I was a good deal annoyed by the wolves, who had scented my blood, and came very close to me; the next day, the 30th, I reached the Fort."

*Private Joseph Sprague survived the massacre making the sixty-five mile trek back to Fort Brooke, but being illiterate, he made no written account of the battle.

* Ransom Clarke convalesced until April 1836 receiving a discharge from the Army in May 1836 after which he drew a full disability pension of $8.00 monthly. Clarke married in 1838 but died 18 November, 1840; survived by his wife and baby daughter. He was twenty-four.

News of the massacre was reported in the Wednesday, January 27, 1836 edition of the *Daily National Intelligencer*, Washington, DC.

"Major Dade, with seven officers and one-hundred ten men, started the day before we arrived, for Fort King. We were all prepared to overtake them the next day…when an intervention of circumstances deferred it for one day—and in the course of that day, three soldiers, horribly mangled, came into camp, and brought the melancholy tidings that Major Dade, and every officer and man, except themselves, were murdered and terribly mangled."

On that same day of the Dade Massacre, Osceola was delayed at Fort King where he had led a band of braves, ambushing and beheading Indian Agent Wiley Thompson. Because of the fort being undermanned, soldiers were not allowed to open the gates to retrieve Thompson's body. His head was impaled on a stick at a Seminole campfire.

Receiving notification of the horrendous assault and loss of Major Dade and his soldiers; President Andrew Jackson ordered General Winfield Scott to Florida to assume command of all U.S. forces in the embattled territory. General Edmund P. Gaines with 1100 troops reached the grisly site of the massacre just northeast of the Upper Withlacoochee two months afterwards on February 20, 1836. They performed what identifications they could, burying the mangled bodies. After the war ended in 1842, the remains were disinterred and brought to be buried in St. Augustine National Cemetery on the grounds of St. Francis Barracks; currently used by today's Florida National Guard.

Immediately after the Dade Massacre before arrival of reinforcements, General Joseph Hernandez was in an unenviable position of trying to defend several regions and plantations under attack by the Seminoles and Maroons. He assigned Captain Winston Stephens to command the Savannah Volunteers to Picolata. Major Benjamin Putnam was first assigned to Darley's Plantation, but feeling it would be impossible to protect against the Indians, moved his small contingent to Bulowville.

John Joachim Bulow, having enjoyed years of peaceful trading with the natives, resisted takeover of Bulowville by the military, convinced the Seminoles would be further angered by his seeming defection of their friendship by allowing presence of troops. After firing a cannonball at the soldiers, Bulow was initially arrested, but later released.

As head of the local militia; the 'Moskito Roarers', Douglas was summoned to the temporary quarters established at Bulowville for Major Putnam for a meeting. A plan of action needed to be formulated for moving settlers gathered at the plantation to the safety of Fort Marion at St. Augustine. Putnam's small force encamped in the yard surrounding the main house was not large enough to withstand an extended attack by hundreds of Seminoles. Food stores were dwindling and supplies becoming critically short with the unexpected arrival of so many settlers seeking refuge at the large plantation.

"I know you were an Army Cavalryman, Captain Dummett; and we are in need of an excellent rider to send to St. Augustine to request troops to provide safe escort for these families. I have observed, however, you appear to be injured and limping badly. My men are infantrymen, so would you have a suggestion for a rider from your militia that you feel confident could make the ride to Fort Marion to request help for our dire situation? Your volunteer must be cognizant of the inherent danger of this mission."

Douglas snapped to attention. "I need no further thought on the matter, Major. I know the man who can outrun and outride the devil himself, and I know he will willingly and gladly volunteer his services. I'll personally select one of John Joachim's fastest and strongest horses for the ride!"

Unbeknownst to those at Bulowville; Micanopy, King Philip, their warriors, and John Caesar's Maroons were deliriously dancing with one-hundred fifteen scalps; still wet and bloody, belonging to Major Dade and his soldiers.

On that same night of December 28, 1835 with no hesitation and draped in darkness of a waning moon, Bartholomew Pons; New Smyrna's brave young mail rider, rode full bore into unknown dangers lurking in the tunnel like blackness of the King's Road. Galloping hell bent north to St. Augustine, he raised the alarm warning settlers unaware of impending attacks. Historians have since bestowed the honor naming Bartholomew Pons: 'The Paul Revere of the Second Seminole War'.

Heeding Pons' request on his arrival to Fort Marion, Captain W. Keogh was assigned to be sent with the St. Augustine Guards to Bulowville to escort the besieged settlers to safety of the fort. He also carried orders to Major Putnam to first secure buried corn supplies from the Anderson Plantation at Dunn-Lawton to keep them from falling into enemy hands. An added benefit of a successful raid would be to provide needed food for the hungry refugees.

TWENTY

January 19, 1836; Battle of Dunn-Lawton

After the arrival at Bulowville of Capt. Keogh and his troops that could be spared from Fort Marion, Major Putnam and Capt. Dummett finalized plans for a stealth party to conduct a strategic raid. Leaving Captain Keogh with infantrymen in charge of providing protection for the refugees at Bulowville; Major Benjamin Putnam led a small group of seasoned troops of the St. Augustine Guard supplemented by militiamen of the 'Moskito Roarers', commanded by their Captain Douglas Dummett, in a foray to the Anderson Plantation at Dunn-Lawton. The mission was to secure any livestock and buried food stores.

Setting out in three boats onto Bulow Creek on January 18th, the two companies sailed down the Halifax; turning into the Tomoka River basin. Tying their boats to saplings then covering them with brush along the riverbank, they prepared for a trek inland to Dunn-Lawton. Soberly vigilant; the men were aware they were likely outnumbered and out gunned by the rampaging Seminole. Each replayed horror stories in their head of unspeakable atrocities committed by Wildcat and Osceola.

Douglas's heart sank passing the Tomoka peninsula extending into the basin, straining his eyes for any sign or remains of Rosetta in the dark. His parent's plantation house was set back in the trees, but some forms should be visible as they drifted past. Sweet pungent smell of smoke burning his nostrils bore witness to the suspected torching of Rosetta. Douglas thought to himself that possibly his mother's dementia might actually be a blessing; for her not to suffer with knowledge of this loss. Scouts sent the day before with a flatboat of supplies met them with reports the Anderson Plantation was in flames. The nearby Williams Plantation had also been completely destroyed.

After securing and hiding their boats along the river, the contingent of seventeen crept inland through dense palmetto hammock towards the Anderson Plantation and buried food stores. Reaching the smoldering house and seemingly deserted grounds, the men found a makeshift corral the Seminole had roughly constructed to hold horses and other livestock. Deciding to hide and rest for the remainder of the night, they waited for daylight to do their reconnaissance.

At dawn, two warriors approached the corral. Trying not to breathe, Major Putnam's and Dummett's small group ducked under palmettos, signaling to stay low hoping the guards would pass them undiscovered; but luck was not with them. Spotting them, the braves yipped and charged; forcing Putnam to fire the first volley. Gunshots killing the two brought the full wrath of encamped Seminoles rushing into the midst of the badly outnumbered militia. After fifteen minutes of heavy fighting against overpowering odds, with most all soldiers and militiamen suffering gunshots and stab wounds, Major Putnam ordered the men to fall back to the river so they wouldn't be cut off from the boats. In retreat, they found since they had landed the tide had gone out; leaving their boats tied aground, yards from the water. With the large force of Seminoles in pursuit, those who were able helped other wounded to the river, pushing and pulling the rafts under heavy fire into the water for escape; the will to survive and

adrenaline blessing them with abnormal strength. Regrouping at
Pelican Island in the middle of the river for a head count, they realized two men had been left behind with the provision flatboat,
now surrounded by screaming Seminoles. One was able to later
make it back to Bulowville; the other was presumed killed.

Douglas Dummett was grievously injured; shot twice in the
neck and stabbed through the left shoulder. He was dragged
through sawgrass and oyster beds by two of his men and thrown
onto one of the rafts, saving his life. Seminoles were merciless at
the river, taking full advantage shooting at the retreating men unable to return fire. Assailed by arrows and gunfire, they hurriedly
loaded their wounded, pushing the unwieldly rafts through shells
and gravel; struggling to deeper water to float the heavy crafts
away from shore.

Arriving at Bulowville around three o'clock, the wounded and
bloody men were helped from the boats by Captain Keough's infantrymen and the militiamen's anxious wives and neighbors.

This listing was made of the killed and wounded in the Battle
of Dunn-Lawton:

Killed: One Negro belonging to Mr. Anderson
Wounded: From the St. Augustine Guards;
    Major Putnam
    Lt. John R. Mitchell
    Lt. N.C. Scobie
    Sgt. Cooper (disabled)
    Sgt. Domingo Martinelli (since dead)
    Pvt. Julius Reynolds
    Pvt. John Simpson
    Pvt. Bartolo Canovas

Pvt. Charles Flora (since dead)

Pvt. Domingo Usina

Wounded: From the 'Moskito Roarers'; Capt. Dummett's Company B

Capt. Dummett

Lt. W.H. Williams

Sgt. Ormond

Pvt. McMurchie

Pvt. Sheldon

Ben Wiggins, a Negro who acted as a guide

Early the next morning, soldiers escorted the weary troupe of nervous settlers and wounded from Bulowville to Fort Marion at St. Augustine.

Delirious and drifting in and out of consciousness during the journey, Douglas was tended worriedly by Mrs. Bousquet as Francesca wavered in various levels of inebriation; resulting in no help to her suffering husband. Douglas's gaping wounds were angrily ragged, and he was feverishly fighting infection. Two shots in his neck and a stab wound clear through his left shoulder had been sewn up to stem the bleeding; but Dr. Bousquet knew he would need further surgery if he survived the agonizing trip to St. Augustine. The buckboard ride up the rutted King's Road was unrelentingly rough and brutal. Fears of further Indian attacks necessitated speed, causing many of the jostling wounded's stitches to break during the painful journey; causing further shock and loss of blood. They were a sad and disheveled lot as they arrived to safety at the fort, but grateful for food, clean beds, and protection for their families. Seminole attacks wrought a terrible death toll for the settlers, and many survivors decided the risk was too great to ever return to what might remain. Flames in New Smyrna lighting the night sky as they fled for the inlet bore testament to the destruction wrought by Wildcat's Seminoles and the massive slave uprising of John Caesar's Maroons. The fires and slaughters were devastating, and burning scent of smoke was stingingly unbearable…and painfully unforgettable.

Almost two months blurred by with Douglas ranting with fevers and raging sweats as his body fought infection. Times of lucidity were tempered by lapses of incoherent rambling.

Released from the hospital's surgical ward to relative safety of his parent's St. Augustine home, he received routine medical care from a local doctor. Mary tended her son constantly; bathing him, changing dressings, monitoring medicines, and forcing food and fluids. Gradually his wounds began healing and strength and clarity of mind returned. Afternoons were spent alternately sitting in the sun and then the cool shade tending flowers of the lanai. Douglas was still young and strong, but cognizant if he did not soon return to physical activity, he would wither.

Dr. Bousquet visited several times to check on Douglas's progress bringing news of settlers who, after losing all, had decided to take their families back north. He had learned from the doctor at Fort Marion of a request for a doctor for the small town of Greenville, SC, and had accepted the position; believing Florida was too dangerous at this time for his young, growing family. Even with all the stress and chaos since Christmas, Connie had given birth to a healthy son in mid-February; naming him Robert after her beloved father. They were excited to find the position in Greenville, but hoped someday to return to Florida.

Taking his last swig of rum, the doctor turned to Douglas.

"I have one request of you for when you are well enough to return to New Smyrna."

"Anything, Doc, I owe you my life!" Douglas was struggling with the sudden wave of emotion.

Gerard laughed. "You don't owe me anything...because there was surely nothing I could do for you. You're alive only by the pure grace of God, so if you weren't a religious man before; you damn sure better learn how to pray, now!"

Nodding in agreement, Douglas grinned at the normally staid man's advice.

"My wife is damned fond of her bay mare, Belle; and there's been more than one tear shed over her since that terrible night, they've been through a lot over the years. I'd be forever grateful if you would watch for her on the island; she'll come to you if you call her name and offer a handful of just about anything green. I'm banking she was smart and contrary enough to keep from getting caught by Wildcat; and Bandit usually follows her pretty closely. They've been good, gentle horses with my wife and girls. They'd be much relieved to know they had a good home at Mount Pleasant."

Douglas nodded, taking Gerard's hand in his.

"Certainly, when I get back, I'll search till I find them. We set them off towards the beach; they probably followed it south till they cut through the woods back towards the river. My best guess is they followed Chieftain and the other horses back to the corral; Big John will take good care of them. When you come back; I'll wager they'll be waiting for you!"

"Thank you, Douglas; my girls will be greatly comforted to hear this. Don't you push too fast; let your body heal before you ask much of it. I think you've spent your quota of miracles!"

With a wink; Bousquet quickly turned, leaving the room.

Displaying the luxury of plenty lacking at Rosetta, the Dummett's city house, known as the 'Governor's House', was a large, imposing structure. Of Spanish design and construction with clay tiled floors and roof, fieldstone and coquina fireplaces, and pink painted stucco exterior; it overlooked Matanzas Bay and Fort Marion. Intricate ironwork dressed windows holding cedar boxes spilling with red geraniums. The courtyard displayed brightly colored ceramic pots bursting with petunias and purslane in the gated patio. Confederate jasmine wound through iron trellises arching over the double front doors, its heady perfume permeating the interior of the high-ceilinged house. Caribbean furniture of exotic, tropical woods gleamed in bright, sunny rooms. Except for an elegant brass bed shipped from Wolcottville, Connecticut; most furniture was teak, rosewood, or mahogany brought from Barbados.

Luckier than most displaced settlers; the Dummetts had means and foresight to keep a house in St. Augustine near the fort. Thomas and Mary were increasingly suffering infirmities of old age with Mary's increasing dementia a constant worry. When reports of nearby Indian raids became more frequent, Thomas made the decision in the fall of 1833 to leave Rosetta and move Mary and most house staff to the St. Augustine residence in the interest of safety. He and Douglas finally made the considered decision to keep the house, but to sell the bulk of acreage of Rosetta plantation to the MacRae brothers. The MacRae's intended to convert the old Addison blockhouse to their home. Most field slaves went with the sale; but Congo Bob and selected others were retained by Douglas to help with his Merritt Island groves. Two nights before the Christmas night raid on New Smyrna; Rosetta, the sugar mill, and machinery were plundered, smashed, and destroyed. A few loyal slaves stayed for a while; most dispersed to join Seminole encampments or the Maroon colony. Though Thomas had received reports of a massive blaze seen from Rosetta, he had not shared that information with his ailing wife who had not been told that most of Rosetta had been sold.

Blissfully unaware of the plantation's fate; Mary occasionally fussed about her home and possessions left at Rosetta, but was exhausted from the necessary constant care and concern over Douglas's debilitating wounds. He was healing, but fevers and infection were always dangerous threats.

TWENTY-ONE

March 1836

Hesitating at his son's bedroom door, Thomas was not sure how to broach heart-rending news he bore carried in a rolled newspaper. Douglas knew by one look at his father's face something awful had happened, he had obviously been crying. The old man straightened his stance, but still couldn't bring himself to look directly into his son's eyes. The room became a vacuum, filled with loud silence.

"I'm sorry, Douglas, to bring you this news… Jim, Dave Crocket, and all those brave patriots at the Alamo are dead!"

"THE TEXAS TELEGRAPH and REGISTER, Published in San Felipe, Texas

THURSDAY, MARCH 24, 1836;
MORE PARTICULARS RESPECTING
THE FALL OF THE ALAMO:

That event, so lamentable, and yet so glorious to Texas, is of such deep interest and excites so much our feelings that we shall never cease celebrate it, and regret that we are not acquainted with the names of all those who fell in that fort, that we might publish them, and thus consecrate to future ages the memory of our heroes who perished at the Thermopylae of Texas. Such examples are bright ones, and should be held up as mirrors, that by reflection, we may catch the spirit and learn to fashion our own behavior. The list of names, inserted below, was furnished by Mr. J.W. Smith and Mr. Navon, and as we obtain more we will publish them. To Mr. Smith, who has rendered good service to Texas, and to Judge Politon, are we indebted for the particulars, as communicated to them by Mrs. Dickinson, who was in the "Alamo" during the siege and assault.

At daybreak of the 6th inst., the enemy surrounded the fort with their infantry, with the cavalry forming a circle outside to prevent escape on the part of the garrison: the number consisted of at least 4000 against 140: General Santa Ana commanded in person, assisted by four generals and a formidable train of artillery. Our men had been previously much fatigued and harassed by night watching and incessant toils, having experienced for some days past, a heavy bombardment and several real and feigned attacks. But, American valor and American love of liberty displayed themselves to the last; they were never more conspicuous; twice did the enemy apply to the walls their scaling ladders, and, twice did they receive a check; for our men were determined to verify the words of the immortal Travis, "to make victory worse to the enemy than a defeat." A pause ensued after the second attack, which was renewed on the third time, owing to the exertions of Santa Ana and his officers; they then poured in over the walls 'like sheep'!

The struggle, however, did not even there cease—unable from the crowd and for want of time to load their guns and rifles, our men made use of the butt-ends of the latter and continued to fight and resist, until life ebbed out through their numberless wounds and the enemy had conquered the fort, but not its brave, its matchless defenders: they perished, but they yielded not; only one (warner) remained to ask for quarter, which was denied by the unrelenting enemy—total extermination succeeded, and the darkness of death occupied the memorable Alamo, but recently so teeming with gallant spirits and filled with deeds of never failing remembrance. We envy not the feelings of the victors, for they must have been bitter and galling; not proud ones. Who would not rather be one of the Alamo heroes, than of the living of its merciless victors? Spirits of the mighty, though fallen; honours and rest are with ye; the spark of immortality which animated your forms shall brighten into a flame, and Texas, the whole world, shall hail ye like demi-gods of old, as founders of new actions, and as patterns for imitation.

From the commencement to its close, the storming lasted less than an hour. Major Evans, Master of Ordinance, was killed when in the act of setting fire to the powder magazine, agreeably to the previous orders from Travis.

The end of David Crocket of Tennessee, the great hunter of the west, was as glorious as his career through life had been useful. He and his companions were found surrounded by piles of assailants, whom they had immolated on the altar of Texas liberties. The countenance of Crocket was unchanged: he had in death that freshness of hue, which his exercise of pursuing the beasts of the forests and the prairie had imparted to him. Texas places him, exultingly, amongst the martyrs in her cause.

Col. Travis stood on the walls cheering his men, exclaiming "Hurrah, my boys!" till he received a second shot, and fell: It is stated that a Mexican general (Mora) then rushed upon him, and lifted his sword to destroy his victim, who, collecting all his expiring energies, directed a thrust at the former, which changed their relative positions; for the victim became the victor, and the remains of both descended to eternal sleep: but not alike to everlasting fame.

Travis's Negro was spared, because, as the enemy said, 'his master had behaved like a brave man;' words which of themselves, an epitaph: they are already engraved on the hearts of Texians, and should be inscribed on his tomb.

Col. James Bowie, who had for several days been sick, was murdered in his bed; his remains were mutilated. Humanity shudders at describing these scenes, and the pen, as a living thing, stops to gain fresh force, that sensibility may give was to duty.

Suspended animation has returned to the instrument of our narration, and we will continue. Mrs. Dickinson and her child, and a Negro of Bowie's, and as before said, Travis's were spared.

Our dead were denied the right of Christian burial; being stripped and thrown into a pile, and burned. Would that we could gather up their ashes and place them in urns!

It is stated that about fifteen hundred of the enemy were killed and wounded in the last and previous attacks.

COLONELS: W.B. Travis, Commandant
                    James Bowie, Texas Volunteers
                    David Crocket, of Tenn.

CAPTAINS: Forsyth, of the regular Army
                    Harrison, of Tenn.
                    Wm. Blazeby, N.O.
                    Grays, Miss. Volunteers
                    Baker, Miss. Volunteers

LIEUT'S: John Jones
                    J.G. Baugh, N.O. (New Orleans)

Robt. Evans, Master Ord., Ireland
Williamson, Serg't Major
Dr. Michison
Dr. Pollard, Surgeon
Dr. Thompson, Tenn.
Chas. Despalier
Eliel Melton, Quarter Master
Anderson, Assist't Qr. Mast.
Burnell, Assist't Qr. Mast.

PRIVATES: Nelson
Nelson (Cl'k of Austin, mer.)
William Smith, Nacogdoches
Lewis Johnson, Trinity
E.P. Mitchell, Georgia
F. Desanque, of Philadelphia
John Thurston (cl'k in Desanque's store)
Moore
Christopher Parker, Natchez
Heiskill
Rose, of Nacogdoches
Blair "
David Wilson, Nacogdoches
John M. Hayes, Tenn.
Stuart
Simpson
W.D. Sutherland, Navidad, Tex.
Dr. Howell, N.O.
Butler "
Charles Smith
McGregor, Scotland

Rusk
Hawkins, Ireland
Holloway
Browne
Smith
Browne—Philadelphia
Kedeson
Wm. Wells—Tenn.
Wm. Cummings—Penn.
Voluntine—Penn.
Cockran
R.W. Valentine
S. Holloway
Isaac White
Day
Robert Muselman, N.O.
Robt. Crossman, "
Richard Starr, England
J.G. Ganett, N.O.
James Dinkin, England
Robert B. Moore, N.O.
Wm. Linn, Boston
Hutchinson
Wm. Johnson, Philadelphia
Nelson—Charleston, S.C.
George Tumlinson
Wm. Deardorf
Dan'l Bourne, England
Ingram—England
Lewis—Wales

Chas. Zanko—Denmark
James Ewing
Robert Cunningham
Burns—Ireland
George Neggin
Maj. G.B. Jamieson
Col. J.B. Bonham—Ala.
Capt. White
Robinson—Scotland
Sewell, shoemaker
Harris—KY
Devault, of MO., plasterer
Jonathon Lindley, Illinois
Tapley Holland
Dewell, blacksmith—NY
James Kinney
Cane
Warner
John Garvin-MO
Wornel
Robbins-KY
Jon Flanders
Isaac Ryan—Opelousas
Jackson—Ireland
Capt. A. Dickinson—Gonzales, TX
Geo. C. Kimball   "
James George   "
Dolphin Floyd   "
Thomas Jackson   "
Jacob Durst   "

George W. Cottrell   "
Andrew Kent   "
Thos. R. Miller   "
Isaac Baker   "
Wm. King   "
Jessee McCoy   "
Claiborn Wright   "
William Fishback"
Millsap   "
Galby Fugun   "
John Davis—Gonzales, TX
Albert Martin—Gonzales, TX

On hearing about the total destruction of Col. Travis's men, and reasonably calculating upon a sudden movement of the enemy, Gen. Houston thought it advisable to fall back to the Colorado; and though this was done with a considerable sacrifice to the citizens of Dewitt's Colony, we do consider that it was the only safe course. It might have been possible that our troops could have checked the enemy at that place, but there being other crossings, the hazard, we think, would have been too great. General Houston's force was small and not well provided with ammunition. Whilst his position at the Colorado gives times for more reinforcements to join him, and so renders our efforts more imposing and the issue less doubtful. The laying waste of all property which could not be removed will convince our enemies that if they overrun our territory, they will get no booty.

Angrily throwing the newspaper from the brass bed across the room, striking and sending a vase shattering to the floor, Douglas fell back onto the pillows, rolling to face the wall, motioning to his worried father to leave him alone. For a few moments; he would allow himself private tears.

Jim Bowie, his invincible friend who had laughed so often in the face of death; who wrestled Louisiana's biggest gators, killed grizzlies and enemies barehanded with only his knife on the western front, who survived innumerable gunshot wounds and stabbings…was slaughtered flat on his back in his bed. On that day, it was the Devil's turn to laugh. Jim's beloved Texas had taken his wife and two babies; and now… it had taken him.

Struggling to his feet, Douglas acquiesced to using a cane leaning against the night stand. At least he was upright, he thought to himself. The hallway was long and his pace slow, but it felt good to be on his feet after so many weeks in bed. Pain at least assured him he was still alive. His parents looked up in surprise as he entered the great room. Both were teary.

Arthritis was wreaking havoc on Thomas. With no way to stop its twisting rampage; rum and laudanum were the only relief from the worsening, crippling pain. Now, father and son shared the same bedfellows.

"It's good to see you up, son," Thomas motioned for Douglas to join him. "How would you like some libation to celebrate the fact we're still standing?"

"I think that's exactly what I need right now. I have been abed long enough! Has Francesca been here? I fear I sleep through her visits!"

Shaking his head, Thomas turned his face away from his son, debating whether or not to tell him the awful truth, not wanting to be the bearer of yet more bad news.

"No, son; I'm sorry. She hasn't been here in more than a week."

Douglas took the crystal snifter from his father, mulling what he had just been told; then tilting it to his lips, allowed the fiery brandy to burn his throat as it coursed warmly to his belly.

"I thought as much. I know I have hardened with the awful events of our lives… and also know Francesca is not the same woman I married. In my heart, I know the best answer for both of us is divorce; we might then each have a chance at happiness. How hard it is to say that word out loud? How harsh it sounds."

Dragging a chair over in front of Thomas; Douglas sat face to face, putting his hand on the older man's shoulder.

"Thank you, Father; thank you for all you've done…and all that Mum has done. I would have surely died without your loving care and tender mercies. Have you had news of Rosetta?"

Thomas lowered his head before looking sadly up into his son's eyes, slowly nodding assent.

" I have not heard news of the MacRae brothers. I am afraid they were caught at the Addison blockhouse."

"I feared as much. I thank God you and Mum sold and left when you did and didn't suffer through the siege at Bulowville. I must quit withering here and return to New Smyrna to see if anything is salvageable, or if any livestock can be reclaimed. At least I know the land remains, I can rebuild from there. Against all odds, I hold hope in my heart that Big John has corralled and been caring for Chieftain and his mares during my interminable recovery and has not given up on my return, and that something of Mount Pleasant remains from the wrath of the savages."

The older man shook his head. "There are times Mary asks about Rosetta; but they are fewer now, and I feel in her heart… she knows. It is better for her here, now…for both of us. The news is most all slaves left in care of plantations have fled to join John Caesar and his Maroons. I fear our way of life has gone up in smoke."

"Father, I will be making my necessary decisions as to how to proceed, and at your grace will continue my rehabilitation here until I feel of sufficient strength and fortitude to return to the endeavors dear to both of us. Surely the government will soon quell the Seminole and slave uprising, and I can return to what's left of my home and enterprise. That is what I pray."

JOURNAL ENTRY, 27 MARCH, 1836

It is with heavy heart I log the fall of the Alamo occurring on March 6th, only nine weeks after Wildcat's brutal massacre in New Smyrna. Though the Texas patriots stood and fought bravely while grossly outnumbered, in the end, all fighting souls were lost. My dear friend, Jim Bowie, Colonel of the Volunteers, was reported by a survivor, Mrs. Dickinson, to have died with great valor. Jim's slave's life was spared in honor of Jim's bravery. As attacking Mexicans swarmed his sickbed, from his pillows Jim emptied both his pistols; then swung his fabled knife fighting as a tiger; true to his reputation until he was killed. Reports say piles of Mexican bodies lay around his bed. Famed frontiersman; Dave Crocket, along with one hundred-forty brave souls were also lost. My greatest wishes are that General Houston soon brings the wrath and vengeance of God upon the merciless head of Santa Ana, and that the words of Colonel Travis come to pass... "to make victory worse to the enemy than a defeat."

Still agonizing over Adeline, Francesca's grief continued to be compounded by nightmares replaying her daughter's horrific death, and the frightening flight from New Smyrna with Wildcat and Osceola close on their heels. She watched her husband as he fought to survive two gaping and near lethal gunshots to his neck and stab wounds from the Battle of Dunn-Lawton, almost bleeding to death during the painful wagon ride from Bulowville to St. Augustine. For almost two months, Douglas hung to life from his grievous wounds; more dead than alive, tended by his parents and nurses they hired. More and more the young wife sought comfort and stress free solitude of her childhood room at her parent's St. Augustine estate; staying away from Douglas for days and weeks at a time. Occasionally she came to check on her injured husband, but only from a sense of guilt. She was now regularly seeking solace in the bed of her former lover from the fort; the now Captain Otero.

TWENTY~TWO

Journal Entry; 30 August 1839

It is with deepest sorrow I log the news of the sudden death of our beloved Father, Henry Thomas Dummett; acquired age of 64 years. I will deeply and sorely miss his wise ways and paternal tenderness. His gentle love and care of our sainted Mother will most surely open Heaven's gates to him. I find myself grateful for Mum's dementia, for she will not understand nor feel the morbid pain of loss. Anna summoned a priest to offer sacraments over the worldly body, and has complied with Father's directives mandating an immediate burial in St. Augustine Cemetery with no outward show of funeral wreaths or ceremonies. I am sorely grateful my sweet sister, Anna, will move permanently into the Governor's House to care for Mum so her life will bear the least disruption at this sad time. Memories of their great love will sustain us.

The Second Seminole War raged seven bloody years, from 1835-1842. Eventually, most all the eastern Native American tribes were transferred by various treaties to reservations in Oklahoma and the West; leaving scattered few bands escaping to the swampy interior of south Florida. For several years those remaining Seminoles carried out sporadic raids against any whites returning to reclaim and rebuild their homesteads; but they had lost the warriors and leaders to mount additional or effective wars to regain their lands. Though the Seminole never surrendered to the United States government, they were defeated. The Second Seminole War was one of our costliest wars in both lives and property lost, and was also the largest slave uprising in our history. Though there was eventual regrowth, the South would not recover the industry and wealth that was lost.

After convalescing in St. Augustine, Douglas left Francesca at her parents' estate. He relocated to Tallahassee for a short time before returning to Mount Pleasant; hiring a group of four former soldiers to ride with him to provide protection on the King's Road to New Smyrna. Though full scale Seminole attacks had lessened; bands of marauders still posed a threat.

First passing Rosetta on their way south, Douglas was disheartened to find nothing left of his parent's house but pieces of blackened wood within stone foundations and scattered metal spikes. Seminoles had tried to burn the sugar mill; succeeding only in destroying the roof, leaving coquina walls charred but mostly intact. Prized steam engines, great sources of pride for his father, had been smashed with parts strewn among other machinery cast into weeds and palmettos. Sections of pipe were missing; most likely taken for weapons. The plantation appeared deserted. Douglas hoped to himself that Congo Bob had taken the hounds with him, and they had not ended up tied to spits over native cooking fires.

Nervously watching over their shoulders with a heightened sense of foreboding, Douglas knew the guards were hoping to reach Mount Pleasant before dark; but he was exhausted and hurting from the rough ride.

"Sorry guys, I suggest we make camp among the mill ruins for the night. We have about forty miles to go, and I don't want to be traveling the King's Road in darkness. I'll take first sentry watch, but I think it wise to forego a fire and just stay as quiet as we can. There's room inside the walls for the horses to be corralled. As well as being concerned about renegades, as I remember, these woods are full of black bear; and we can't afford to lose our mounts!"

Bedrolls and mosquito netting were unrolled inside the thick, coquina walls, giving the small party some respite against biting bugs and merciless mosquitoes. Sleep was fitful, even in the deathly still of night; each twig snap signaling unseen danger. All were thankful for the first rays of dawn peeking through the dense forest.

Douglas consented to building a morning campfire to fortify the men with mugs of hot coffee with their jerky. He knew they faced another grueling day on horseback, but if they rode hard, weather cooperated and they weren't slowed by unforeseen perils, they should reach New Smyrna by dusk.

Even in full daylight, sections of the King's Road plunged into darkness, the roadway tunneling through canopies of overhanging trees and bushes so thick they blocked the light. Invisible whips of cutting branches reached out, slicing their faces as they rode. The journey was harrowing, but luckily, no Seminoles were encountered. Finally the vista began changing, trees thinned allowing glimpses of the Hillsborough River to their left as the roadway widened entering New Smyrna.

The devastation was complete with the town in rubble. Approaching what had been the main street, he could discern locations of where buildings had been by wreckage and scattered stones of foundations. New Smyrna was now nothing more than an overgrown ghost town, its bones being picked by long-legged birds arguing over the remains. Anything of use or value had been plundered.

Continuing south, Douglas thought for sure his eyes were deceiving him. There in the gloaming and barely visible in the rising river fog, Mount Pleasant stood, tall and white across the water. She was not unscathed, but she was standing. Coaxing the tired horses reluctantly into the slow moving river, they swam across to the island, stumbling up the slippery bank. Douglas turned to look back at the ruins of the settlement, now still and quiet, overcome by nature's ruthless advance. Screams and embers of that Christmas nightmare of seven years earlier were now silent, cold, and buried.

"Well, Massa Douglas!!! I was beginnin' to think you was never comin' back!!"

Recognizing Douglas and relieved the intruders meant no harm, Big John strode grinning from his hiding place around the south side of the house.

"GOOD GOD, JOHN; AM I GLAD TO SEE YOU!! Douglas dismounted into the arms of the old slave. Big John lifted the younger man, hugging and swinging him in enthusiastic circles.

Quickly scanning the homestead, Douglas noted smoke streaks tracking up the outer walls from the windows on the first floor. Other than that, there didn't appear to be further damage to the house.

"Are you alone...where's Etta?"

"My Etta gone, sir! She gone most a month, now. Her big heart filled up full of sadness, I think it busted of clear sorrow. She buried out there by Miss Addie's bird. She loved that chile, so I knowed that would make her happy. All dem others lef; but me and Etta knowed we're too old and dis our home. Dos 'noles tried to burn dis house, but me and my Etta got de fire beat out. Dere's a big hole in de floor front of de fireplace, but that's all. Dey come back after chasing you, but my Etta hid your big fiddle and Miss Mary's candlesticks in our cabin under de bed wif de quilts. They took most everything else but some cookin' pans we tossed in de brush, and left after dey started de fire. We laid Miss Addie's statue down in de grass and covered it wif fronds so dey didn't see it. It's still layin' down, but it's not broke!"

"What about Chieftain?" Douglas feared the answer.

"He okay, Massa Douglas; I keep 'em out of sight out back in de south corral. He come back to his girls, but he only have three now, but these past years Mister Chieftain done his duty with dos mares and sired some real pretty colts and fillies, eight now and one 'bout to drop. Two of Miss Francesca's mares gone from dat night, I think they got scared from all dat whoopin' and hollerin' and got loose and ran. They be on this island somewhere…iff'n the bears ain't got'em. Only have two cows and three goats left, de others too stupid to run, so them Injuns got'em. Oh, and I rounded 'bout a dozen chickens and two roosters, have a pretty good flock now, but dere's more guineas in de palmettos cause I keep finin' eggs on de ground! My Etta had a good store of beans all canned up in jars, and melons and squash in de garden, so wif fishin' and shrimpin' and all… I been eatin' okay."

Big John leaned close to Douglas's ear and whispered, "Your gold is safe, sir. Dey didn't find it." Douglas nodded in understanding and relief.

"I knowed you got away in dos boats, cuz when de 'noles showed up back here, dere weren't no yellow scalp on de belts!!" John grinned, patting Douglas on the head.

"I'll never be able to repay you for all you've done, John. I'm truly sorry about Etta."

"She be in a better place now, sir, and she be lookin' real purty. I put her silver ear bobs on her so she be all dressed up for Heaven. She loved dos ear bobs! I build me a bench out dere by her grave; sos I can sit with her and we can watch dat old river together. She loved dat river."

Douglas draped his arm over the old slave's shoulder; then turned to face the weary horsemen.

"Gentlemen, I welcome you to Mount Pleasant. You are welcome to spend the night and return to St. Augustine on the morrow, unless you have need of further employment. I will need hired hands to help restore my groves and men at arms to provide protection, so please think about it and discuss it with your families when you arrive home. New Smyrna will rise again with those willing to brave the wilderness to work and build. There is no more beautiful or bountiful place on earth. Water and tie your horses, then come inside. Tonight, we have a roof...and fried chicken!!!! "

Big John lit a fire in the fireplace, balancing a large, cast iron skillet over the flames on two stones on one side, while a pot of water hung from a tripod next to it. Soon enough, chicken was crackling and spattering lard in the pan, emitting a delicious scent over the circle of famished men.

"Iffin dis chicken don't fill yur bellies; Big John been crabbin' today!"

"Grab a plate and don't be shy, I'm so hungry, as my friend Jim used to say; my big ones are eatin' my little ones!"

To a hearty round of applause, John dumped a heaping bowl of soft shell crabs into the boiling water, but cheers broke out when Douglas held up a bottle of mahogany colored rum; bowing with an exaggerated flourish.

"Gentlemen, I give you magic elixir from the late but beautiful Rosetta…surely, it is truly the nectar of the Gods!"

Tall tales and drunken laughter pierced through curling fog as the men finally let down their guard to feast and drink. Stories went late into the night until one by one, the weary travelers kicked off muddy boots before passing out onto bedrolls spread about the main room floor. Ragged snores rising in unison competed with a chorus of frogs from surrounding trees, until the night was deafening.

In following years, Douglas threw himself into expanding his orange groves planted on the northern end of Merritt Island, the peninsula situated perfectly on rich, fertile land between Moskito Lagoon and the river. Trees blossomed strong and bountifully in the perfect humidity between the waterways, bearing delightfully sweet fruit.

Dummett Groves grew and prospered; their citrus commanding highest prices from consumers in the north willing to pay premium money for the juicy orbs. Douglas Dummett became one of the largest exporters of oranges in wilderness Florida.

Settlers ventured back into Florida, ever vigilant against attacks by remnants of Seminole bands refusing to leave, instead retreating to the Everglades; their tribes and families decimated by years of war against the US Army. By 1842, most native tribes had been coerced from their homes to the western reservations, many dying during that long, forced exodus in our country's shameful…'Trail of Tears'.

TWENTY~THREE

1842
Leandra

"I was nigh on sixteen first time I laid eyes on Captain Douglas Dummett. He was ridin' a tall black stallion that fancy walked like he was steppin' on hot coals. His buckskins was fairly bustin' with muscles, and his hair...well, it was blowin' light in the sunshine and was the color of lemons in the shade. He was the purtiest white man I ever did see. Mammy Sue say the Captain had powerful tragedy in his life, and sadness rode his shoulders like a widow's cloak".

"Massa Woodruff, afore he was shot and killed by that Injun boy, served with him on the 'Moskito Roarers', and said the Captain was a fine man and the best Injun fighter he ever seen. The Captain came that day to Spring Gardens to soak his wounded leg in the magic healin' spring and to tend to business with the widow Woodruff."

"Me and Prissy ran ahead to the water and ducked down, hidin' in the reeds along the bank to watch him. He had his back to us when all a sudden he started strippin' off all his clothes; layin' them on a rock till he was clear nekkid! Priss pulled her apron up to cover her face, squealin' over and over, "Oh, my! Oh, my!! Knowin' we most likely get lashed for lookin' at a white man, but I couldn't look away. All of a sudden like, he just turned straight around smilin' right at me. I pulled Priss up by the arm and started running for the house, trippin' and draggin' her through the scrub 'cause that silly girl would not take that apron down! We ran breathless all the way to the cookhouse; then fell on the floor in a fit of giggles. We quit and stared down at our hands all quiet and guilty like when we saw Mammy Sue standin' in the shadows with her big, wooden stew spoon. Mammy looked more scared than mad, and told us she saw big trouble for the Captain in the tea leaves. But all I knowed was, when he looked at me... there was summer lightnin' in his eyes!"

On Woodruff's Spring Garden Plantation, (now Deleon Springs) a short walk through jungle and scrub palmettos led to an idyllic Eden where palms, tangerine colored hibiscus, and heady jasmine circled the perimeter of a natural, limestone cauldron. Cold, crystalline water shot upwards from the dark blue abyss, mysterious in its origins, bursting to the surface in millions of tiny bubbles. Even with a distinct mineral odor of Sulphur; it was a favored hole of ancient turtles and large gars; and locally famous for its healing properties. Great blue herons and snowy egrets flaunted their finery strutting along stone edges, joined by chattering guineas and ibis. With such a smorgasbord of game; giant alligators napped satisfied around the springs, sunning between and atop fieldstone boulders; the prehistoric predators safe in their armament.

Soaking in the cool mineral springs had a very cathartic effect on the young man's wound. In conjunction with cold stones carefully placed and stacked along his leg, most swelling could be controlled between treatments. Mammy Sue was revered for her African drawing poultices passed down through her family, much like Granny Moon's. Preparing several poultices at a time, she tied them in small burlap bags for Douglas to take home for additional applications as needed. When steeped in strong, black tea made from yaupon asi holly leaves, they were applied to festering injuries to draw recurring infection to the surface where boils could be lanced and drained. A paste of ground nicotiana packed tightly into the wound worked to kill infection.

Without an armed spotter, keeping a wary eye on surrounding gators made it impossible for Douglas to fully relax in the water. Finally, climbing dripping and shivering from the spring, he drip dried in the unrelenting sun, reveling in its warmth before pulling on his breeches. Smiling to himself, he thought of the two girls that had been watching him from the reeds and fled; mortified he had seen them spying.

He found himself strangely fascinated by the taller girl, her slim, nubile figure accented by darts and pleats of a gingham dress pulled up high as she ran barefoot across the grass; revealing slender, muscular legs. African heritage was evident in her dark skin and long, curly black hair, but her finely chiseled features indicated presence of Seminole or Cajun blood. She was young and beautifully wild with defiant eyes…and Douglas was intrigued.

Riding Chieftain to the burned skeleton of Spring Gardens' house, he was greeted by Jane Woodruff, waving from a small cabin behind the ruins. She was still wearing widow's weeds after the death of her husband at the hands of a young Indian boy they had raised. Still a handsome woman, stress of wilderness life and grief were showing on her face. Her long brown hair plaited into a single braid was coiled and pinned atop her head.

"Douglas, it's so good to see you, again. I hope your leg and other wounds aren't paining you so much, anymore. Come sit down in the shade where there's a bit of a breeze. It's much cooler here on the porch than inside. I'll have Mammy Sue get us some lemonade."

"Thank you, Jane; the mineral springs definitely help."

Anticipating the request, a smiling Mammy Sue appeared with a pitcher of the tart drink, obviously proud of her offering.

"Just the way you like it, Missy, fresh squeezed and jus' enuff sugar to take de pucker out!"

"That's the way I like it, too," Douglas laughed.

The two rocked on the shady porch sipping the lemonade and engaging in light conversation until the actual subject of Douglas's visit was addressed.

"Jane, I am truly sorry about Joseph's death, he was a valued militiaman and a good friend, and sorry you have decided to sell Spring Gardens to return north. I come prepared with what I hope you will consider a fair offer for many of your slaves before you send them to auction. I intend to replant Mount Pleasant, and have groves needing work on land I purchased down at Merritt Island before the war. A few of my older slaves returned to New Smyrna; but I need young, strong backs for stonework, reclamation of citrus groves at Merritt Island... and I wish to build a log cabin there on the lagoon." Taking a breath, he continued. " Were it not for expenses and loss of crops after seven years of Seminole wars, I would willingly buy Spring Gardens from you. Speculators are returning to Florida flush with cash, and once statehood is granted, it will bring revitalization and rebirth. You should receive a good price for this beautiful land. "

Jane Woodruff nodded at Douglas, forcing a brave smile while dabbing her eyes with a torn and soiled handkerchief. Her words began tumbling out.

"Douglas, I am sorry to display myself as such a weak woman, but I am frantic over recent news from Enterprise that they are in the throes of a smallpox outbreak. Nine slaves and one little white girl have already died with others showing the spots. I cannot bear one more loss in my family! I thought I could return and rebuild. It was Joseph's dream for our children to have this God forsaken land, this piece of paradise that he loved... but that so cruelly took his life. I have no heart left to stay, and all I can see is what was lost and cannot be replaced. My beloved is buried here, scalped by the very savage he raised with only a tender hand; and six of our beautiful children dead of the Yellow Fever. That is the hardest to bear. I will take my two remaining children back to the bosom of our family in Pennsylvania to live, and when I look back at Spring Gardens in my memory, I will only grieve leaving my loved ones buried in this uncivilized territory."

Douglas knelt at the distraught woman's side, pulling her sobbing into a hug against his shoulder. Regaining her composure, she continued...

"I intend only to take a couple drivers and a few house-servants and their children. Our livestock is mostly all dead by the distemper, so I have no real need of wranglers. Most young field slaves ran off with the Seminoles and that devil, John Caesar. I would hope to keep families together, if that is possible for you, as the ones left have been loyal in these awful times. I have made arrangements with our solicitor in St. Augustine to handle the sale and all business matters of this wretched plantation, but I will accept your draft for your selection of slaves. If God is willing, we will be leaving within a fortnight, so it's best we get this done."

"Along with field slaves, stone men, and blacksmiths; I specifically would offer a good price to buy Mammy Sue, as I need a good cook. I have Clarice, and she tries; but I miss Ma Etta's recipes and kitchen abilities that I recall were similar to dinners I have enjoyed at your table. Also, a girl I saw at the springs this morning. She was tall with long, curly hair; I don't remember seeing her here, before."

Before she could stop herself, the Widow Woodruff inadvertently stiffened, glancing sideways at Douglas, barely able to hide her expression of disgust; correctly imagining his intended purpose for the slave girl.

"That would be Leandra Fernandez. Her mother was a green-eyed Seminole woman I suspect of being a French Cajun bastard. She bedded with one of our field slaves who brought her to live as his woman here at Spring Gardens before the wars, but she died of the pox when her child was about seven. He ran away to join the Maroons leaving the girl with Mammy Sue to tend. Yours is not the first male head she has turned since she blossomed into womanhood. I must warn you, she is rebellious and high spirited and will not be easily broken. She was competent in housekeeping and helping Mammy Sue with cooking...and has always been a favored playmate with my children; so she has not been turned out for field experience... if that is your desire. Though I should tell you, I felt she was unnecessarily attentive when the tutor came to instruct with the children's lessons. She's healthy and strong and should be old enough to breed. You have a good eye for horseflesh, so let's get this done."

Catching the edge in her voice, Douglas nodded in agreement; embarrassed his old friend's wife had read his carnal intent. The now silent widow Woodruff set down her glass, using both hands to slick her hair back behind her ears before leading the way to slave quarters for his selections to be made. With deals finalized, arrangements were made for Big John and Moses to bring wagons in three days to transport the slaves and chattel to their new home at Mount Pleasant.

Swinging atop Chieftain, Douglas turned to wave goodbye to Jane. Without response or gesture, she turned, disappearing into the house in an angry swirl of black skirts.

TWENTY-FOUR

Sparks and pungent smoke curled upward through darkly shadowed oaks as a fire crackled, blazing in front of the slave quarters. Negroes began gathering, sitting on straw bales loosely arranged in a haphazard circle around limestone banked flames; their damp faces reflecting the orange fiery glow. Their chorus of voices and mostly makeshift instruments combined in strange African melodies, remembered from similar tribal circles in that far-away land. Congo drums and tom-toms had been fashioned from leather hides, stretched, tied, and tacked over barrels and kegs of varying sizes; determining timbre and depth of tones of each drum. Flutes had been carved of palm and stringed instruments were fashioned from available implements. These nighttime songs and ritual chants were important in passing down memories to their children of homelands, their village tribes, and ancestors. Without written records; stories, music and dance were the most prevalent methods to celebrate and preserve their African culture and history for future generations born in this foreign land.

Carrying his drink onto the porch where he stood in shadows watching the dancers; Douglas was amazed at how wild and free they were. Their movements were so different from proper English holds and stiff steps of formal dances his mother had taught him as a boy. Teaching of basic dance steps was virtually mandated as a rite of passage for children of privilege, and Thomas Dummett's holdings, moneyed family, and military rank ensured his children were included in the upper echelon of

British elite. Douglas's favorite had always been the elegant and romantic Viennese waltz; finding it exciting to watch two bodies so perfectly fluid, gracefully synchronized, and floating in each other's arms.

These primitive African dances were earthy and strangely primal. Negresses who appeared staid in daylight drudgery, transformed into stomping, writhing seductresses by night's campfire.

He found himself transfixed by Leandra, unable to look away from her. Entering the circle shyly at first, as she danced she bent over releasing her hair from its demure scarf, whirling it in curly mayhem. Relinquishing all inhibitions she became lost in the pounding rhythms, exposing long lean legs as her skirt swung wildly to the incessant beat as she stomped; twirling and spinning, pumping her elbows into distorted angles. Draping her thin scarf as a prop, she began pulling it across her body in deliberate, overtly seductive movements. Her dance ended to appreciative applause of other participants and onlookers; then, for a fleeting moment, she turned to glance provocatively over a bare shoulder, looking directly through the darkness at Douglas with those unbelievable eyes.

Her brief, but obviously intentional smile to the porch took Douglas by surprise, causing him to catch his breath and step backwards. He was mesmerized by how lovely she was in the flickering firelight, how freely and beautifully she danced, a wild thing unfettered by false modesties. But mostly, he couldn't believe the profound effect she had on him; and the thrill of an almost forgotten awakening from deep inside. He was more than entranced, and deep in his heart…he felt he was in trouble.

When exhausted dancers took the sidelines, laughing and wiping sweaty faces, they gulped from a communal dipper of sangria wine fermented from plantation fruits. Big John stepped into the circle alone, his commanding presence demanding silence until he began patting his chest and thighs. Soon, all were on their feet, joining him in the rhythmic rocking and slapping of their bodies with the syncopated clapping of hands. Blending hauntingly, their voices joined in the impromptu singing of the Negro ballad; *'Bring Me Some Water, Sylvie!'* Perfectly synchronous, their song melded, drifting with the spiraling smoke, slowly, smooth and dark; lifting the slave anthem as a lament. Big John's bass resonated with pain felt of the lyrics, and after the sad song ended, the gathering broke up as revelers wandered to their quarters. Smudge pots, ignited from the campfire before buckets of water extinguished it, were carried and placed under elevated chickee huts to thwart ravenous bugs. Quiet fell over Mount Pleasant as night darkened and inhabitants succumbed to sleep, lulled by relief of cooling river breezes.

Feeling the rum's languid effect and listing slightly, Douglas slowly maneuvered the stairs to his room where his tub waited, half filled with now cool water.

"CLARICE! I need some hot water to warm this bath!"

"Yassir, I'll get it right now!"

"Tell Moses I need him!"

Douglas sprawled across the four-poster; contemplating and enjoying the old familiar warmth of desire. He was surprised his arousal wasn't just familiar lust; but the actual feeling of desiring a woman, again. Anticipation of her was exquisite agony. Opening his eyes, he realized Moses had appeared in the doorway.

"Go to the slave quarters. Bring the girl, Leandra, to me."

"Yessir, I be fetchin' her right back!"

Clarice came into the room, sidling two buckets of boiling

water hanging from a yoke through the narrow doorway. Carefully pouring the hot liquid while swishing it with her hand, she blended and warmed the water in the big copper tub.

"When the girl gets here, make sure she's washed before sending her up."

"Yes Massa Douglas, I'll see to it she be real clean."

After what seemed to be an interminable length of time, Douglas began drifting in and out of a fitful sleep, interrupted by visions of Leandra's mesmerizing dance, her wild black hair…her hauntingly beautiful green eyes. A noise at the door startled him awake…and there she was.

"Come here where I can see you."

The girl stepped hesitatingly across the darkened room, stopping where a patch of moonlight knifed through the window onto the floor. She was scared, but stared defiantly, chin up at the man who now stood before her. Wearing a freshly laundered, gauzy white nightgown; the scent of orange blossoms wafted around her. Translucent enough to reveal a thin but curvaceous black silhouette under the light cotton, her shift was cut low enough to outline tantalizingly rounded cleavage. Suddenly self-conscious; she nervously tugged the bodice up in an attempt to cover herself.

"Over on the bedtable there's a candle and matches. Light it and bring it over here." Douglas was enjoying her nervousness.

Leandra did as she was told, carrying the flickering candle mounted in a blue china bowl carefully across the floor. Handing it to Douglas, he set it on a low stool by the tub, its warm glow illuminating a small circle of quivering light, deepening the shadows in the corners of his chamber.

"Let down your hair." Douglas waited while she hesitantly

reached up with both hands to untie the scarf, letting her hair fall in curly masses over her shoulders and down her back.

"Turn, for me."

Barefooted, Leandra slowly turned in place; fixing her gaze to his.

"I remembered you and your friend were quite interested in watching me from the reeds at Spring Gardens, so I wish to satisfy your curiosity by having you help me bathe."

The girl, embarrassed at the memory, momentarily dropped her eyes from his.

"No, don't look at the floor; I want your amazing green eyes on me."

With that, Douglas opened and removed his robe. Handing it to her as he stepped fully naked into the tub, slowly lowering himself into the warm water, his arousal was fully on display. His gaze never left hers.

"My mother's handmade soap is on the dresser." Douglas grinned to himself at her discomfort.

Leandra retrieved the fragrant bar, shyly reaching to hand it to him.

"You can start by washing my back!"

Kneeling behind the tub, she dipped the bar into the water, slowly rubbing the soft soap across his back. Marveling at the muscles rippling across his shoulders; she began rinsing with a large, copper ladle he handed her, slowly and deliberately soaping then pouring the warm water along and over his arms, using her hands to gently wipe off remaining lather. Her delicate fingers lingered, tracing his defined biceps and gnarled scars on his left shoulder.

"Good… now, take off your gown and wash my chest."

Rising to obey, Leandra pulled the filmy gown over her head, dropping it to the floor leaving her standing topless in sheer pantaloons. A sudden shallowness of her breathing took over; not from fear...but in unfamiliar, strange anticipation. She knelt this time beside the tub, leaning down in front of Douglas, reaching across his chest with the soap, one breast dipping into the water as she stretched, aware of his eyes smoldering on her body and the effect she was having on him. Stroking across the hardening of his nipples, she coyly answered his stare looking up from under long, black eyelashes, shyly returning his smile. Suddenly unable to resist temptation any longer, he reached, lifting her to him; ravenously smashing her breasts to his mouth and pulling her squealing, laughing, and splashing into the tub with him. The beautiful slave girl responded with a feral passion of her own, opening a surprising and wondrous new world to them both.

In the distant darkness of the jungle...a black panther screamed.

TWENTY~FIVE

By the end of the Seminole Wars in 1842, Douglas had been able to repair most damages to Mount Pleasant in New Smyrna, and while amassing and purchasing slaves to work his groves; he had bought the stunning fifteen year old slave girl, Namona Leandra Fernandez, who was becoming an integral part of his life. Surprisingly, and against all that was culturally acceptable in the pre-Civil War South, they fell deeply in love. Bowing to social mores' of the times, Douglas built Leandra her own house in the line of slave quarters behind the main home of Mount Pleasant so not to offend sensibilities and prejudice of the small settlement's citizens, and to maintain the appearance of decorum. Douglas was elected judge in New Smyrna, and as long as he didn't flaunt Leandra or try to legitimize her, gossip stayed in the shadows and he remained a respected member of the community.

Having served as the first Postmaster at Tomoka from 1833-1836, Douglas Dummett became a member of the Legislative Council of the Territory of Florida serving as a representative of St. John's County from 1843-1845. Later, after statehood was granted, he became a member of the Florida House of Representatives from Moskito County in 1845.

1843

From the mist hovering above the water, the moon rose tall in lavender skies, its majesty reflecting a thousand times skimming across the slowly moving river. With the sky darkening; three blue herons squawked flying over in formation chased by a contingent of noisy geese, whitewashed by the now brilliant, blue-white lunar orb. Douglas leaned against an oak porch pillar, lifting his face to the cooling river winds, the splendor and tranquility of Mount Pleasant always amazing him. Turning, he smiled at Leandra resting comfortably in a rocker, bare feet pulled up under her. A long patchwork skirt, lovingly embroidered at the hem, tucked loosely around her legs. The lustrous dark hair he loved splayed over her shoulders, gleaming in the low light as she slowly brushed its length; smoothing and untwining thick, myriads of curls.

"This is my favorite time of day," he reminisced. "Mum called it the 'violet hour', the time when day gently turns to night. If we are particularly blessed this evening, maybe mullet will draw the dolphins to chase them into the river and entertain us with their ability to fly!"

Leandra smiled back, eyes closing enjoying the refreshing night air, moist against her skin. Rocking, she began humming a melody learned in her youth, blending rhythms of her African father and songs of her Seminole mother. Musically haunting, Douglas was surprised but pleased at how similar it was to old English and Scottish hymns his own mother had sung when he was a boy.

Turning his face into the breeze, he surrendered his senses to the delectable scent of Confederate jasmine surrounding the veranda, its tiny, star shaped flowers bursting with sweet perfume.

"Come inside with me, my lovely. I'll brush your silken hair," he flourished with an exaggerated bow.

"Sure, you will," she cooed, recognizing his tone…and exactly what it entailed! Slowly she rose from the rocker, stretching and walking ahead of him to the bedroom, exaggerating the sway of her hips knowing how it tantalized him.

Breaking into a run, she beat Douglas into the bedroom and dove headlong, squealing onto the big four poster. He chased behind grabbing her ankles, dragging her struggling and laughing to the foot of the bed. Locking her gorgeous eyes into his, she stopped thrashing, smiling seductively up at him as she rolled onto her back. Propping herself up on her elbows, Leandra untangled her legs, and with agonizing slowness, pulled up her skirt, spreading her knees; exposing her promise of warm, silken pleasure.

"You are surely a vixen, because you have put a hex on me!"

Suddenly silent, she straightened her arms pushing herself up, raising her mouth to reach his, pulling him deeply into her.

Journal entry: May 4th, 1843

*The misted morning shrouds the dawn in shades of deepest pink,
with Herons' cries to scarlet skies…
over water, black as ink.
The Moon falls away to another day, leaving Heavens of azure hue.
A lost breeze sings through white geese wings…
and their feathers turn to blue.
But when the sunshine wearies, deep purple claims the light.
A Heron screams as a blue Goose sings…
as they fly into the night.*

He didn't want to admit it, but repair work on Mount Pleasant had been rough for Douglas. Ragged wounds from the

Battle of Dunn-Lawton had been slow to heal, with many nights spent in agony. Rum numbed most of the pain, but caused problems of its own; leaving his mornings fogged and blurry. Orange groves planted on his property acquired in Oak Hill had matured enough to produce excellent fruit, but showed the need for more cleared land to expand the groves. After destruction of his trees by the Seminole; several sweet orange trees planted by Minorcan slaves of the Turnbull Colony were found growing wild. Those few trees survived the onslaught because they were not part of obviously tended groves. Only a few of those remaining overgrown trees were located, but they were enough to provide grafting stock for new groves.

His cold bud grafting method of sweet orange seedling shoots to Florida's native sour orange trees was producing delightfully sweet fruit, bursting with delicious juice. Overwhelming northern demands for the delectable oranges were padding Dummett's bank accounts, but rapidly outstripping supply. More land was necessary and bought further south at Merritt Island on a sheltered peninsula between the river and Moskito Lagoon; more trees, more work...more slaves. Dummett Groves became the largest shipper of citrus in Florida; the strain eventually becoming recognized world-wide as the start of 'Indian River Fruit'.

Douglas worked on building an isolated outpost cabin in the groves at Merritt Island on the lagoon about forty miles south of New Smyrna and almost thirteen miles north of Port Canaveral. Rustic and basic, it was constructed of logs cut on the property, providing snug but comfortable living quarters when he traveled down to oversee work at the groves. Serving another purpose, it was far from gossiping tongues of New Smyrna. The welcome privacy allowed Leandra and him to eat together on the front porch, and freedom to walk hand in hand far from prying eyes. Lavender evenings were spent lost in one another; unashamedly swimming nude and making love in deep purple water of the lagoon.

Making sure necessary creature comforts were stocked and a pot-bellied wood stove installed, Douglas ordered copper pans and a mattress from Jacksonville; over stuffed with down to be used over intertwined ropes suspended from cedar bedposts and framework. A freshwater spring gushed close by with additional barrels collecting rainwater set in under steeply angled eaves of the cabin. Mazes of berry bushes tangled and climbed across a low, rocky ridge a short sand path walk about 100 yards behind; bursting with succulent blackberries, raspberries, and huge luscious strawberries. Oranges were the primary crop of the prolific groves; but there were also grapefruit, lemons, kumquats, and limes.

Those days were some of the happiest of their lives, with isolation of Merritt Island allowing the couple total freedom to live as they wished. When governmental duties mandated his return to New Smyrna, Leandra reverted to being his property; relegated to slave quarters of Mount Pleasant until cover of darkness. Here at Merritt Island; they were free to just be a man and woman in love.

Douglas spent hours teaching her steps of the gracefully swaying Viennese Waltz; with skirts swinging high in the turns, Leandra twirled in classically proper hold in his arms to his perfect baritone emphasizing songs sung to the rhythm of 3/2 time. Teaching him the Seminole Stomp Dance from the Green Corn Ceremony learned from her mother, they would dance in wild abandon, spinning and stomping; he in a breechcloth, she natively topless in long, brightly colored, geometric patterned Seminole skirts. With shell shakers tied to their ankles; the rattling accentuated rhythms of their punctuated movements. Flashing seductive smiles at him over smooth, bare shoulders, she carried the bloom of youth provocatively in the body of a woman.

His cello playing became intensely passionate when he played for her. With elbows high and eyes closed, his head jerked with the rise and fall of the music like a man possessed. Clutching the neck of the instrument against his left cheek, he alternated between manic fingering at the frets to the bow coming to life in his hands; drawing and pushing as an extension of himself, pulling a sexual crescendo from inanimate strings! The outside world be damned; their sensual existence at the groves was Utopia.

TWENTY~SIX

1844

In the two years since he bought her as a coltish girl, Leandra was developing into an alluring, beautifully elegant woman; curves and roundness replacing gangly girlish angles. Douglas encouraged her continuing education, expanding her initial years of lessons overheard and practiced with the Woodruff children from teachers brought to Spring Gardens Plantation, along with intense Bible studies tutored by Jane Woodruff. Illegal for Leandra to be formally schooled in the south, she devoured books from his library, reading in island privacy Mount Pleasant and Merritt Island groves afforded. Her intelligence and desire to learn made her a quick study, the unexpected depth and dimension adding to her charms. Douglas found himself increasingly enthralled by her…the emotions perplexing him at the same time.

After a night of torrid lovemaking in his bedroom of Mount Pleasant, Douglas fell back on the plush pillows, spent and sweating even though the February night was cool. Leandra rolled to him propping her head on his chest, reaching across to hug him, her arm dark against his skin, counting the breaths as his breathing slowed. With closed eyes he returned her embrace while stroking the length of her hair, languishing in the sense of calm and contentment she brought him.

Suddenly lifting his hand, she placed it down on her belly,

causing him to open his eyes and questioningly turn to her; pulling his hand away.

"Mammy Sue says I am with child." She spoke quietly and deliberately, her eyes pleading into his, unsure if her news would please or anger him. "No other man has lain with me."

Sitting up, Douglas flipped the coverlet off his legs, the surprise of her announcement showing on his face. Lifting her chin with one hand, he placed the other gently onto her tummy. With the initial shock passing; he now broadly smiled into her searching eyes.

"When?"

"She says late into summer...before fall."

Douglas grabbed her tightly to him, "It's about time! Thank God, IT'S ABOUT TIME!!!!"

Jumping out of bed in obvious glee, spinning with arms outstretched, Douglas turned to Leandra, now sitting up with hands over her mouth in surprise at his reaction.

"I DON'T KNOW WHAT TO SAY!!! I DON'T KNOW WHAT TO DO!! MY CELLO, I NEED MY CELLO!!"

Douglas raced down the stairs with Leandra following hesitantly behind, not sure of his intent.

Grabbing the instrument, he carried it out onto the porch, bracing it between his knees. With his left hand low on the frets drawing the bow across the strings with his right; music danced through the night air across the river in an impromptu concerto of exuberant trills and runs.

Wakened from sound sleep from his cot in the slave quarters, Big John listened to the jubilant music swirling through the night; rolling over, he smiled.

Journal Entry; February 4, 1844

Tonight and forthwith there will be music at Mount Pleasant, and I will insist that only joyful noise be heard from this plantation in hopes God himself hears my pleas for a healthy child; and that once again I will know the happiness of my baby's cry!

In March 1844, Douglas received request paperwork for a Writ of Divorce issued from the State of Georgia where Francesca was living in Savannah. Without contest or remorse, he signed; finally ending their marriage.

There was plenty of gossip for the small settlement of New Smyrna. Though she was staying on the island at Mount Pleasant during her pregnancy, news of Leandra's burgeoning belly was common knowledge. Some speculated one of several young buck slaves was the father; but those who had seen the way Douglas doted on her…knew the truth.

Spring and summer brought numerous trips to the groves with the couple enjoying complete privacy of Merritt Island and skinny-dipping in the lagoon afire in colors of sunset. Douglas loved her pregnant body, kissing her belly where little feet pushed and stretched her skin, marveling at the feel of his baby's kicking and laughing at bouts of uterine hiccups. He was as much in love with the child as he was with her. She delighted in gathering orange blossoms and elderflowers, crushing the petals until they released fragrant oils to make perfume or for scenting bathwater. Blackberries and blueberries were picked for jam, pies and wines; with plump, fresh strawberries sliced atop shortcakes.

After cooking, elderberries were safe to eat in pies or jellies, and were doubly useful because the edible flowers were used in making a light wine similar to champagne. Masses of elder blossoms dipped in sugared-flour and fried in hot lard into delicious elderflower fritters became one of Douglas's favorite sweet treats.

With the pregnancy becoming too heavy for Leandra to comfortably travel, Douglas put Mammy Sue in charge of her care, ordering every whim be catered. Evenings he would sit by her bed brushing her hair; other nights bringing the requested cello; losing himself in passionately played concertos by Bach and Handel. Leandra laughed, swearing the baby kicked to the rhythm of the music.

AUGUST 18, 1844

"Massa Douglas, you need to get yourself outta here, lessen you want to borne dis baby, youself! You go back to dat big house, us womenfolk be takin' care of bizness, here!"

Mammy Sue pushed Douglas towards the front door of Leandra's small house.

"What can I do? Can I help?"

"You want to help some? Prop all de windows open to get some breeze in here. I be bubblin' molasses outta mine ears iffen it don't cool off! Dis August heat don make birthin' any easier for Missy Leandra, neither!"

Douglas set to work, opening all hurricane shutters over windows in the two-room house, securing them against outer walls with loops of rawhide nailed to the wood. The system was primitive but effective, allowing some shade cooled breezes to cross ventilate the stifling house. There was a noticeable and immediate drop in the inside temperature.

Douglas paced outside, only leaving briefly to retrieve a bottle of rum from the main house. Leandra's labor was long and difficult with this first child, her screams ripping late into the night, until finally; cries of a baby signaled a successful delivery. Running inside, he was greeted by a profusely sweating Mammy Sue in a bloody apron, but she was grinning as she placed a bundled, wailing, creamy-skinned baby into his arms.

"What is it? WHAT IS IT, MAMMY??"

"You got you a son, Massa Douglas! A strappin' big boy…and he bright!"

"Leandra???"

"She fine, sir, just pooped out! Come on in."

Douglas stepped tentatively into the bedroom where Leandra sat propped against a pile of clean, white pillows atop a freshly changed mattress stuffed with moss. A canopy of mosquito netting wound through a leather loop hanging from the ceiling draped over the iron bed. Her long black hair was loose, splayed out in an explosion of curls against the pristine linens. Her eyes were closed. The pregnancy had brought a new dimension of womanhood to her; a softness to her features and fullness to her breasts. He had never seen her looking so beautiful. Lifting the netting to sit on the bed, he unbundled and admired his son, counting tiny fingers and toes. Leaning to kiss her, Leandra opened her eyes; strikingly emerald in the low candlelight. Touching Douglas's face, she smiled that radiant smile of all new mothers.

"Are you happy?" Her question was tentative.

"I am going to name him Charles, after my grandfather!"

"But, are you happy??"

"I am the happiest man in the world!!" Tears glistened as he bent to kiss her. "I'll be right back."

Carrying his new son through the dewy grass to the river, he turned, lifting Charles to face the moon and stars.

"Dear God, thank you for this great blessing of fatherhood you have bestowed on me once again. This is Charles; protect him, Lord; let him grow into a fine man worthy of your grace. Let him be kind, morally strong, and physically healthy. Let him love; as he is loved. Let him live in a peaceful world, and when he is an old man on the porch of Mount Pleasant; let him be graced watching his grandchildren at play. With this prayer, I beseech you. Amen."

With Charles safely snuggling at Leandra's breast, she opened her beautiful eyes, briefly smiling as Douglas kissed her on the head before walking outside. Lighting a cigar, he turned to look through the doorway at mother and swaddled son softly illuminated by lamplight; wishing the scene could be captured in a portrait to always be remembered. Slowly blowing smoke rings, he walked alone to his dark house.

Journal entry; August 18, 1844

God has given me a son, a fat, healthy boy I will name after my grandfather and my father. He will be Charles Thomas Dummett; heir to Mount Pleasant, father to my grandchildren; inheritor of my dreams and fortune. My promise to him on this blessed night is that he will be loved as no other child and given every opportunity his humble father can provide. He will be taught to read and write with an education befitting his status as my son, and he will be exposed to music, languages, and the classics. He will be taught matters of etiquette, culture, and courtesy to further his life in society. He will learn to be kind and gentle with God's creatures, and to respect all gifts from Mother Earth. He will be an honest man and others will respect the value of his word. He will prosper and be generous. He will be a free man. These are my hopes and most earnest intentions for my son, and I pray to be a worthy father of whom he will always be proud.

TWENTY~SEVEN

March 3, 1845; Journal entry

I mark this day with great jubilation! The legislature has granted Florida statehood with her becoming the 27th state in this grand union of the United States of America. This day has long been anticipated and greatly coveted since Spain first conceded this 'land of flowers'.

December 1847; Journal entry

Missive from my sister Elizabeth sends news of great joy of the birth of their third child, a son to be christened with his father's name, William Joseph Hardee, Jr. He will be called Willie! This addition of a new baby ensures Beth's life is quite busy with one year old Anna, and two year old Sallie still in nappies! William's army career requires much travel and all are grateful for Auntie Anna's help with the children in St. Augustine during his missions. Anna has said in confidence that Elizabeth is frail and sorely exhausted.

1848

Leandra rolled onto her side, sleeping the guileless slumber of the innocent. Douglas propped himself on his elbow, listening to her breathing, admiring her naked form, outlined and glowing in the moonlight. As many times as she had come to his room, to his bed, he was always taken by her beauty... and his profound reaction to her. This old four-poster was like a raft for them, he thought; a raft to bind them together in solace, floating them through gathering storms, and riding rough waters of prejudice and hate. She was his true love, his soulmate; a gift he thought he'd never have again. But southern propriety and law of the land would not allow him to take her for his wife. She had borne him a beautiful son, and now again; her body was ripening and rounding with the promise of another baby to grace their lives. Welcome to them, but unspeakable bastards in the eyes of those around them; recognized as property, chattel...nothing better than animals. His standing in the community, his judgeship, even their very lives could be at risk if he publicly revealed his true feelings. Illicit acts with slave women were tolerated and even condoned; but there could be no official commitment to her, no proud acknowledgement of their children, only life in shadows behind closed doors...and together in torrid nights in this bed.

His brain racing, Douglas sat up, recognizing the need to record verses into his journal before sleep could come; knowing the words would disappear before morning light. Quietly closing the bedroom door behind him, he went barefooted to his high-backed desk, opening the inkwell putting quill to paper. On this night in this hour, anguish for what he knew could never be, overflowed from his poet's heart.

Journal entry; April 3, 1848

LEANDRA

This African beauty of mahogany,
*   doth rend my heart and tear at me... but satisfies all dreams*
*   to be.*
So, I'll cast my fate to blinded sight! Evoke emotions of the night!
*   I'll laugh with this woman of reckless heart, and dance in*
*   dreams of bliss!*
*   I'll burn in the fire of her passion...*
*   and drown in the depth of her kiss.*
But I must rise no further than I can fall... measure love, not
give it all!
*   For this woman of passions bright and passion bold...*
*   she is to have... but not to hold.*

Finishing his journal, Douglas limped to the bedroom window to check the incoming river tide. Pulling billowing curtains aside, he was startled by Leandra's touch on his arm as she joined him, kissing his shoulder as she stood beside him in the darkened room. Suddenly, she leaned forward peering out the open window.

"Who is that?"

"Where?"

"There... along the bank, someone's sitting on the bench."

Straining his eyes, Douglas struggled to focus on the large form, outlined by low light of a now clouded moon.

"I think it's Big John; it must be him... probably talking with Ma Etta."

"But, it's so late; he's always in bed before this. Mammy Sue complains she can hear him snoring from her cabin before the frogs and crickets start singing!" Leandra was obviously concerned.

"I'll take a walk down, you go back to bed." Pulling on breeches and boots, Douglas bent to kiss her belly before leaving the room.

Once outside, the night air proved more damp and chilly than the interior of the house. Taking a deep breath, overpowering sweetness of jasmine bushes caused him to cough as he made his way across the wide yard. Grateful he had grabbed a jacket off the rack; his boots left a trail in the wet grass as he approached the bench. Now he could definitely tell it was Big John, his broad shoulders facing the river, holding a small bouquet of roses and white lilies on the lap of his overalls.

"I saw you from the upstairs window, figured you were out here talking to Ma Etta."

Douglas leaned to brush oak pollen off a wing of Addie's egret statuary before sitting down on the bench beside the old slave.

"What's wrong, John, didn't she want the flowers...being her obstinate self?" Douglas smiled at his recollection of Etta's bossiness before turning to look at the man who hadn't answered.

Big John sat stoically silent, his wise eyes staring blankly at the river. He had gone to be with Etta; both now free in the Promised Land.

Douglas sat for a few minutes before closing the old man's eyes; then taking one of his wizened hands, held it in his, tracing a lifetime of callouses in the huge palm. Leaning his head against the slave's shoulder...he wept.

"Well, John, these hands lifted me onto my first horse; and both of my children, Adeline and Charles have ridden on these strong shoulders as I did as a boy. I know Ma Etta has been calling you for some time...but I am selfishly going to miss you."

Tucking one rose into the old man's shirt, Douglas placed the remainder of the fragrant bouquet on Etta's grave; then sat heavily on the bench with John until dawn.

Big John was buried beside Ma Etta by Adeline's white egret; his death causing the entire plantation to go into mourning. Grief brought a new depth of timbre to the cello; with Douglas's raw emotions lamenting his loss through music. Leandra watched through bedroom windows as night after night, with starlight glinting on his blonde hair, Douglas sat on the riverside bench leaning over the gleaming instrument, his bow sending pure melancholy into sad skies.

A few weeks later, Bartholomew Pons swam his horse across the river, galloping to Mount Pleasant with a missive from Anna Dummett detailing Mary's failing health; forcing Douglas to make the decision to journey to St. Augustine. Not sure of his mother's reaction, the desire to let Mary meet her grandson before she died convinced him it was now or never to make the trip with Leandra and four-year old Charles.

"Leandra, I want you to prepare for a journey. We are going to take Charles to meet his grandmother; we'll travel overland to Enterprise to catch the steamboat to St. Augustine. It will be an easier trip for you than the long ride up the King's Road. Take the green taffeta suit I had made for you; it compliments your beautiful eyes! It's my hope Jacob Brock is still captaining the 'George Washington' on that route. It will be good to see him again after so many years."

Leandra had misgivings about the taffeta suit; unable to fasten the skirt over her greatly expanding belly, she was relieved the blouson jacket hid the buttons that wouldn't pull closed. Tomorrow would be spent on horseback...she didn't relish the trip, but had no choice in the matter. With time of the essence, they couldn't chance a broken carriage axle; horses would be faster on the unforgiving roads.

Leaving the plantation at dawn, the lightly packed small entourage first traveled north on the King's Road until turning west to Enterprise on the St. John's River. Accustomed to quiet of the plantation; a miserable night was spent in a hotel smelling vaguely of urine… next to a saloon hosting a loudly singing crowd celebrating an engagement. More squalid than Douglas remembered; the only way to cross the town's rutted, pot-holed streets without sinking knee-deep into the mud was by maneuvering across boards thrown haphazardly atop the muck. Morning brought welcoming blasts of a steamboat whistle heralding arrival of the *'George Washington'*.

Tall, brass buttoned, and impeccably uniformed; Jacob Brock presented much the same except now his black hair and drooping mustache shone silvery white.

"GOOD GAWD, DUMMETT!! I heard Osceola damned near killed you at Dunn-Lawton!! "

Brock's enthusiastic handshake pulled Douglas into a back-slapping hug.

"He gave it a good try, we lost some fine men; but my mother's prayers must have protected me."

"Come on aboard, it's good to see you with my own eyes. I heard those heathens shot you twice in the neck and then, Goddammit…stabbed your shoulder through and through!"

"You heard right!"

"My Gawd, Douglas. Ask your Momma to say a prayer for me!"

"Actually, that's why I'm making this trip. We just received a missive from my sister that Mum's dying."

Shaking his head, Brock stroked his mustache, checking the horizon before glancing back, putting his hand on Douglas's shoulder.

"Sorry to hear that, son. Your mother is a fine woman; please take my regards."

Pausing in uneasy silence, Brock nervously tugged at his ear before spitting over the rail.

"I hate to broach another sad subject at this time, Douglas; but have you had any word on the alligator you've sought?"

"Over the years I have had reports on sightings ranging from Jacksonville to Cape Canaveral. One hunter even tried to pass off a skeleton head with a knife he must have impaled into the skull for the reward, but it wasn't my Bowie. It seems gold brings out the charlatans. If I may, I would appreciate your permission to hang another poster onboard. That big bull is crafty, and I believe he is still alive; for surely I would feel the relief of his death in my heart."

"Certainly; if you would leave several posters with me, I will have them hung again at each of our landings and waystations."

"Thank you, Jacob. Your offer is most appreciated; I'll have them delivered to your stateroom."

The cruise north on the St. John's to St. Augustine was thankfully uneventful. Leaving the horses tended by Moses on the lower deck; Douglas, Leandra, and Charles settled into the privacy of a small stateroom, away from curious eyes. Soon, lulled by rhythmic paddlewheels slapping the river and the rocking sway of the boat; the three napped cuddling together in restless sleep until awakened by the steam whistle screaming their arrival at Picolata.

Opting to wait for the more remote stop at Picolata instead of disembarking at busy Palatka docks; the overland horseback ride to St. Augustine was not as familiar, but Douglas felt it would be quicker and would draw less attention. Thickly forested hammocks and pine-barrens kept the ride interesting, providing a more comfortable trip through shade blocking hot afternoon sun. With outskirts of St. Augustine becoming visible in the distance, Douglas was shocked at how the city had grown and spread since his last visit. Approaching downtown, turrets of his parents' 'Governor's House' came into view; its glass windows glowing golden orange from reflection of the setting sun; now just dropping behind the western horizon.

Massive, ornate, and lushly landscaped with tall Queen and Silver Palms, hedges of Elephant Ears and Philodendron; the 1791 'Governor's House' dwarfed neighboring buildings. Mary's signature pink Floribunda Roses flanked wide iron entry gates that were opened for the riders by uniformed guards; the horses' hooves clattering across the courtyard of clay tile pavers. Handing Charles down to a slave, Douglas dismounted into a crowd of baying hounds; then busied helping Leandra from her horse.

Nervously tucking errant curls behind scarf ties of her bonnet, the young woman wiped her face with backs of her hands; then shook road dust from her long skirt.

"Do I look alright? Do you think they'll accept me?" Leandra was wishing to be anyplace but St. Augustine at this moment.

"You look lovely; but I want you and Charles to wait out here until I come get you. I need a few moments alone with my mother and sister."

Climbing the veranda steps, Douglas noticed for the first time the large black funeral wreath hanging on the front door. Opening the door, he was greeted by his teary-eyed sister, Anna; who threw herself into his hug. Heavy skirts of her voluminous mourning dress swished along the floor, her long blonde hair braided and wound into a bun held by tortoise-shell combs, her only adornment a large, pearl cameo brooch at her throat. Patrician and ivory-skinned; Anna was a younger version of her beautiful Scottish mother.

"I'm so sorry, Douglas; Mum just passed this morning. She's in state in the parlor."

Clinging in their embrace; the brother and sister spent a few moments of tears in each other's arms before composing themselves to walk arm in arm to the parlor.

Mary's white satin-lined, rosewood casket sat open on a large, black-velvet draped library table in the center of the room. Dressed in a pale pink dress overlaid with pink lace, her flawless face showed evidence of unfamiliar rouge; garish against her light skin. Boughs of orange blossoms were tucked beside her corpse in the casket; their sweet scent competing with the strong incense burning in silver holders at each corner of the dais. Tall, twisted-armed candelabras stood as sentries around the room; their candles casting eerily moving shadows in the high ceilinged, heavily curtained room.

Quietly strumming the guitar; Mary's hair-lipped slave, Daniel, stood sadly in the corner. Douglas recognized the music as haunting Scottish hymns his mother sang when he was a boy; her pure soprano passed from her ancestors originating from the moors of her homeland. He was grateful she had the foresight to teach those songs to Daniel, and with a twinge of guilt; wished he had been more attentive in learning them.

Returning to the main hall and taking both of Anna's hands in his, Douglas's eyes searched hers.

"I have someone I want you to meet, dear sister; actually two.

I'll get them and pray you recognize the love I have for them, and beseech that you will, in time, feel the same. My heart; that has been so long closed and empty; has finally been reborn with joy and overflows with love once again."

Leandra and Charles were summoned into the Spanish mansion, the young woman hesitantly stepping forward with Charles peeking from behind her full skirts.

"Anna, I would like you to meet your nephew; my son Charles. And this is his mother; Leandra."

Masking her shock in deference to her brother; Anna initially forced a smile looking into the frightened dark faces, but then softening; extended her hand to Leandra.

"Welcome…I see why my brother is so taken with you! Who is this handsome young man behind you?"

Charles stepped shyly from behind his mother, snapping his heels and bowing curtly in the military manner taught by his father.

"My goodness; such manners!" Anna responded with a deep curtsy. "Come to me, child; I can see your handsome father's face in yours. I am going to be your most favorite Auntie Anna!"

Responding to his aunt's warm greeting, Charles stepped into her hug. Beaming, Douglas was relieved and grateful at his sister's response.

Anna stood, straightening her skirts, fixing her younger brother with a wry smile. "Well, Douglas, it's probably better this news waited until after our parents were gone…because it surely would have finished Father! Come into the dining room, I'll have Beulah bring us something to eat. You all must be famished. Charles, do you like cookies?"

They all laughed at the young boy's vigorously shaking head.

"Beulah will be pleased to hear that, as her cookies are widely acclaimed here in St. Augustine!"

The next two days passed in a blur with the burial and evenings around the dining table laughing at old stories. When family friends arrived to pay their respects; Leandra and Charles retired to their upstairs quarters, wisely staying out of sight. Acceptance by a loving sister was one thing; acceptance by southern society was drastically different.

"Before you leave, dear brother, I have something Mum wanted me to give to you. She gave me her engagement ring and asked me to give you her wedding pearls and earbobs Father gave her… for when you take another wife. Anything else you desire will be gladly given. Also, my intent now that Mum is gone is to convert this home into an inn in hopes it will become self-sustaining. These past months I have already begun opening the dining room for Sunday dinners for officers from Fort Marion. They are most appreciative of Beulah's cooking, and many purchase her pies to take with them back to their quarters."

Smiling into his sister's anxious face, Douglas pulled her close.

"You, my darling sister, shall be the most beautiful and successful innkeeper in St. Augustine…and Beulah's pies will be hailed far and wide as the stuff of lore!"

Greatly relieved at her brother's willing acceptance of her plan and laughingly kissing both his cheeks and forehead; the two embraced as they had as children.

"Anna, your love is the greatest gift; so I hope you will not feel me ungrateful for asking for one more of Mum's prized possessions. Charles has shown great interest in the cello; so I want him to receive instruction to learn string fingering of the guitar until he is able to handle the larger instrument. I, of course will send him to boarding school in the north for his formal education when he is older; but until then, would you consent to allowing me to have Daniel. He has memorized many of Mother's Scottish melodies I would like for him to teach Charles. I remember him as a gifted guitarist and feel he would make an excellent tutor for my son."

"I will miss him, Douglas; but he has tutored others who will remain, and surely our dear mother is smiling at this request. It brings me joy to know your son will carry her legacy of music as you did. I'll sign the ownership transferal papers tonight; you'll have the documents to take with you on the morrow's journey to Mount Pleasant. I'll have Daniel gather his belongings. He has no woman or children, so there should be no grief or hesitance on his part."

TWENTY~EIGHT

1848~1855

In the following years, three daughters were born to Douglas and Leandra at Mount Pleasant; Louisa in 1848, Kate in 1852, and Mary in 1854. Those were happy years on the plantation, filled with music and laughter of children. The family thrived as Douglas's carefully tended citrus trees provided abundant harvests and prosperity, with Dummett Groves becoming one of the largest exporters of fruit to northern states. In 1850, President Zachary Taylor died in the White House, V.P. Millard Fillmore ascended to the Presidency; and P.T. Barnum presented Swedish opera sensation, Jenny Lind, in New York City. Herman Melville published his novel, *'Moby Dick'* in 1851. Franklin Pierce was elected President and Harriet Beecher Stowe's landmark novel, *'Uncle Tom's Cabin'* lit the fire of abolition in 1852.

With the Seminole Wars reduced to small sporadic raids, the settlement of New Smyrna was rebuilding with an influx of homesteaders bringing assorted talents and strengths to the small community.

Charles was always at his father's side; watching, learning, grooming to be the next master of Mount Pleasant. Accompanying Douglas to the groves at Merritt Island from the time he could walk, Charles was a natural horseman and by the age of eight...a fearless sailor. By twelve, he had mastered grafting and could expertly tell by the look and feel of an orange if it was at the perfect stage of ripeness for picking and shipping. A doting older brother;

he adored his little sisters who trailed behind him, marching in mock parades of curls and giggles. Days were spent playing under watchful eyes of Leandra and Clarice in the manor house and around the extensive yards of Mount Pleasant; but mother and children retired to her small house in the slave quarters to sleep… except for those nights she was summoned to Douglas's bed.

June 10, 1853; Journal entry

It is with utmost sadness I record the untimely death of my dear youngest sister, Elizabeth Hennery Dummett Hardee, having achieved only thirty-three years of life; the last spent in wasting illness. William arranged a full military burial befitting his station and rank. She is laid to rest in St. Augustine National Cemetery. Anna shall continue caring for Beth's four motherless children ranging in age from three to eight at the inn until William's battlefield duties are complete.

Closing his journal and stepping from his stifling den to the cooler front porch, Douglas shaded his eyes focusing on a woman and two children walking up his lane from the landing dragging a squealing pig. Two hounds ran baying to intercept, barking and circling the three strangers stopping their progress. His whistle brought the dogs running to him.

"Mrs. Shive; welcome to Mount Pleasant! I didn't recognize you at first. Come sit down; I'll have Clarice bring us some orange juice. You have had a long walk from Oak Hill in this beastly heat!"

"Thank you, Captain Dummett; that would be appreciated. Mr. Malloy was kind enough to row us across the river. This is my son and daughter; David and Margaret."

Eleven year old David stepped forward to shake hands while

eight year old Margaret curtsied. Dirt farmers; they were rent-
ing Jane Murray Sheldon's cabin on Jane's father's property;
the original Murray homestead between New Smyrna and Oak
Hill. Recently arrived from Philadelphia; the Shives intended to
buy the small claim from the Sheldon's who had bought Tom
Stamps' plantation in New Smyrna after the Seminole War, and
had moved to town to finish construction of their hotel atop the
foundation of the old fort. Though a poor family, the Shive children were polite and well mannered.

Suzanne Shive tied the loudly complaining pig to a porch
post, shaking a cloud of dust from her faded skirt before bending
to sniff roses decorating the steps. Standing no more than five
foot, she and her children were blonde, tanned and barefoot. A
plowing accident had left her husband hobbled, leaving most of
the homestead heavy work to her and David. Young and pretty;
Mrs. Shive appeared more like an older sister than the mother.

Gratefully accepting the sweet cool juice, Mrs. Shive and the
children quickly emptied the proffered glasses. Setting the tumbler down and dabbing her lips with her skirt, she took a deep
breath before broaching the reason for her visit.

"Captain Dummett; last night a big cat got into our coop,
killing all my chickens. I was hoping you might be willing to
trade this pig for a few layers…and a rooster? Others along the
way didn't have any to spare."

Briefly assessing the skinny pig tied to his porch and turning
to the worried woman, Douglas's smile brought an expression of
relief to her face.

"That's a fine pig, Mrs. Shive; I'll look forward to some quality bacon. AMOS; gather about a dozen layers and a rooster for
Mrs. Shive…and a sack of oranges; and have Charles ready his
sail boat."

"Thank you, Captain; but that is much more than the pig is worth!"

"Nonsense; there is no price too high for good bacon and ham! Besides that, Mammy Sue and Clarice will render lard to cut into their pie dough and flavor their fry cooking through the next several months…all from that one pig! I am already looking forward to fried pies! What kind of cat do you think it was… panther…or could it have been a bear?"

"No sir, tracks weren't that large. My husband believes it was a bobcat."

Moses came from the barn carrying two kicking gunny sacks of irate hens, clucking their displeasure at the indignities of being sacked; and a third with a rooster. Kojo followed dragging an overfilled bag of oranges.

"My son, Charles, will sail you home. You would not make it before sunset if you tried to walk, and I could not allow you and your children to chance these woods in the dark. My best to you and your husband, Mrs. Shive; I can sympathize with the pain and infirmity of a leg injury…as I have long endured."

"We thank you for your kindness, sir. We will say an extra prayer for your leg."

Mrs. Shive climbed easily into the boat. Douglas lifted Margaret to her with her brother and the fluttering, noisy bags; waving as the small craft tacked south from the bank. Watching them leave, he summoned Moses and Kojo; untying and handing the lasso around the pig to the older slave.

"Moses, make sure our henhouses are secure and the goats and pigs are herded into the barn at night. There's a bobcat lurking…and he has developed a taste for an easy dinner."

Mammy Sue came out onto the porch gathering juice glasses, dabbing her face and neck with a wet handkerchief.

"Lawdy, Massa Douglas, it shore be hot over dat stove!"

"Well, Mammy Sue; put whatever you're cooking on the back burner. I need to row over to the General Store to see if my order has arrived from Savannah. I should be back before dusk."

"Yassir; I keep the stock bubblin' and wait to drop those dumplins till I see you at the launch."

Just as promised, Douglas pulled his rowboat up onto the shallow river beach next to Charles' small sail boat at dusk, tying the anchor rope to a tree at the top of the bank. Carrying a large box, he was obviously pleased with the contents.

"LEANDRA!! GIRLS!!! COME SEE YOUR GIFTS!!"

Excitedly running across the yard towards him; seven year old Louisa and three year old Kate squealed with anticipation at this unexpected surprise.

"WHAT IS IT, PAPA?? WHAT IS IT??"

"You'll see soon enough, go get your mother; we'll open it in the living room!" Douglas was enjoying their excitement every bit as much as they were.

Leandra walked in through the kitchen, carrying baby Mary on her hip.

"Okay, girls...I'll cut the twine and you three can open the box."

They gasped as the box ripped open revealing numerous bolts of jewel-toned silks and velvets, colorfully embroidered brocades, white eyelet lace, and bright taffetas. Flinging their arms around him, Louisa and Kate jumped in excitement at the beautiful materials. Douglas removed two parcels, hurriedly taking them to his den before they could be opened.

"They're beautiful, Papa. BEAUTIFUL! "

Beaming at their reactions, Douglas smiled at Leandra who was stroking the luxurious fabrics in amazement.

"Where did these come from?"

"I had them ordered from Paris. They were shipped into Savannah and I've been awaiting their arrival. You and our girls will be princesses of Mount Pleasant in the loveliest gowns in Florida. We have a new Irish family in town; the blacksmith, Michael Malloy, and his wife Catherine; who is a talented seamstress by trade. She will sew dresses for you and the girls, and vests and frock coats for Charles. Mrs. Malloy has agreed to allow me to send a boat for her in the morning to come to Mount Pleasant to take necessary measurements, and for her to suggest designs for the most stylish fashions. As heirs to Mount Pleasant and Dummett Groves, I want them to be appropriately dressed befitting their station."

Carrying pots of chicken and dumplings and green beans, Clarice and Mammy Sue came scurrying from the kitchen as if on cue. Mounded plates of steaming sourdough biscuits served with bowls of orange marmalade and stacks of bright red sliced tomatoes completed the dinner offering; but an unmistakable scent of cinnamon and spices brought dessert promises of pumpkin pie, now cooling on the kitchen window sill.

"Now, we feast! Then, Charles and Daniel can entertain us with their new selections."

JOURNAL ENTRY; 15 DECEMBER 1855

I am full with blessings of love and joy. Though but eleven, Charles is big of build and showing marvelous aptitude for music; amazing us with his talent and passion for the guitar. My heart breaks at the thought of sending him so far to school, away from his adoring mother and me, but he must learn refinement of his studies before entering Yale at fifteen. He has been accepted for boarding at the private preparatory Episcopal Academy in Chesire, Connecticut;

*and will receive advanced studies in English, Latin, and Greek, phi-
losophy, mathematics, and science. The campus is quite lovely, over
one-hundred acres as I recall from a visit while at New Haven. He
is a kind and loving brother, this night sitting on Kate's bed, playing
and singing 'Silent Night' to hasten her journey to sleep. His sweet
voice is a comfort to us all, but Kate will miss him most. Of all his
talents, I am most pleased with his good heart and gentle soul.*

Christmas 1855 was a happy time with gifts and feasts for
all. Sunday school children presented a Christmas pageant to the
appreciative gathering of New Smyrna's townspeople who joined
in singing the familiar carols. The small community was growing and thriving, tentatively recovering from the devastating
Seminole Wars. Plantation slaves at Mount Pleasant were granted
an extra day off for the holiday, with men receiving new shirts and
each woman two colorful bolts of material. Children celebrated
with individual bags containing candies and one bright coin each.
Slowly turning a calf carcass on the iron spit, voices harmonized
with Moses' passionate baritone in the ballad … 'Wade in the
Water'. Listening from a wicker porch rocker, Douglas rocked
with his eyes closed, admiring the choral blend accompanied by
gourd banjos and primitive flutes. He was completely oblivious
to the actual meaning of the words describing escape; too interested in his own children's squeals of delight at antics of a mostly
white, six-week old shepherd/husky puppy Charles named 'Boo'.

"*Who's that yonder dressed in blue? Wade in the Water.
Must be Children that's coming through, and God's gonna trouble
the Water.*"

TWENTY~NINE

1856

Six pelicans soared in perfect formation with wings out-stretched; riding the breeze, skimming a mere two feet above the river. One by one lifting skyward until arcing over, folding their wings, nose-diving; crashing in ungainly splashes into the water. Emerging with fish flopping from their beaks; they carried their bounty to the banks, tipping their heads back, gobbling and swallowing dinner whole.

Douglas watched in amusement from the porch as the pelican parade continued south before he turned back into the house. Catherine Malloy was in the living room pinning final fittings for Charles' clothes for him to take to school. He would be fitted for uniforms there, but he needed coats and wool leisure clothing for Connecticut's brutal winters. Charles was obviously embarrassed with the presence of Mrs. Malloy's thirteen year old daughter, Maggie, watching the measuring process. A year older than Charles, Maggie was a mirror image of her Irish mother; both flaunting curly hair the color of flames, rosy cheeked fair skin… and flashing blue eyes.

Dancing around their brother, Louisa and Kate flounced in new crinolines; laughing at Charles who stood as a nervous scare-crow with arms outspread as Mrs. Malloy fussed, pinning paper patterns to his shirt.

"Alright, I believe that's enough for this fine day!" Mrs. Malloy began stuffing pincushions into her sewing basket, readying to leave.

"Please, have some lemonade and sit a few minutes. I so rarely have visitors to talk with."

Catherine nodded, accepting Leandra's offer of a cool drink, happy at the invitation to sit down to visit with a young woman close to her age.

"Mount Pleasant is very beautiful; we often admire it from town, particularly at sunset when the color of the house changes to lavender!"

Leandra laughed at the description. "Douglas is most proud of this house, so I don't think I will tell him townspeople admire her most when she's PURPLE!"

Charles went outside, shortly returning with Boo; squirming in his arms.

"OH...A PUPPY!!" Immediately enthralled, Maggie gladly took the excited dog; hugging him and giggling at his kisses.

"We have some new baby goats if you'd like to see them?" Charles summoned his courage to make the offer.

"I LOVE GOATS!! PLEASE, MAMA?"

Catherine shook her head in resignation.

"Go quickly, but we need to be leaving soon. You know your papa doesn't take kindly to late dinners!"

Mary toddled to Charles raising her hands up to him.

"SEE DOTES?"

"Yes, sweet girl, we're going to the barn to see the 'dotes'." Laughing, Charles lifted his little sister over his head, sitting her onto his shoulders, straddling his neck. The five left with handfuls of cookies from Mammy Sue, followed by Boo; gleefully chasing and terrorizing their bare feet. Maggie bent to sniff the fragrant roses, admiring the luscious shade of pastel pink.

Their hilarious laughter in the barn paddock with the jumping goats ended with Kojo's arrival summoning them back to the house. Mrs. Malloy was ready to leave and Amos was readying the rowboat to take them across the river.

"Thank you for showing me the goats and letting me play with Boo. It was the most fun I've had in a long time!"

Reaching the porch, Charles lowered two-year old Mary to Leandra to help her down. Impetuously picking one of the beautiful roses, he shyly extended the blossom to Maggie; suddenly aware of the deep red richness of her hair...and the light speckling of freckles across her nose.

Wordlessly lifting the delicate flower to her nose, she closed her eyes to absorb the scent; then with a fleeting smile over the bloom, turned to chase her mother to the boat in a whirl of a gingham skirt and scarlet ringlets.

Watching her go, in that moment...twelve year old Charles fell in love.

On subsequent visits in following months while Mrs. Malloy was busy sewing, Charles escorted Maggie around the plantation usually surrounded by little sisters. Taking every opportunity to be together; the two played and chased, riding horses on the beach; talking of dreams for the future, and at every parting; he gave her a rose.

Walking along the river just before Thanksgiving; the couple came upon Adeline's memorial.

"What is this statue? It's beautiful?" Maggie stroked the wide marble wings of the egret statuary before joining Charles on the old bench. "Is this a family cemetery?"

"It's for my half-sister, Adeline; she died before I was born. The two stones are for Big John and Ma Etta; my father's slaves from when he was a boy. Big John built this bench; I remember him carrying me on his shoulders...and thinking he was the biggest man I had ever seen!" A smile of remembrance fluttered across his face.

"What happened to Adeline?"

"I really don't know much, Father doesn't talk about her; but I was told she was taken by a big gator. Father tried to fight him to save her, but it was too late. Big John dragged Father out of the water or he would have gotten pulled under, too. Father carried a big dagger a friend made for him that he stuck in that gator's head...he still posts a reward for anyone who can kill it and bring him the skull with that knife. Some nights he sits on this bench to talk to Adeline and Big John...and he cries."

"That's so sad, Charles, I'm so sorry." Taking his hand in both of hers and with tears turning her blue eyes liquid; she leaned to him with one soft, perfect first kiss.

"We best be headed back to the house, looks like a storm's a brewin'!" Charles stepped shyly backwards, scanning to see if anyone had seen them.

"CHARLES!!! CHARLES!!!" The reverie of the moment was interrupted by shrill screaming of his younger sisters.

Eight year old Louisa, four year old Kate, and Mary, now two; were playing in a beached canoe by the river launch. Their movements had caused the small craft to slide down the muddy bank into the river...now they were adrift, the outgoing tide pulling them toward the inlet and the ocean beyond.

"GO GET FATHER!" Charles yelled at Maggie over his shoulder as he started running along the riverbank, adjacent to the frightened girls huddled in the boat.

"HOLD ON, I'M GOING TO GET AHEAD OF YOU!"

Panicked at the realization his sisters could get swept to sea, Charles ran through the fear and pain stabbing his chest, jumping over roots and thrashing through palmettos to a small river beach about 200 yards south of the inlet. Winds were picking up now, and rain was stinging his face. He knew sharks were waiting at the inlet for the turning tide to deliver food fish, and memories of witnessing bloody feeding frenzies were making him sick to his stomach. At the beach he could see whitecaps in the roiling inlet just north of his location; waves wash-boarding between the shores; then his sisters came into view from around a bend. With no further thought, he dove headlong into the river to get ahead of the canoe. It was impossible to swim against the current, struggling to stroke across, he grabbed at the boat as it swept past him, catching the stern line dragging behind it.

Maggie's screams alerted Douglas and Moses who were now racing towards the inlet on horseback. Skidding his horse belly deep into the surf; Douglas heaved a rope toward the thrashing boat, now dragging Charles alternately submerging then surfacing, choking and spitting behind. Two tries were unsuccessful, but on the third Charles snagged the lasso. Wrapping the rope around the saddle horn; the two men backed the horse pulling the ricocheting canoe and children onto the beach. On this day, the ocean lost. Relieved, Douglas hugged his crying daughters, pulling Charles' face to his.

"Let's get home, your momma's waiting, I don't want to keep her worrying."

Maggie rode up followed by Boo, relief showing on her face at the sight of the drenched band safely ashore. Offering a hand to Charles who swung up behind her, they rode in silence, the gravity of danger they had been in now fully sinking in. Douglas and

Moses lifted the girls onto the horses with them for the sobering ride back to Mt. Pleasant in the slackening rain.

Sliding off the horses at the house, the bedraggled troupe ran into waiting arms of their relieved mother. Maggie and Charles were confronted by Cate Malloy who was nervously pacing in the yard, anxiously waiting for her daughter's return. Grabbing Maggie by the arm, she hustled her to their canoe at the landing, knowing the angry scene they were going to face with her husband at this late hour. Charles ran to untie the craft, leaning down with a smile to hand Maggie one of Mary Dummett's pink roses as he pushed the small boat into the current. Strongly paddling towards the opposite shore, the worried mother began admonishing her daughter.

"This has to stop, Maggie, you know how your father feels; we have talked to you about this. Charles is a nice boy…but he's a slave…and you two aren't children anymore."

With that warning and fearing the reaction of her husband, Mrs. Malloy snatched the distinctive rose from Maggie's grasp, throwing it into the river.

"Listen to what I say, girl! It is for your own good."

November 22, 1856; Journal entry

My heart is surely eased this night, having felt the fear of loss of my darling children. Though angry the girls disregarded my constant admonitions about playing by the river, and Charles' attention only on Miss Malloy instead of his little sisters, I am filled with only gratitude for God's tender mercies in the outcome of the day. My heart overflows with the knowledge my son is good and brave, surely knowing he was sacrificing his own life in attempting to save his sisters.

JENNY CONNER KEELEY

I must soon make penance for my feelings tonight...for I am truly prideful in my blessings. Thanksgiving will give us pause to rejoice and be thankful for all gifts bestowed upon us...especially our dear, dear children, now safe in their beds.

THIRTY

December 24, 1856; Shive Family Massacre

December 30, 1856; Journal Entry

It is with most sadness I log the horrendous massacre of the Shive family occurring on 24 December 1856, just south of town at Jane Sheldon's rental cabin at Oak Hill. Two of Jane's sons, Dolph and Henry, were duck hunting at the lagoon. Knowing Mr. Shive was still hobbled, the boys being of blessed heart stopped to share the bounty of their good hunt with the family. They found to their great distress the still smoking ruins of the cabin. Mutilated and scalped bodies of Mr. Shive and his boy were found outside in the yard near the water. Mrs. Shive's body was located behind a small hill. It has been determined Mrs. Shive suffered unspeakable indignities before her death at the hands of the savages. Bones of their little girl were found burned within the foundation remains. With poor Dolph retching from the horrors they witnessed, the boys ran to fetch the only other settlers at Oak Hill; E.K. and John Lowd and their uncle, Arad Sheldon, who after a cursory examination of the scene, determined a Seminole raid was responsible for the carnage. They loaded the devastated bodies of the poor Shives into a wagon, bringing them to New Smyrna for Christian burials. A volunteer company was summoned from Mellonsville to pursue the renegades, determined to number nineteen. The posse tracked the godless band for seventy miles, their trail clearly marked by the Shive's possessions discarded along the path of their disgraceful flight. But with several days head start; they could not be overtaken and disappeared into the glades. My heart is sickened knowing Mrs. Shive's and Margaret's long, blonde braids now hang as proud trophies from a savage's belt.

THIRTY ONE

1857

Charles thrived in Connecticut at school. The Episcopal Preparatory Academy excited his curiosity in learning, introducing him to foreign worlds and unfamiliar concepts. He absorbed and grew, bringing great pride to Douglas and his family at home at Mount Pleasant. A small embroidered pouch of silk containing a red ringlet from Maggie was always tucked into his vest. She sent sporadic letters, but Charles's missives were intercepted by her father.

"LEANDRA...come see this sunset!"

Leandra exited the doorway in time to see a pod of dolphins leaping past the house. Colored varying hues of purple in the reddening light; they glistened diving over and under the water, fishing in perfect unison. A line of opportunistic pelicans soared just above them, eyes searching for any fish that might scatter, escaping to the surface.

"It's a full moon tonight. When the girls are in bed, let's take a ride to the beach." Douglas turned to her with that smile that always quickened her heart.

"I'll see to it they're bedded early!" she answered coyly.

The evening passed with clattering of dishes from the kitchen and Mammy Sue's rich voice singing an unfamiliar spiritual. Douglas carried the cello to the porch, carefully rosining the bow before sending music waltzing across the river. Boo was never far from the girls, following Leandra leading her small tribe across the dusty backyard to her neat house. The three girls were tucked, snuggling together into one feather bed with the now large dog spinning at the foot, rumpling and clawing the quilt into just the right nest. Canvassing the room one last time, he flopped down to immediate snoring.

Mammy Sue settled in with them, rocking back and forth in the big nursing rocker with her eyes closed; alternately humming and singing, the songs accompanied by rhythmic creaking of the floorboards.

Tree frogs signaled approaching rain; but for now, the night was clear and beautiful.

Douglas met Leandra out front with a mare prancing with excitement to be taken for an unexpected night ride. The pathway to the beach followed a deer trail through the woods, intermittently lit with bolts of moonlight surprising through oak branches and palm fronds.

Stars and moonlight transformed the beach to a crystalline ballroom, idyllic for two lovers dancing alone across the pure white sand. Douglas hummed a waltz, laughing as Leandra exaggeratedly swung her skirt to the music as she twirled in his arms, her head perfectly back and turned to the side in the classic style he had taught, her movements gracefully following his as they counted and spun in three quarter time... stepping and whirling across the endless beach.

Their nights were perfect and private; away from disapproving eyes, away from archaic laws, away from anyone or anything intruding on their happiness.

"Let's go home; I want you in my bed."

Galloping through darkness, the two lovers tied the horses to front rails, running and laughing like thieves up the stairs. Clutching and rolling until finally exhausted, naked on the cool sheets, arms and legs draped over each other in spent passion; Douglas kissed her sleeping face then quietly rolled away from her.

It had been a while since words had come to him, but this night had fired his creative juices…and he didn't want to lose the thoughts and poetry to sleep. Leandra was always inspiring to him, but tonight it was this place of paradise providing inspiration. Shuffling a neat stack of paper, leaning over his desk by candlelight, words and emotions he felt of Leandra and New Smyrna flowed easily from his quill.

Journal Entry; October 4, 1857

'THE SMYRNA SERENADE'

Come to New Smyrna, waltz upon this land
   created by Neptune's pearls… crushed to alabaster sand.
Spread your wings with Seagulls, soar on the ocean breeze.
   Dive with rays and dolphins…ballet with manatees!
Close your eyes and take a breath of Smyrna's fresh salt air;
   commingled with scents of jasmine and blossoms of oranges,
   there.
Crabwalk with dancing sandpipers performing the 'Pelican Promenade'.
   Let the surf's soul rhythms lull you with the 'Smyrna Serenade.'
Listen to your heartbeat matching breakers on the shore,
   And know you'll always love her…New Smyrna, forevermore.

THIRTY TWO

1860

---

12 March 1860

> *To Charles Dummett*
> *Yale University*
> *New Haven, Connecticut*

My dearest Charles,

It is with deepest regret and sorrow I must write you of this news of my betrothal. By the time you receive this letter, I shall be traversing to the territory of Kansas to be married in Wichita by arrangement of my father. The man to be my husband is a parson, known to be a good and saintly man of pious habits. He is twenty-four years of age, seven years older than I and wiser accordingly. A million tears could not deter my father from his decision, even knowing the fondness my heart holds for you. He insists this is the best and only course of action for us both, to each marry our own kind…but it does not feel that way.

Do not forget me, Charles, for I shall remember you always as my first true sweetheart.

> *With abiding love,*
> *Maggie*

"Momma, when will Charles be home?" Six year old Mary was getting bored with waiting.

"Soon, sweetheart, Yale is very far away. Your brother has a long journey by clipper ship and steamboat and then the rest of the way to New Smyrna by horseback. Don't worry; your Papa will have him here by Easter. Louisa, come help Kate with her buttons. I'm trying to get Mary's hair braided!"

As on cue, Boo started barking, barreling for the landing, heralding the arrival of the travelers. Unable to contain their excitement, Leandra and the girls followed, running across the yard to meet them.

"Oh, land sakes my handsome boy; you've grown more than a head since you were home last year on your fifteenth birthday!" Charles smiled down at his mother, his growth spurt now putting him as tall as his father at over six foot.

"Well, who are all these beautiful young women?" Charles laughed as he was assailed by his giggling sisters, all jockeying for hugs. Little Mary was now six, Kate eight, and Louisa at twelve was as tall as Leandra.

"Alright, alright, boy, we'll play ball tomorrow!" Boo was joyously jumping and clawing at Charles, whining and ecstatic to have his boy home and the whole family together.

"Mammy Sue has been working all day pitting cherries for cobbler to welcome you home. You must be half starved from your journey!"

"I am, Momma, to quote Father…" My big ones are eatin' my little ones!"

Laughing, the small family walked arm in arm across the yard to the house, glowing with lantern light. Mammy Sue and Clarice were hurriedly setting the big dining table and lighting candles for the homecoming feast. The frivolity carried late into the evening with Charles, Douglas, and Hair-lip Daniel serenading with dueling trios of cello, violin, and guitar. Leandra and the girls danced while Mammy Sue clapped in time from a rocking chair until Mary climbed into her lap, pillowing her head against the old woman's ample bosom, falling soundly asleep. Motioning for the others to follow her to their small house, Douglas picked up his exhausted daughter to carry her to her bed.

"Charles, I'll be back directly, we can talk then."

After Leandra and the girls were settled, Douglas returned to the manor house where Charles was waiting at the table, nervously picking at a dish of cobbler. Douglas poured himself a horn of rum, surprising Charles by pouring a second one for him, setting the stein in front of the boy he sat heavily next to him.

"This trip you have been unusually quiet, son. Is there something on your mind?"

Charles stared at the cherries in his bowl before picking up the rum and downing it. Douglas could see he was fighting tears.

"I have been dismissed from Yale, Father; our lies have been discovered by the Dean and my classmates, and they know the truth of my parentage. I am now caused to be the source of great merriment to some, and cruel derision by others I considered to be my friends. Talk in the North is of war with the South…and my heart is confused as to where I should stand in such a conflict! Do I stand with you, my white father…or do I fight for the flag that comes to liberate my slave mother? Do you love her…or is she just your chattel? Are we all chattel to you?"

Douglas was stunned by the words gushing from his son.

"Son, when you're old enough we will talk of love…"

"Love…or ownership? No, Father, I will tell you what I have

learned of love. My Maggie has been sent away so my love will not sully her for a white husband…a man 'of her own kind'! What am I, am I not a man? What love is it that makes me a son not allowed to have a room in my father's house, or to sleep under his roof! What kind of love dictates one man shall be owned by another?"

Slamming his stein onto the table, Charles angrily stood, tearfully knocking the chair backwards, sending it crashing onto the oak floor. "Good night, Father. I'm going where I belong, to the slave quarters with my momma and sisters…my own kind!" With that, he stormed out.

Douglas sat alone with his rum, mulling his son's words in the now quiet house until the last table candle snuffed. Slowly climbing the stairs in darkness to his empty bed, he fell into a restless sleep.

It was the quiet that woke him, a crushing sense of doom. Night birds and tree frogs had stopped their songs; crickets chirping in the damp night became suddenly silent. Feeling unease in the air, Douglas sat up focusing his eyes at the moonlit window.

The single shotgun blast from the yard shattered all their lives. Running barefoot to the crumpled form in the grass, Douglas cradled his son; rocking and moaning, oblivious to others now sobbing around him, fighting those attempting to take the lifeless body from his grasp.

Charles was buried in the yard of Mount Pleasant overlooking his beloved river, the gravesite surrounded by massive live oaks he used to climb. His funeral was private, attended only by his mother and sisters, plantation slaves, and Boo. Douglas; devastated and stoic, tearfully conducted the short service.

"In this most terrible of times, agony of loss has taken my

words; so I will use those of Greek philosopher Aeschylus; "There is no pain so great as the memory of joy in present grief. He who loves must suffer, and even in our sleep, pain that cannot forget falls drop by drop upon the heart. And in our own despair, against our will, comes wisdom to us by the awful grace of God."

Before the thick marble slab was placed atop the crypt, Douglas tucked the silk pouch containing the red ringlet into his son's hands crossed above his heart.

Boo's mournful howls echoed nightly through the trees, the disconsolate dog's wails puncturing already wounded hearts.

Journal Entry; April 23, 1860

My beautiful boy, Charles, just four months shy of his sixteenth year, is dead by his own hand. God has forsaken us, taking our son in penance for our sins against law and nature; but why does love elicit such cruelty from a loving God? Why did He not take us instead of our innocent son? Why did I not know the depth of his suffering? Was it inability of his youth to ignore cruelties by those who could not see his mighty heart for the color of his skin? Was it angst caused by talk of war and secession that would force a rending choice he could not make? We will never know the answers; for he has taken them with him.

I can't believe you did this…can't believe it's real.
I love you…and I miss you. I don't know how to feel!
What went on in your mind? Why couldn't you confide?
Why didn't you tell me you were planning suicide?
What burning drive made you want to cut short your years?
Was it the sudden ending…of many hidden fears?

Why did you do this, son? Was it for some welcome relief?
Or was it to cause us a never ending, revenging grief?
This act was cruel and selfish; you threw away your dreams.
Did you suddenly stop loving us, because that is how it seems.
I'm angry…and I'm bitter. Was it me…or was it you?
I cry, but I can't find the tears…though my heart is ripped in two.
Now, no one will ever know, never find out why
or what possessed you, my darling boy…to want to die.
I cannot believe you did this, cannot believe it's real.
I love you…and I miss you…I just don't know how to feel.
I don't know how to feel….

Unable to bear memories or further heartache at Mount Pleasant, Douglas moved Leandra, their three daughters, Boo, and a few select slaves to his isolated groves at Merritt Island; away from disapproving eyes of New Smyrna, and away from memories too hard to bear. Remaining slaves were sent to auction.

THIRTY THREE

1860-1865

Times after the Seminole Wars were hard for New Smyrna, but the small settlement slowly grew, trickling in population by tough and resilient pioneers who returned and rebuilt; their spirits resurrecting the land they loved. Though life was difficult, those who returned thrived as best they could; tilling the rich soil and planting crops while holding on to their southern ways and culture. Slavery was the evil necessary to achieve that end. During the Seminole Wars, most Florida slaves had fled plantations to join and fight with the Seminoles or Maroon colonies, intermarrying with natives and establishing families living as freedmen. Mercenaries and slave-hunters relentlessly pursued them, capturing and returning many to plantation owners who were able to pay. Slave hunting was not a noble profession, but proved to be lucrative. Returning with a vengeance; heartbreaking and dehumanizing slave auctions once again marred the landscape of Florida.

Impassioned voices of Abolitionists leading fiery debates in northern state legislatures and on the floor of Congress raised strident pleas against the inhumanity of slavery. With rifts widening throughout the country and desperate to protect their commerce; southern states of South Carolina, Mississippi, Florida, Alabama, Georgia, Louisiana, and Texas banded together, seceding from the Union to form the separate Confederate States of America.

Jefferson Davis was elected to serve as their President in 1860. With the advent of the Civil War in 1861, declared to save the Union, many southern families trying to rebuild from previous losses during the Indian Wars now found themselves without men to provide labor and protection. The Confederacy needed all men of fighting age to bear arms for the preservation of the South and their way of life, leaving their families to fend for themselves. Women became heads of families that had always been patriarchal, surviving by learning to shoot and hunt, to plow, to become livestock wranglers, business partners, and protectors of the children and homesteads. Southern homes were not only in danger from Union troops but also from Confederate deserters and hungry rebel soldiers.

JANUARY 10, 1861; Florida's Articles of Secession

We, the people of the State of Florida, in convention assembled, do solemnly ordain, publish and declare: That the State of Florida hereby withdraws herself from the Confederacy of States existing under the name of the United States of America, and from the existing government of said States, and that all political connection between her and the government of said States ought to be, and the same is hereby totally annulled, and said union of States dissolved, and the State of Florida is hereby declared [11] a sovereign and independent nation, and that all ordinances heretofore adopted, in so far as they create or recognize said Union, are rescinded, and all laws or parts of laws in force in this State, in so far as they recognize or assent to said Union be, and they are hereby repealed.'

APRIL 12, 1861

Confederate troops led by General Beauregard opened fire on Fort Sumter, a Union fort on Charleston Bay, South Carolina, beginning the Civil War.

APRIL 13, 1861

Fort Sumter fell. Major Robert Anderson surrendered the fort to Confederate officers.

APRIL 15, 1861

Republican President Abraham Lincoln issues proclamation calling for 75,000 volunteer soldiers to put down the South's insurrection.

THURSDAY, MARCH 20, 1862

With Union troops taking Fernandina, Jacksonville, and St. Augustine on the east coast of Florida, two Federal gunships; the *Penguin* and the *Henry Andrew* were sent by Flag Officer Dupont of the South Atlantic Blockading Squadron to accompany the larger *USS Keystone State* to blockade the inlet at New Smyrna. With the fall of three major port cities, Moskito Inlet became a vital supply line for the Confederacy; providing food, quinine, arms, and ammunition for their soldiers. Needed ladings were transferred from large vessels in the Bahama Islands to smaller, faster boats that could easily slip past blockading Federal ships into the inlet. Those supplies were unloaded to be hauled overland to Confederate Army distribution points at Cabbage Bluff and Enterprise; then further disseminated by wagons and river boats. The blockade runners were reloaded for their return trip with goods and cotton to sell to raise money for the South from Caribbean and European buyers.

Following Dupont's orders, the larger *Keystone* anchored outside the inlet while Acting Lieutenant Commander T.A. Budd on the *Penguin,* and the *Henry Andrew* under Acting Master S.W. Mather, nosed into the inlet across the bar to anchor along the east bank of the Hillsborough River. Their orders were to establish an inside blockade; to guard a large quantity of live oak owned by the Swift Brothers Company that was stacked and stored on government land on the east shore of the river awaiting transport; and to capture or destroy any Rebel vessels they came across.

Between 1816 and 1874; the Swift Brothers from Falmouth, Massachusetts, engaged in cutting thousands of Florida's huge live oaks. Continuing except for times during the Seminole and Civil Wars, the relentless harvest provided millions of board feet of the preferred wood for use in ship building, and was much in demand by the Federal Navy and Union forces. The Naval vessel *USS Constitution* was nicknamed 'Old Ironsides' after her live oak hull survived numerous cannon fire hits during the War of 1812. Not only was the wood incredibly hard and strong, the sweet fall acorns fed a wide spectrum of birds and fowl providing food for many mammals, including squirrels and rabbits, black bear and deer. Live oaks usually grow to 40'-60' and spread 60'-100' at their crowns with trunks and branches sinuously curved and limber to survive hurricanes by bowing and waving without snapping.

The *Henry Andrew* was to protect the valuable cut wood from incendiary attacks by the Confederacy, with further instructions for the *Penguin* to find and capture two blockade running vessels rumored to be in the river unloading ammunition; The *Kate* and the *Caroline*.

Once over the bar and into the inlet, they anchored in the Hillsborough River (renamed the Indian River in 1901) along the east shore (approximately ¼ mile south of the present site of New Smyrna's north bridge). Albert W. Kelsey of the *Henry Andrew* wrote notes about the expedition after the ship was berthed. Kelsey went ashore with Captains Mather and Budd to pay a visit at the Sheldon Hotel, buying chickens and other supplies to feed the crews.

After the end of the Second Seminole War, Jane and John Sheldon completed building their forty-room rooming house in 1859 atop the ancient, massive coquina foundation overlooking the river.

FRIDAY, MARCH 21, 1862

Kelsey wrote a memorandum, recalling Friday, March 21, 1862, as a beautiful day with a morning trip ashore where they picked ripe beans and Oleander blossoms. That evening, the *Penguin's* Captain Budd came aboard the *Henry Andrew* with news received from a Negro pilot from salt works near Oak Hill. Being sympathetic to the Union and amenable to bribes, the man willingly reported the small steamer, *Kate,* was waiting for the opportune time and tide to evade the guards and run the blockade. She was reportedly tied, hiding in brush not far from the *Henry Andrew.* Another Rebel steamer, *Caroline,* was also reported as having gone into Moskito Inlet from Nassau on 17 March, 1862, and was unloading arms.

A Union expedition was launched with 43 men in four or five small boats from the *Henry Andrew* and *Penguin* to find the blockade runners. They were commanded by Lt. Budd and Acting Master Mather, with the eighteen mile trip south down river to Oak Hill being uneventful, cool, and relatively enjoyable for the crews. Finding nothing, they turned back north to New Smyrna where their larger ships were at anchor. The men were in good spirits with no concern over Confederate troops, as their scouting reports showed no activity in the area. Unfortunately for them, the reports were wrong.

The Third Florida Volunteers of the Confederate States commanded by Captain Strain, knelt concealed in brush along New Smyrna's stone wharf, waiting for the small boats of Union soldiers to pass as they returned. The Confederate troops were guarding food and cotton stored in sheds at Clinch Street, not intending to engage, but when the lead Union boat approached the beach dangerously close to their position... southern rifles proved deadly. The ambush was sudden and lethal.

* CONFEDERATE RECORDS dated March 23, 1862; Affairs at Smyrna, Florida

"Report of Col. W.S. Dilsworth, commanding forces of the Department of East and Middle Florida. Headquarters, Provisional Forces, Department E. and M. Florida, Tallahassee, Florida
April 4, 1862.

Major, I have to report a most successful skirmish which took place at Smyrna on the 21st ult., Captain D. B. Bird,

Third Florida Volunteers C.S. (Army) commanding post, the skirmishers commanded by Captain Strain, Third Regiment and Lieutenant Chambers of Captain Owens' independent troop of cavalry.

The enemy landed, or attempted to land, from gunboats *Penguin* and *Henry Andrew*, in launches when our men fired into them. The enemy retreated to the opposite side of the river and abandoned their launches, five in number.

Captain Bird reports seven killed, three prisoners and about (unclear) wounded. Among the killed were Captain Mather of the *Henry Andrew* and Lieutenant Budd of the *Penguin*. A runaway Negro slave also was captured, who had piloted the enemy into the inlet to Smyrna, and who was to be hanged.

The skirmish I regard as quite a success; not a man on our side killed or wounded.

Smyrna is the place where arms, etc., for the Confederate States have been landed and the enemy were seeking to capture them. The enemy are preparing to advance from Jacksonville to Baldwin to cut them off there.

I have the honor to subscribe myself, respectfully, your obedient servant,

W.S. Dilsworth
Colonel Commanding

Ma. T.A. Washington, Assistant Adjutant General, Pocotaligo, S.C."

*FEDERAL RECORDS dated March 24, 1862 regarding the Smyrna ambush:

"Letter to Honorable Gideon Welles, Secretary of the Navy:

Flagship *Wabash*, off Mosquito Inlet, Fla. March 24, 1862.
Sir; I have to report to the department some casualties that have occurred to officers and men belonging to two vessels of my fleet—casualties as painful as they were unexpected, but the loss of gallant lives has expiated the error of judgement which enthusiastic zeal had induced.

The department was informed after the capture of Fernandina that so soon I should take possession of Jacksonville and St. Augustine I would give my attention to Mosquito Inlet, fifty miles south of the latter, which, according to my information, was resorted to for the introduction of arms transshipped from English ships and steamers at the British colony of Nassau into small vessels of light drought.

I accordingly ordered the *Penguin*, Acting Lieutenant Commanding T.A. Budd, and the *Henry Andrew*, Acting Master S.W. Mather, to proceed to this place—the latter to cross the bar, establish an inside blockade, capture any Rebel vessels there, and guard from incendiarism large quantities of live oak timber on the Government lands, cut and ready for shipment, to which the department has called my attention.

On reaching here myself, on the 22nd, I was boarded by the executive officer of the *Penguin*, and informed that Lieutenant Commanding Budd, with Acting Master Mather, had organized an expedition from the two vessels, and had moved southward through the inland passage leading into Mosquito Inlet, passing Smyrna, with four or five light boats carrying in all some forty-three men.

Soon after this report, which I heard with anxiety, the results were developed. It appears that after going some fifteen or eighteen miles without incident, and while on their return and within sight of the *Henry Andrew*, the order of the line being no longer observed, the two commanding quite in advance, landed under certain earthworks which had been abandoned or never armed, near a dense grove of live oak with underbrush, and a heavy and continuous fire was unexpectedly opened upon them from both these covers. Lieutenant Commander Budd and Acting Master Mather, with three of the five men comprising the boat's crew, were killed. The remaining two were wounded and made prisoners.

As the other boats came up, they were also fired into, and suffered more or less; the rear boat of all had a howitzer, which, however could not be properly secured or worked, the boat not being fitted for the purpose, and could therefore be of little use. The men had to seek cover on shore, but as soon as it was dark, Acting Master's Mate McIntosh returned to the boats, brought away the body of one of the crew who had been killed, all of the arms and ammunition and flags, threw the howitzer into the river, passed close to the Rebel pickets, who hailed but elicited no reply, and arrived safely aboard the *Henry Andrew*.

On hearing of this untoward event, I directed Commander Rogers to send off the launch and cutters of his ship, to the support of the *Andrew*. The boats crossed the bar at midnight, and the next morning the vessel was hauled close up to the scene of the attack, but no enemy could be discovered.

The bodies of Lieutenant Budd and Acting Master Mather were received under a flag of truce, and the commanding officer, a Captain Bird, who had come from a camp at a distance, made some show of courtesy by returning papers and a watch, as if ashamed of this mode of warfare; for these were the very troops that with sufficient force, means and material for a respectable defense had ingloriously fled from St. Augustine on our approach.

I enclose a copy of my instructions to Acting Lieutenant Budd, the original which was found on his person and was one of the papers returned by the Rebel officer.

Lieutenant Commander Budd and Acting Master Mather were brave and devoted officers; the former commanded the *Penguin* in the action of the 7th of November, and received my commendation. The latter, in the prime of life, was a man of uncommon energy and daring, and had no superior, probably, among the patriotic men who have been appointed in the Navy from the mercantile marine.

> Very respectfully, your obedient servant,
> S. Dupont
> Flag Officer Commanding South Atlantic Blockade Squadron
> Hon. Gideon Welles, Secretary of the Navy, Washington."

[See official records Union and Confederate Armies, Series 1, Volume VI, page 111.]

APRIL 27, 1862

Confederate troops or sympathizers, under cover of night, conducted a guerilla raid and incendiary attack on 30,000-40,000 board feet of live oak and red cedar. Stacked at New Smyrna near Moskito Inlet awaiting shipment by the Union; the valuable wood was being guarded by the U.S. Steamer *Henry Andrew.* The crew was unable to put out the firestorm, with the huge stockpile being a total loss.

SUNDAY AFTERNOON; JULY 26, 1863

"AUNTIE JANE!!!! AUNTIE JANE!!"

Jane Sheldon wiped her brow with the back of her hand, smearing flour from her pie crust dough on her forehead and into her white hair. Chunks of sweet potato caramelized in bubbling molasses in a heavy iron skillet atop a massive pot-bellied stove.

"HOLD YOUR BRITCHES, BOYS!! AUNTIE'S GOT TO STIR THESE SWEET TATERS SO THEY DON'T STICK!!"

Yelling back at nieces and nephews playing stick-ball in the side yard, the old woman dipped a long handled, wooden spatula into the molasses. Flinching as she burned her lips tasting the hot syrup, she gave a quick stir scraping pieces stuck to the sides into the sweet, dark brew. Sweeping perspiration off her face with her apron, she bent over checking the large turkey, browning nicely in the oven from religious basting with sweet cream butter, freshly churned for her guests' Sunday dinner. Green beans picked earlier from her garden in the north-west yard stewed on the back burner in a large pot; cooking in the southern way with bacon, vinegar, onions, and liberal spoonfuls of sugar. Freshly baked tart rhubarb and strawberry pies cooled on the window sill; causing spirited discussion between squirrels watching from the shade of a cedar tree branch, and a blue jay perched on the porch railing.

As a longtime dream of Jane and John, the Sheldon Hotel had finally been completed in 1859; at that time the largest hotel south of St. Augustine along the east coast. Perfectly located sitting high atop the coquina bulwark in a treed and shady, park like setting along the west bank of the Hillsborough River, the large forty room structure caught cooling river breezes through the many tall windows, providing both home and shelter for grateful travelers… and for the Sheldon's own growing, multi-generation family.

Joy at completion of their hotel was short lived. In 1862, John Sheldon, who had been a renowned Federal scout during the Indian wars; ran the Union blockade to meet with their son, Rudolphus, in Bimini. 'Dolph' Sheldon was trying to return home from school in the North, but before they could sail; his father contracted yellow fever and died. 'Dolph' was eventually able to make it back through the dangerous blockade to New Smyrna under cover of darkness.

"NOW, WHAT ARE YOU YOUNGUNS YELLING FOR???" Jane called through the kitchen window to no one in particular.

Now in her fifties, Jane smoothed wispy hairs at her temples, tucking them back into combs holding her neat bun. Walking out of the steamy kitchen, she surveyed the gleaming, long needle pine harvest table that was perfectly polished and set for Sunday dinner. Straightening hibiscus, their large blooms leaning in her mother's Dresden vase, she stepped back to admire the sunny room; greeting the widow Dora Lourcey and her two young children who were choosing seats at the table. Dora had brought John Dressner; a young man as her guest from Tallahassee. Jane's sons; sixteen year old 'Dolph' and twenty year old Henry, crippled since birth with a malformed spine, were the next to come down the stairs to the comfortable dining room. For all appearances, Henry Sheldon was discounted as helpless and incapable, cruelly nicknamed 'Hunchback Henry'; but in reality, he was a daring and efficient blockade runner in his small sailboat. Pleased at her guests' arrivals, the portly mother turned to look out the side windows, suddenly aware the children's laughter had stopped. Their ball was rolling to the base of a palm, with the usually raucous band of young cousins standing strangely quiet, pointing towards the river.

Limping to the front windows while cursing her gout swollen big toe under her breath, Jane saw two Federal gunboats; the side-wheeler steamer *Oleander* with schooner *Beauregard* in tow had both anchored close, just opposite the hotel ; nosing in, facing her. It wasn't unusual to see Union boats in the river searching for blockade runners, but she had never seen this type of maneuver. Suddenly in unison, both boats began swinging broadside towards the bank. Realizing cannons were being brought around aiming at the town; she immediately knew their horrible intent.

"RUN!! RUN TO THE WOODS!!!" Children began scattering, dragging younger siblings, all running now towards safety and cover of the dense hammock to the west.

Just as she yelled the warning to children in the yard, a cannonball came screaming toward the hotel, crashing through the dining room windows and flying to the back of the room, grazing the dining table. Luckily, the ball was a dud and didn't explode, sparing the diners. Splintering the upright piano standing in its path against the west wall, the prized instrument was reduced to kindling tossing ivory keys throughout the room.

Panicked, the adults grabbed what food stuffs and supplies they could, cramming them into carpet bags and long skirts. Chasing after the children, they ran deeper into the woods, hiding out of range of Union artillery.

Relentless shelling decimated New Smyrna until an afternoon thunderstorm brought a temporary stop to the cannon fire. During the lull, men and boys went back salvaging more food and blankets for the drenched and frightened townspeople, sheltering under trees and broad leafed bushes. At dusk, Jane first tried lighting a smudge fire to bring relief from the biting bugs and to dry their clothes; but the curling smoke column betrayed their position, causing Union guns to be aimed in their direction. With no smoke to repel the merciless mosquitoes, she resorted to a Seminole trick, showing the miserable survivors how to scoop mud with their hands, smearing it over every inch of exposed skin. They were a wet, dirty, pitiful group... but they were alive.

On that balmy July Sunday, the 'Northern Army of Aggression' obtained retribution for the 1862 ambush against their soldiers at the stone wharf by the 3rd Florida Volunteers. New Smyrna was shelled into oblivion. Anything surviving the cannons was looted or set afire by troops. Douglas Dummett's beautiful and gracefully columned Mount Pleasant that had survived Wildcat's attempt to burn it Christmas night of 1835 could not stand against the concentrated Union barrage, falling to charred ruins.

With complete destruction of all buildings in New Smyrna by the Union onslaught, the Ora Carpenter family relocated to Osteen; Dora Lourcey and her children returned to their homestead north of town at the juncture of Murray and Spruce Creeks.

Jane Sheldon and her two sons walked over five miles inland to a
pine ridge (now Glencoe) where they were assisted with building a
cabin of palmetto thatch where they lived until the following year;
subsisting on wild game, berries, and foraged root stock. Jane had
listened well to her elders, learning in her youth about plant iden-
tification; those that were edible, those that were poisonous, and
those that could be used for medicinal teas, potions, and tinctures.

With the death of her husband; John, of yellow fever and destruction of her home and possessions in the shelling, 1863 held
another blow for Jane and her boys. She received news her eldest son, George; a Private in Company H, 2nd Regiment of the
Florida Volunteers attached to the Army of Northern Virginia;
had survived the carnage in Manassas in the Battle of Bull Run,
only to succumb to pneumonia in the hospital in Richmond.
George Sheldon was twenty-seven.

AUGUST 12, 1863

Report of Lieutenant-Commander English, U.S. Navy,
commanding *U.S.S. Sagamore,* regarding the attack upon New
Smyrna, and reporting the capture of sloop *Clara Louisa*, and
schooners *Southern Rights, Shot*, and *Ann,* to Acting Rear-Admiral
Theodorus Bailey.

"U.S. Gunboat *Sagamore,* Key West, August 12, 1863

Sir: On the afternoon of the 26th July, I attacked New Smyrna
with the U.S. dispatch steamer *Oleander* and schooner *Beauregard*
and boats belonging to this vessel and the schooner *Para*, which
vessel was stationed off blockading that place. The *Oleander* took

the *Beauregard* in tow, crossed the bar and anchored abreast the place giving it a good shelling, the boats going up past the town. We captured one sloop loaded with cotton, one schooner not laden; caused them to destroy several vessels, some of which were loaded with cotton and about ready to sail. They burned large quantities of it on shore, which we could not prevent. Landed a strong force, destroyed all the buildings that had been occupied by troops. In landing the party was fired upon by a number of stragglers concealed in the bushes. The conduct of all connected with the expedition was praiseworthy. From the handsome dash in which it was made I attribute our success, particularly in coming off without having anyone injured. The sloop I sent to Port Royal with the *Oleander,* the schooner I have brought to this place for adjudication. Having operated with Rear-Admiral Dahlgren's vessels, I made a report to him of the affair, as well as to the Secretary of the Navy, which letters I have sent north by the *Oleander.*

I have stationed the *Beauregard* at the Haul Over, 13 miles above Cape Canaveral, where cargoes have landed and others taken in, with orders for him to proceed to Jupiter Inlet when it is necessary to communicate with the bark *Pursuit* for stores.

I found it impossible to close Jupiter Inlet; therefore consider it important to have a vessel of some kind stationed at that place constantly.

I am, very respectfully, your obedient servant,
Earl English, Lieutenant-Commander

Acting Rear-Admiral Theodorus Bailey
Commanding Eastern Gulf Blockading Squadron."

THIRTY FOUR

AUGUST 1, 1863

"MASSA DOUGLAS!! MASSA DOUGLAS!!!"

Drying a large copper pot, Leandra stepped through the cabin's front door, her three daughters trailing curiously. Now fifteen, eleven, and nine, each was a beauty in her own right. Amos ran up onto the front porch, out of breath and obviously upset.

"WHERE'S MASSA DOUGLAS?? I GOT'S TO TELL HIM NEWS!! BAD NEWS!!!"

"For Heaven's sake, Amos; WHAT IS IT??"

"THOSE YANKEES DONE SHOT UP AND BURNED NEW SMYRNA!!"

Hearing the commotion, Douglas came around the side of the house from the garden.

"What about Mount Pleasant??"

"SHE GONE, SIR... ALL GONE!! DEY BLASTED HER TO DE GROUND!!!"

Leandra dropped the pan, covering her face with her hands. "OH, DOUGLAS!!"

"WHEN, WHEN DID IT HAPPEN??? IS ANYONE LEFT ALIVE???" Douglas was doing his best to wrap his head around the awful news.

"BOUT FIVE DAYS HENCE!! DEY DOCKED FRONT OF MISS SHELDON'S HOTEL, DEN SWUNG DOS BIG

CANNONS ROUND AND SHELLED DE TOWN! DEY LOOTED AND FIRED ANYTHIN' LEFT STANDIN'! MOST FOLKS RAN TO DE WOODS TO HIDE. DON'T KNOW HOW MANY KILLED!"

"Come sit down, Amos, I'll get you something to drink." Leandra handed him her towel to wipe his face, patting Douglas on the chest before hustling inside to get water for the exhausted slave.

Douglas followed her, sitting heavily at the table, stunned at the news.

"Tomorrow, I'll sail up to check Mount Pleasant. I have to see for myself if it's completely destroyed or if there's anything left to salvage."

"But, it might not be safe. What if Yankees are still there?"

"I'll be alright, I'll see them long before they'll see the 'Flying Fish'; I'll take the sail down around Oak Hill and paddle in along the mangroves."

Knowing argument was fruitless, Leandra set to preparing a satchel of supplies for his scouting trip. Pulling the Hawken off the wall, he began oiling the long gun with a vengeance while his brain raced trying to formulate a plan for what this news meant for his family. Would they be safe here in isolation on Merritt Island, or would the Yanks venture south and find them?

Douglas's arrival to New Smyrna confirmed Amos's report. Union soldiers and boats had pulled out leaving one moored at the inlet to thwart blockade runners, but their damage had been done and New Smyrna lay deserted in ruins, some still smoking. Mount Pleasant had also been reduced to rubble with many trees blackened and fallen. Tears of relief filled his eyes when he finally saw Charles's crypt was undisturbed covered and hidden by palmettos...one place of peace left in the mayhem.

"Maybe there is some humanity left in this horrible war," he thought to himself.

Feeling it was safe to cross from the island, Douglas paddled his small craft over to the mainland. Small spirals of smoke still rose through the trees, mementos of the panic and horrors wrought by the Federal gunships just days earlier.

Dolph Sheldon waved to him from atop the old fort ruins, barely recognizable with his face and clothing sooty and muddy. Completed in 1859, the massive Sheldon Hotel built by his parents on the fort foundation now was nothing more than a pile of charred boards lying among the coquina walls of the buttress. Long a dream of the Sheldons; the hotel survived realization by only four years.

Dolph climbed down from his vantage point to help beach Douglas's canoe. After hugging in greeting, the young man tied the craft to a root protruding from the bank.

"Is Jane okay...the townspeople?"

Dolph nodded replying with a smile, "Well, Captain, you know my Mama is a tough woman. She's hangin' on like a hair in a biscuit!" Douglas chuckled at Dolph's descriptive visual of his mother.

"All are still alive, a couple are wounded that stayed behind to cover while womenfolk and children ran, but most everybody has split up to find safer places further inland for their families, at least until we kick the ass of those blue coats. We been building a log and palmetto thatch cabin out by Glencoe, up on the ridge by where our boys buried their cannon and extra arms. Mama thinks it's far enough inland the bastards won't find us. Bugs and skeeters 'bout chewed us alive in the swamp, and Dora Lourcey's little boy got snake bit; but it's better than bein' shot by them damn Yankees. We was able to round up some chickens, a heifer, and two goats; and there be wild game and taters aplenty in the hammocks. I've been salvagin' what I can from the gardens and cellars that the Yanks didn't steal…Henry found a stand of wild butter beans and poke greens that hawgs have been feedin' on, so we ain't been goin' hungry. "

"Tell your mama my next time up I'll bring a boatload of fruit. Soldiers haven't found us yet, so we have plenty we can share from our groves. "

"Real sorry 'bout Mount Pleasant, Captain Dummett; she was sure a beauty." Dolph Sheldon was the same age and build as Charles when he died, but his sixteen year old eyes were now sadly the eyes of an old man, the responsibility of his mother and crippled brother weighed on his shoulders.

"As soon as I can get Mama and Henry settled and stocked up, I'm joinin' the army and makin' those blue coats pay for what they done here!"

Douglas hugged the boy one last time, abruptly turning to hide his suddenly welling tears.

"I'm heading back to my girls; don't want to be gone too long with all these sentinels around. You take care of yourself. Give your mama my love."

With that, Douglas untied his cat boat, sliding expertly onto the river, grateful to be catching the incoming tide carrying him south towards Oak Hill and Merritt Island beyond. Dolph watched the small boat and the rhythmic rise and fall of the paddle until it was lost in the dusk and rising fog. Slinging a burlap bag over his shoulder with a pot, two forks, three spoons and a teapot he had scrounged from the ruins, he turned for the treacherous hike back to Glencoe ridge.

*Rallied by a patriotic poem from the letterhead of one of his older brother George's letters; "Let Ball and Grapeshot fly, Trust in God and Davis, but keep your powder dry!"; teenager Dolph Sheldon joined the fight for the Confederacy becoming a Private assigned to Company H, 5th Battalion Cavalry of the Florida Volunteers. He survived the war, living to be 89. He is buried in the Edgewater Cemetery.

THIRTY FIVE

1865

March 23, 1865; Journal entry

Another log of sadness for our family; my dear sister Elizabeth's son, William Hardee, has been killed at the Battle of Bentonville, North Carolina in proud service of the Confederacy. My heart breaks for his father as I know the depths of grief he feels in the loss of his only son. It is a tender mercy my beloved Beth did not live to feel this pain. Willie was a brave and good boy of seventeen.

"CAPTAIN DUMMETT!!! CAPTAIN DUMMETT!!" Hunchbacked Henry Sheldon pulled his canoe alongside the dock waving a rolled newspaper. "LEE SURRENDERED… THE WAR IS OVER!!! THE WAR IS OVER!!!"

Jubilation with the news spread through the slave quarters like a rising tide, men came running from the groves, hugging and celebrating with their wives and children. Finally clustering together into a large group, they moved as one towards Dummett's cabin. Climbing onto the porch, he turned to face the celebrating crowd of slaves now filling the yard.

Moses was the first to speak. "Massa Douglas, I been wid you most my life, most us here been wid you at Mount Pleasant and here at de groves. We be free now, and most be wantin' to go to make our own way. We be hearin' bout railroad jobs in the north payin' a fair wage, even to darkies."

Motioning the men closer to the porch, Douglas took in a deep breath; then began speaking in a quietly resigned voice.

"This day has been long expected. If you choose to leave, that is your decision to make. I can make you this offer...for those who choose to stay; I will allow those families to remain in the cabins with a plot for your own gardens and a small salary in exchange for your labors in the groves. The more hours worked, the more salary earned. Those few left who have been loyal servants to my family and are too old to work the groves may live out your lives in your cabins, I would ask only that you assist me with house chores, cooking, and communal gardening. Salary I offer cannot meet that of the railroad, but here at least you have shelter and food for your families. I will ferry those leaving across to the mainland with good wishes and ten dollars gold when your decisions are made."

Most of the younger slaves chose to leave, carrying meager possessions in burlap bags and knapsacks. After tearful hugs with those who remained, the rag tag parade made their way to the launch to be rowed across the river, bound for a long walk over the river Jordan to a promised land called Detroit.

Journal entry; April 9, 1865

Though we Southerners find no joy in this day, we can at least be grateful this bloody, wretched war is over. General Robert E. Lee has surrendered his Army of Northern Virginia to General Ulysses S. Grant at the McLean house in the village of Appomattox Court House in Virginia. The fall of the South will affect us all, especially our commerce without labor of the Negroes, and will change our lives forever. I am in better position than most as my trees do not require replanting each season to maintain a saleable crop, and will work myself as needed. God bless the Confederacy, and God bless the sons of the South who will return to destroyed homesteads and fallow fields; many of them wounded and missing limbs.

Rolling over in bed he touched Leandra's sleeping face. Rousing, she smiled into his eyes. "Are you going to leave me, Leandra? For if you do I will surely wither and die."

"Never will I willingly leave you; you are my heart and a most loving father to my children, and as much my husband as any legal ceremony could bestow."

Holding each other, the quiet moment was interrupted by a rising crescendo of wails from the cabins. Taking a moment to splash water on his face, he pulled on breeches before stepping outside. Clarice and other women were tearfully embracing, their faces contorted by shock and grief, raising and shaking their hands as if to beseech the heavens. Mammy Sue collapsed to her knees, eyes closed in her wrinkled face as she prayed.

"WHAT'S GOING ON OUT HERE? " Douglas was stymied by the sudden emotional display of grief by everyone in the yard…even the men.

"HE BE DEAD, MISTA DOUGLAS, THEY KILLED HIM!! PRESIDENT LINCOLN DONE BEEN SHOT!!" Clarice fell to the ground, distraught and foaming at the mouth, her arms and legs jerking awkwardly in seizures. Several surrounded her flailing form; picking her up and carrying her to her cabin.

Douglas went back to Leandra who was sitting horrified in the bed.

"It's going to be alright, today they can mourn, but I'm going to have a drink!"

Journal entry; April 15, 1865

Lincoln has been shot and killed while attending a Shakespearean play at the Ford Theater. Actor John Wilkes Booth and other Sons of the Confederacy set in motion a plot to kill the vile man and his top staff; Secretary of State Seward, Vice President Johnson, and the bastard Grant. Booth's derringer was true; affecting a fatal wound behind the president's ear. Grant and his wife, Julia, would have been in the box with the Lincoln's had they not changed plans at the last hour and did not attend. Seward was surprised and repeatedly stabbed at his home, but he has survived as family members thwarted his attacker. Unfortunately Johnson evaded his assassin and will be sworn as President, so it seems the Devil is protecting his own! What a sad, sad time in history our country is enduring.

I shall be forever thankful my small family is sheltered on this beautiful island, far away from the madness of civilization.

Journal Entry; June 30, 1865

Eight brave Southern patriots, conspirators in the assassination of Lincoln and attempted assassinations of Seward, Johnson, and Grant have been apprehended and tried by a military commission. Their sentences are as follows: Edman Spangler sentenced to six years in prison; Dr. Samuel Mudd, Samuel Arnold, and Michael O'Laughlen received sentences of life in prison; Mary Surratt, George Atzerodt, Lewis Powell, and David Lee Herold shall be hanged.

Journal entry; July 7, 1865

Mary Surratt, George Atzerodt, Lewis Powell, and David Lee Herold were hanged in front of the Old Arsenal Building in Washington, DC in front of a crowd of one thousand. They hung for twenty-five minutes before their bodies were cut down. I pray for their brave and patriotic southern souls.

THIRTY SIX

MAY 6, 1870

"Come on girls, I don't want to wait until the sun is so beastly hot we can't stand it! Get your bonnets on!"

Leandra hustled the girls while gathering burlap bags for each of them.

"But Mama, I don't want to go berry picking, my thumb still hurts!" Fifteen year old Mary held up an injured finger hoping for a sympathetic reprieve from the thorny task.

"You're just fine; get your sack…if you don't help….no blackberry pie!" Leandra handed her a bag and a sunbonnet.

"Can we take Boo, Momma?"

"I don't know, Douglas, do you think it's too hot for him?"

"Let the old boy go, he'll enjoy the walk; he'll find a shady spot and rest if he needs it."

"Alright, come on Boo!"

Twisting to rise from the porch, Boo's hips were tender with arthritis, but his spirit was willing.

"Have you got your pistol?"

Leandra sighed, "No, we're just going down to the berry patch."

"Take it, I'll feel better…humor this old man!"

Eighteen year old Kate, the image of her mother, ran teasingly ahead onto the trail. "Last one to the patch has to dump the thunder pots for a week!"

Twenty-two year old Louisa bumped into Douglas as she chased out of the cabin after her sisters. Laughingly she turned, "Sorry Papa!!"

Douglas stood on the cabin porch, smiling to himself at the sudden race brought on by Kate's challenge. The girls disappeared out of sight around the bend as Boo, feeling all of his fifteen years, limped behind.

It was a beautifully blue day, perfect for replacing two shingles on the roof a recent rainstorm has revealed were askance. The job only took about twenty minutes but long enough to work up a sweat in the humid air. Douglas climbed down the ladder and drew a bucket from the well, dumping cool water over his head. Moses and Amos joined him, bantering about the heat. Though most had gone their own way, a few of Mt. Pleasant's slaves had agreed to stay as free men working shares for Douglas at Merritt Island. Giving each man a plot of acreage to grow their own food, the former slaves traded their labor in the citrus groves for individual cabins and a small salary.

Talking by the well, the three men were startled by a shot from the woods, followed by shrill screams of the Dummett daughters. Kate was the first to come into sight with Mary and Louisa fast on her heels. The men went running to the front of the cabin where they could finally make out the horrifying word the girls were yelling.

"BEAR!!!... BEEAAAR!!!"

Jumping onto the porch scrambling into the cabin for his rifle, Douglas raked at his collar trying to breathe. The girls were panicked and breathless; screaming that Leandra had drawn the she-bear's attention while yelling for her daughters to run. They saw Boo lunge at the bear as she charged, momentarily drawing her attention. Standing to her full height, she swung with a mighty paw, her claws ripping his belly, throwing Boo against a tree.

His heart pounding, Douglas ran onto the trail joined by Amos and Moses; Moses with a shotgun, Amos brandishing a machete.

About 100 yards down the path through the hammock Boo lay whimpering beside the trail; the old dog ripped open and his back broken. Just beyond him they saw the massive hulk of the black bear lying atop a motionless form, a brightly patterned Seminole skirt splayed over twisted, distorted legs extending from underneath the carcass. The bruin had died from the pistol shot, but not before fatally mauling Leandra.

Douglas threw himself belly down to reach her, wiping blood from her beautiful face, talking to her. Rolling the beast off Leandra, Amos and Moses quietly left Douglas to close her green eyes, rocking her against his chest... alone in the woods with his grief and anguished cries.

Moses went back to Boo, stroking his bloody fur, talking lowly to soothe the frightened dog.

"You did good, ole buddy; now Moses gonna stop the hurtin'." With a quick motion of his knife, Boo's suffering was ended.

Leandra and Boo were buried next to Adeline's marble egret, brought from Mount Pleasant, on a bluff at their favorite picnic point overlooking Moskito Lagoon.

The next weeks were lost in a drunken fog. Withdrawn and inconsolable, Douglas was insane with grief. In desperation and at a loss as to how to deal with their father, eldest daughter Louisa summoned their Aunt Anna, now a very successful innkeeper in St. Augustine.

During another night of nonstop drinking, Douglas stumbled

to Moses and Clarice's cabin, kicking open the door. Moses jumped from the bed, alarmed at the sudden intrusion and the pistol in Douglas's shaking hand.

"WHAT YOU DOIN'SIR?! WHAT YOU DOIN HERE IN DE MID OF DE NIGHT??" Moses was fixated on the gun now being waved wildly about. Stepping towards Moses, Douglas flipped the revolver around offering the butt handle to him.

"TAKE THIS MOSES, TAKE THIS AND KILL ME! PUT ME OUT OF THIS MISERY! PLEASE...KILL ME!!!"

"Mista Douglas, I not goin' to SHOOT you, I DON BE NO MURDERER!!"

"MOSES, CAN'T YOU SEE, IT WON'T BE MURDER... I'M ALREADY DEAD!! I'M ALREADY DEAD!!" Moses gingerly crossed the small room, taking the pistol from the sobbing man, pulling him to his shoulder.

"Come on, Mista Douglas. Moses be taking you to yor bed, now. Come on. Come on."

Falling heavily onto his mattress, Douglas lifted his grizzled head to look at Moses.

"How pathetic am I; I don't even have the courage of my sixteen year old son."

Passing out and falling into a fitful sleep, Douglas snored drunkenly into his pillow. Pulling off the broken man's boots, Moses covered him with Leandra's embroidered coverlet. Surveying damage in the room from the rum fueled rampage, he kicked pieces of the smashed cello into the corner... and backed out of the cabin.

The scent of coffee roused Douglas, causing a multi-colored whirling pain in his head. Suddenly retching, he made it off the bed, stumbling onto the porch before convulsing in dry heaves.

Reeling, he steadied himself against a post to keep from falling, he tried to stand but dropping to his knees, dry heaved from the weeks' long binge. Anna followed him outside, unflinchingly throwing a bucket of water splashing over his head; then derisively threw a towel at him.

"Brother, you are a shameful sight of a man! We are in need of a serious conversation about my nieces, but first go clean the stink off." With her voice softening, Anna offered a bar of lye soap and a mug of coffee to her older sibling. "After we get some vittles into you, I'll shave that mess off your face and we'll see if there's still a human being under there harboring some measure of civility!"

With that, Anna turned back into the cabin to heat a stew carried in by Clarice and a put a pot onto boil to moisturize a shaving towel. Without argument, Douglas dragged himself to the well, taking off his clothes to bathe, returning to the cabin draped in a towel. Slipping on the clean shirt and breeches laying out on his bed, he resignedly sat at the table, quietly finishing a bowl of stew; then moved to sit in a chair Anna had pulled into the sunlight at the doorway. Expertly wrapping the steaming towel around his head, she took full advantage of her captive audience and his inability to speak.

"Since you're still off your head with grief and not taking care of business, I have been talking with the girls and we have come to the following decisions. Mary and Louisa have expressed their desire to come to St. Augustine and live with me at the inn. It's time they met their cousins and were afforded an expansion of their education and horizons the city and I can offer. They sorely miss their mother and this old spinster will do her best to offer love and gentle care to help fill that void. Kate chooses to remain with you, helping with the administration of the groves. She is eighteen, excels at arithmetic, and is of good mind. In your fog you may not have noticed, but she is mightily taken with affection for your former slave, Andrew Jackson. He seems a fine honest young man and an industrious sort, and also has moon eyes for Kate."

Removing the towel, Anna lathered her brother and proceeded to shave him. She continued in the silence.

"Do not argue these decisions, my brother. Keep forefront in your mind your sister means to have her way…and she is holding a razor at your throat!" Smiling, she patted his face dry. Douglas stood up and embraced her.

"Thank you, good sister. Until I can pull myself from these awful depths, I will abide by your good and generous decisions."

"Come in girls and gather your things, we are off for St. Augustine!"

Douglas sailed them to New Smyrna where arrangements were made for a coach and liveryman. With tears and hugs they waved goodbye to their father and sister from the carriage until it disappeared northbound on the King's Road.

Kate and Andrew jumped the broom at her father's citrus groves on Merritt Island in 1872, surrounded by family and friends. She carried lilies, hibiscus, and orange blossoms, but wore her grandmother's pink roses in her hair.

THIRTY SEVEN

March 27, 1873

Early light shone cool yellow over the glades, the waking
sun filtering haphazardly through layers of fluttering moss and
branches. Douglas was on his second cup of brandied coffee, the
fiddle-back rocker creaking on the warped, grey porch boards.
Closing his eyes to listen to the morning songs of larks and mockingbirds; buzzing of mosquitoes was accompanied by various
unidentified but plentiful Florida pests. A bullfrog added a baritone to the cacophony of the birds' soprano lilts, while the songs,
all diverse, blended beautifully in concert, stirring the beginnings
of a poem. With his journal opened atop a water barrel beside his
rocker, he dipped his quill into the ink well, tapping a blob loose
against the rim of the bottle.

Journal entry; March 27, 1873

Mother Earth doth sing to me with birds in breathless harmony.
When evening embers fade to violet sky,
In purple grace…the Dolphins fly!!
Waves the color of emerald eyes, roll as languid summer sighs;
rising and falling to sea gulls' cries
…eternal as Love that never dies.

Closing the book, he leaned back heavily urging the rocker to motion.

"Damn," he thought to himself, scratching his chin. "Are those boards creaking...or my bones??"

Aging had not been kind to Douglas, not sparing his handsome looks. Now his blonde hair glistened silver and white with fringes of bangs falling over his sun furrowed forehead. His leathery brow had fallen, hooding his eyes though they remained blue and sharp. He maintained a vigor and humor that belied his age, but on this morning he was truly feeling the years. Arthritis aggravated by hand to hand combat in his youth, back-breaking work in the groves, and swollen wounds made pain his now constant companion. Some of the aches could be deadened with spirits, but that brought a steadily debilitating stupor to his days. A cool breeze teased his hair as he meditated, eyes closed, rocking back and forth....only moving his arms to occasionally swat at two or three incessant mosquitoes molesting his face.

"MISTA DOUGLAS!! MISTA DOUGLAS, SIR!!!" Panting up onto the porch, eyes wide with excitement; Moses grabbed onto a porch post, bent over at the waist trying to catch his breath.

"I JUST SEEN HIM, SIR, I JUST SEEN HIM!!! DAT GATOR!! DAT ONE WID THE SILVER HANDLE STUCK IN HIS HAID!! YOUR GATOR, MISTA DOUGLAS!!!"

"WHERE? Moses, calm down man, now...TELL ME WHERE!!" Douglas fumbled with his boot strings, cursing his stiff fingers.

"HE HEADIN' FOR THE BIG BEND, BY WHERE MISS LEANDRA IS LAID TO REST! IT'S HIM, MISTA DOUGLAS!! IT CAN'T BE NO OTHER GATOR!!"

"GET MY HAWKEN OFF THE RACK!!!"

Moses ran panting into the house, grabbing the oily rifle off its place of honor above the fireplace.

"HERE TIS, SIR!"

Douglas stood; one boot still undone, making a cursory check of the long gun, making doubly sure it was loaded even though he knew it was.

"LET'S GO!! SHOW ME WHERE YOU SAW HIM, MOSES!!"

"Iff'n we run down to deriver by de salt lick, he should be 'bout comin' 'round the big bend! He be comin' right at us in dat spot iff'n we can get dere afor he do! You have a good shot, fo sure!!"

Sprinting for the river; the two elderly men's hair caught and snagged in low branches that whipped and cut their faces as they ran. Jumping and plowing through thick marsh grasses and rocky terrain, oblivious to spiny stickers of sand spurs and cutting edges of saw palmettos, Douglas ran like a man possessed. Finding strength of his youth he had forgotten in his legs, he was surprised he felt no pain. Innately he knew this would be his last chance to kill the beast that wrought so much horror, grief, and night sweats to his life. Reaching the riverbank, Douglas leapt, skidding down a muddy gator slide on his butt with Moses right behind. Holding the heavy firearm high over his head with both hands, he slipped down onto a small, rocky beach at the water's edge. Regaining his footing at the bottom, he scanned for a vantage point to brace the rifle.

"CHECK OVER THERE!!" Douglas motioned Moses to go further up river to spot the gator as he steadied himself, balancing the Hawken in the 'Y' of a tree branch, sighting the big gun onto the tannic water, searching for the giant lizard.

"HERE HE COME, MISTA DOUGLAS!!! HERE HE COME!!"

Suddenly, forty years of tears, sweats, and torturous nightmares culminated in this moment... there he was. The massive bull's head with the unmistakable curved handled silver knife buried to the hilt in his skull came slowly, deliberately around the bend, thrust and propelled by an almost taunting waving of his long, armored tail, wake rippling to the banks.

Tilting the Hawken till his scaly nemesis was perfectly in the sights, taking a deep breath; Douglas exhaled slowly, set the rear trigger; then squeezed the front hair trigger. Standing in slippery mud, the recoil of the thunderous blast from the big gun against his shoulder knocked the old man over backwards, but his aim was true. Launching fire from Hell, the trusty long barrel spewed death straight into the hallowed target. Bellowing, the enormous gator lurched in the water; bloody bubbles spewing from the cavernous wound, but revenge was not complete. Pitching the rifle onto the bank; Douglas waded knee-deep into the shallow black water toward the thrashing dragon, deftly firing one shot after another, alternating two pistols. Each concussion knocked the saurian in different directions, throwing chunks and scales flying off the beast. With one final roar, the dying monster sank wheezing and gurgling; partially submerged onto the sandbar of the bend. Wading to the mortally wounded animal, he braced his boot on the alligator's head, rocking and pulling the Bowie knife from its bony encasement with both hands; the blade releasing with a sickening, sucking sound.

Douglas's celebratory dance was that of a victorious madman. Gleefully raising and waving the dagger over his head as an offering to the Gods; joyously whooping, spinning, high-kicking in soaked boots, splashing to the bank through bloody water.

"MOSES!!! GO GET THE MULE CART AND SOME HELP TO DRAG THIS BIG BASTARD OUT OF THE WATER!!! I'M GOING TO SKIN THIS DEVIL; THEN WE'RE PUTTING HIM ON THE BIGGEST SPIT IN FLORIDA!!! TONIGHT, WE CELEBRATE!!!"

"WHOO-EEE!! I BE GETTING' IT!! YASSIR, MOSES BE GETTIN' DAT OLE MULE CART!!!" The elderly Negro turned, scrambling and climbing back up the bank towards the house, his bib-overalls covered in mud.

The pain hit Douglas out of the clear blue, like a board swung full force crashing into his heart, momentarily blinding him. Grabbing his chest, he barely broke his fall with the other arm. Stumbling as he fell, scooting himself to a sitting position at the base of a live oak, he clawed at his collar…struggling to breathe.

Willfully slowing and calming his breaths, the weight eased slightly on his chest, excruciating pain subsiding to a heavy throb. Raising his head, he glimpsed sudden movement in the shadows of the woods ahead of him. A colorful Seminole skirt swirled among the leaves from a narrow waist, revealing lithe dark legs and bare feet. Frantically wiping at his eyes with the back of his hand, he struggled to focus, trying to make out the face. Leandra smiled teasingly, swinging her curly masses of long, black hair as she spun and danced among the trees. Intermittent shafts of sunlight in the shade lit her smile, her unforgettable green eyes beckoning in that way he remembered. A little blonde girl and a tall, handsome young man walked towards him, hand in hand; Leandra close behind them.

"Adeline?" "Charles??" "Oh, come to me, my darling children!" Laughing as she skipped to her father, Adeline threw her arms around his neck as he squeezed her to him, crying into her hair. Charles bent to hug him; helping him to his feet as Leandra smothered him with kisses, smiling into his eyes as she brushed tears from his cheeks. Kissing each one, Douglas felt pure joy in their reunion. No more pain…no more anguish…

Adeline pulled his hand as he stood. "Come, Papa, it's time to come home. We're all going home!"

BIBLIOGRAPHY

With thanks to the many authors and historians who helped paint this picture of our history. Their painstaking research on this tumultuous time in America and specifically Florida helped bring the trials, flavor, grief, and joy of the Dummett family to life.

- A LAND REMEMBERED; a novel by Patrick D. Smith
- THE SEMINOLE WARS: America's Longest Indian Conflict; by John Missall and Mary Lou Missall
- THE PASSIONS OF ANDREW JACKSON; by Andrew Burstein
- THREE ROADS TO THE ALAMO: The Lives and Fortunes of David Crockett, James Bowie, and William Harret Travis; by William C. Davis
- MANHUNT: The 12-Day Chase for Lincoln's Killer; by James L. Swanson
- IMAGES OF NEW SMYRNA BEACH; by Lawrence J. Sweet
- HOPES, DREAMS, & PROMISES; by Michael G. Schene
- THE CIVIL WAR; by Robert Paul Jordan
- THE AGE OF JACKSON; by Arthur M. Schlesinger, Jr.
- TRAIL FROM ST. AUGUSTINE; by Lee Gramling
- THE BLACK SEMINOLES: History of a Freedom Seeking People; by Kenneth W. Porter, revised and edited by Alcione M. Amos and Thomas P. Senter
- CANAVERAL LIGHT; a Novel by Don David Argo
- INDIAN ORATORY: Famous Speeches by Noted Indian Chieftains;

Compiled by W.C. Vanderwerth

- RHETT BUTLER'S PEOPLE; A Novel by Donald McCaig
- HISTORY OF NEW SMYRNA; Compiled by Gary Luther
- FLORIDA'S GHOSTLY LEGENDS AND HAUNTED FOLKLORE: South and Central Florida; Greg Jenkins
- NEW SMYRNA: An Eighteenth Century Greek Odyssey; by E.P. Panagopoulos
- EXPLORING FLORIDA 100 YEARS AGO: St. Augustine, the Keys, Kissimmee River, West Coast; compiled and annotated by Stuart D. Ludlum
- 1846 PORTRAIT OF THE NATION; National Portrait Gallery, Smithsonian Institution
- FLORIDA, AMERICAN REVOLUTION BICENTENNIAL 1776-1976: An Account of the First Discovery and Natural History of FLORIDA; by William Roberts
- LAST COMMAND: THE DADE MASSACRE; by W.S. Steele
- THE TWILIGHT OF SAILING SHIPS; by Robert Carse
- OLD DAYS, OLD WAYS: Eighty Years of New Smyrna Memories; by Lois Tipton
- NARROW DOG TO INDIAN RIVER; by Terry Darlington
- NATIVE AMERICANS; by Turner, Smithsonian Books
- NEW SMYRNA, FLORIDA, ITS HISTORY AND ANTIQUITIES; http://ufdc.ufl.edu//UF00055148/00001 University of Florida Digital Collections
- A GUIDED TOUR OF HISTORIC NEW SMYRNA; a pamphlet by Gary Luther and the Southeast Volusia Historical Society, Inc.
- THE CLIFTON COLORED SCHOOL CIRCA 1890; Black Florida History, North Brevard History, Titusville, Florida; http://nbbd.com/godo/history/CliftonSchool/
- DIGNITY IS RENEWED FOR FORGOTTEN GRAVE; Article

by Jean Morgan, Daytona News-Journal

- OAK HILL HISTORY; http://www.volusia.com/
- RESTLESS LIBERTY: The Fall of Florida's Maroon Haven and the Largest Slave Rebellion in U.S. History, 1835-1838; by Daniel Barcia, A thesis submitted to the Department of History in Partial fulfillment of the requirements for the Degree of Bachelor of Arts with Honors, Harvard University, Cambridge, Massachusetts, 12 March 2015
- NEW SMYRNA BEACH HISTORICAL TRAIL, VOLUSIA COUNTY, FLORIDA; Reocities.com project
- THE DADE MASSACRE, DEC. 28, 1835; Online Florida history, eyewitness account by Seminole leader Halpatter Tustenuggee (Alligator, the white man called him) and News article of the battle reported in the Daily National Intelligencer, Washington, D.C. in the Wednesday, January 27, 1836 edition.
- TEXAS TELEGRAPH AND REGISTER: March 24, 1836, report and listing of the dead at the Alamo; https://drtlibrary.files.wordpress.com/2009/03/sc-telegraph-andtexas-rister-1836
- MERRITT ISLAND NATIONAL WILDLIFE REFUGE; pamphlet by U.S. Fish and Wildlife Service
- APRIL 6, 1832: BLACK HAWK WAR BEGINS; www.history.com/this-day-in-history/black-hawk-war-begins/print
- INDIAN TREATIES AND THE REMOVAL ACT OF 1830; The Trail of Tears; https://history.state.gov/milestones/1830-1960/Indian-treaties
- DeLEON SPRINGS STATE PARK, Spring of Healing Waters; informational pamphlet from www.FloridaStateParks.org
- SUGAR MILL RUINS; Pamphlet by the New Smyrna Beach Area Visitor's Bureau
- Wikipedia searches on New Smyrna history

- BULOW PLANTATION RUINS HISTORIC STATE PARK; Pamphlet by FloridaStateParks.org
- FLAGLER AVENUE HISTORIC & WALKING AREA; Pamphlet by the Community Redevelopment Agency, New Smyrna Beach, FL
- NEW SMYRNA, FLORIDA IN THE CIVIL WAR; Assembled by Zelia Wilson Sweett, 1963; A Volusia County Historical Commission Publication
- THE STORY OF THE DUNLAWTON PLANTATION; Harold D. Cardwell, Sr.
- RUINS OF THE EARLY PLANTATIONS OF THE HALIFAX AREA VOLUSIA COUNTY, FLORIDA; by Edith Penrose Stanton under the direction of The Volusia County Historical Society
- TREK TO FLORIDA; Broome Stringfellow
- OLD TOWN BY THE SEA: A PICTORAL HISTORY OF NEW SMYRNA BEACH; Bo Poertner
- WAR, ROMANCE, SCANDAL IN DUMMETT GROVE PAST, by Marguerite Drennen from the Daytona Beach Sunday News Journal article dated April 26, 1958 by County News Editor Wayne Chandler

HISTORY EPILOGUE

Mother Earth sings her best songs at New Smyrna.

Glistening along the east coast of Florida, this alabaster sand barrier island beckons as paradise just south of Daytona. Vivid yellow-orange Atlantic sunrises are upstaged only by brilliant sunsets firing the Indian River and Mosquito Lagoon ablaze in vibrant reds, pinks, and purples. Palms and sea oats shimmy in tropical breezes, teasing with scents of magnolia, sweet jasmine, and orange blossoms. Fuchsia bougainvillea winds high through treetops while yellow hibiscus stand as lanterns in the shade. Ancient live oaks spread arthritic limbs draped by snowy egrets and mossy shawls of tattered grey…Confederate grey; for this is the historic South.

New Smyrna's rich history has been well documented by numerous authors and scholars. We've learned about early local Timucua (Tee-moo-qua) Indians, their shell mounds and societies; of Spanish explorer Ponce de Leon landing on the east coast of Florida in 1513 claiming it for Spain…and we've read many controversies about origins of our mysterious fort bulwark and sugar mill ruins.

Establishing an historical timeline of colonization of Florida and other early American events during research, the following information and dates were ascertained to form a framework of facts to help background and build the story…WHERE DOLPHINS FLY.

1513-1763: *Florida became a territory of the Kingdom of Spain; claimed by Spanish explorer Ponce de Leon in 1513. During this 250 year possession; Spanish missions were built down the east coast of Georgia and Florida under the direction of Franciscan Friars. Their purpose was to evangelize native tribes. With Florida being turned over to England in 1763, the missions were abandoned with the Spanish Friars leaving to establish new missions in California.

* Due to the construction and design, some local historians believe the 'old fort' coquina and stone bulwark on the river waterfront of New Smyrna was in the process of being built by Spaniards in the 1600's when it was overrun by natives before completion. Their hypothesis is the soldiers then fled north where similar construction on the Castillo de San Marcos was started in St. Augustine in 1672. The core of the coquina, bastion style fort was completed there in 1695 at the Matanzas Inlet.

1727-1733: *British cartographer, Henry Popple, was sent to map the American colonies including Florida, by the Lord Commissioner of Trade and Plantation in 1727-1733. Maps were needed to mediate disputes arising from competing property claims of English, French, and Spanish colonists .The charts also included information from an important survey from 1722 by Colonel John Barnwell annotating important landmarks and points of interest of the southern frontier. Several substantial Spanish missions along the east coasts of Georgia and Florida were noted.

*Though New Smyrna did not yet exist as a settlement; the Popple maps show the location of what appears to be

Ponce Inlet, with the native Ais village of Caparaca located just south of said inlet on the mainland near a large stone bulwark foundation. It is assumed to be our old fort buttress as there are no others in the vicinity along the river. Inland a few miles, west of the Ais village; the Spanish Mission Atocuimi de Jororo is specified on the map. The Friars of this mission attended to the Jororo tribe ranging in the area between the current St. John's, Indian, and Halifax Rivers.

*The Popple Maps are part of the collection of the British Museum in London, England, and predate the Turnbull Colony.

*With conflict growing between Spain and the British crown; Spain offered freedom to any slaves who would join them in fighting the British in Florida. Hundreds ran away from southern plantations to become Freedmen receiving Spanish military training. Accustomed to tropical climate and familiar with the territory, the slaves became invaluable as translators with native tribes.

1763-1783: *The 1763 Treaty of Paris ceded Florida from Spain to the Kingdom of Great Britain. Their possession lasted twenty years.

*With the end of Spanish rule in 1763 and the pullout of their troops; Spain deserted the Freedmen who had aligned with them against the English. Forming a colony deep in central Florida; many Freedmen intermarried with natives and became known as Black Seminoles or Maroons. The colony grew to an estimated 1000-1600; becoming a haven for runaway slaves. Their leader in the early and mid 1800's was the great orator and ruthless warrior tactician; slave John Caesar.

*With Florida now under British rule; the Spanish Franciscans deserted their monasteries in Georgia and jungles of Florida to establish missions in Spanish California. The elegantly arched stone structures were left to ravages of nature.

1768-1777: *The Turnbull Colony was established in New Smyrna in 1768-1777 as the largest British colonization attempt in the New World; almost three times larger than the Jamestown settlements of 1607. After nine brutal years for the colonists, mostly indentured from the Mediterranean region…the Turnbull Colony failed.

New Smyrna was the vision of Scottish physician Dr. Andrew Turnbull. Obtaining a land grant in 1765 of approximately 60,000 acres to establish his Florida colony, he named it New Smyrnea after his wife's birthplace in Asia Minor, now Turkey. Returning then to the Mediterranean; he contracted with workers who signed to be indentured for set periods of years. Of the original 1403 colonists; only 1255 survived the ravages of scurvy during the voyage to New Smyrna in 1768. Promised living conditions, pay, and freedom after their contracted servitude were never honored. Instead, colonists endured nine years of horrific treatment, back-breaking labor, whippings and starvation from Turnbull and his barbarous overseers. Desperate for assistance; colonists met with freedom fighters from Georgia, discussing whether to abdicate and join American patriots in their revolution fighting for independence from the Crown.

Instead; in May 1777, ninety colonists risked their lives leaving the plantation to seek asylum; walking sixty-two miles to St. Augustine bringing their stories of atrocities to the attention of British Governor Patrick Tonyn. Heart rending depositions about conditions at New Smyrna detailed beatings, deaths by stoning, rapes, and murder. If a colonist presented proof to Turnbull or his overseers that his time of indenture was fulfilled and asked to be released, many reported being chained and flogged until they signed new contracts pledging additional time to be served. During those nine years of inhumane servitude of the 1255 colonists who survived the sea journey; another 964 died at New Smyrna with another 69 men, women, and children dying after leaving New Smyrna but before the Governor's investigative report of 15 January 1778 was completed. Governor Tonyn eventually granted the families asylum, setting aside a section of St. Augustine for them to settle. With the colony's failure, Florida's jungles soon overtook the intricate canals, irrigation systems, and cleared fields; returning the land to palmettos and native flora. Turnbull reportedly lived on the plantation until it was overrun by natives. Eventually tried and briefly jailed before being released when Britain ceded the troubled territory to Spain in 1783; he retired with his family to Charleston, South Carolina.

1776: *With American colonies fighting for freedom from the British Crown in the 1776 Revolution; patriot conflict continually spilled into the southern wilderness of Florida.

1783-1821: *Unwilling to bear continuing costs of war; Great Britain ceded Florida back to Spain in 1783 after the American Revolution.

1807: British Marine Officer Major Thomas Dummett and his wife Mary; brought their children and slaves to America in 1807, abandoning their sugar plantation in Barbados, fleeing bloody uprisings after Britain's abolishment of slavery. To avoid capture and almost certain hanging, Thomas Dummett was carried aboard ship concealed in a wine cask. Living between New Haven, Connecticut and their home known as the 'Governor's House' in St. Augustine; Thomas continued as a successful businessman.

1818: * In 1818, responding to reports that Seminoles were harboring runaway slaves; Andrew Jackson led 3000 Army troops in a murderous and fiery raid against the north Florida village of Mikasuk, initiating a cruel assault on indigenous people who had fled southward from Georgia. This started a cycle of three, bloody Seminole Wars; the First in 1817-1819; the Second 1835-1842; and the Third 1855-1858.

1821: * With fighting and costs spiraling out of control for the Spanish during Seminole Wars; tensions further increased because of US Army incursions into Florida led by General Andrew Jackson. Soldiers hunted runaway slaves returning them to their plantation owners, as well as attacking Spanish forts. Jackson was also exacting revenge and wholesale slaughter against native tribes for their attacks against whites.

Spain ceded Florida to the US under the Adams-Onis Treaty. The deal gave the wilderness territory to the United States in return for forgiving Spain's $5,000,000 debt.

1825: Thomas Dummett bought the abandoned 2000 acre

Rosetta Plantation in the Florida territory near current day Ormond Beach. Rosetta had been developed in the late 1770's by John Moultrie, but was deserted when Florida was ceded back to Spain by the British in 1783. Moultrie had successfully grown and processed indigo, rice, corn, and sugar cane. John Bunch acquired Rosetta in 1803; his heirs sold the plantation to Dummett in 1825. Thomas Dummett also purchased part of the adjoining Addison plantation known as Carrickfergus and additional lands of the failed Turnbull property to augment acreage, eventually growing Rosetta to approximately 4600 acres.

May 28, 1830: Indian Removal Act

Fleeing from a relentless invasion of European pioneers eager for eastern land; Native Americans re-established homes in northern Florida, only to be continually pushed further south. Our government decided to use the Army to move all native tribes onto reservation lands in Oklahoma...and to eliminate any refusing to leave. Andrew Jackson proved to be merciless not only with his sword in battle, but also with his pen as president; pushing the Indian Removal Act through Congress.

1830-1835: Douglas Dummett found a plot farther south of his parents' acreage at Rosetta (near Ormond) in the fledging settlement of New Smyrna where he built his plantation; Mount Pleasant. His forty-three acre parcel on beachside extended about from current day Flagler Avenue south to Third Avenue; along the Indian River (formerly the Hillsborough River). Situated on a large shell midden; old maps show the plantation house was built where Callalisa Creek branched off the Hillsborough. Acquiring additional lands at Oak Hill and Merritt Island, he planted citrus groves devising a method of cold bud grafting melding sweet oranges with Florida's native sour oranges... beginning the Indian River Citrus strain. He became one of the largest exporters of citrus with northern demand commanding highest prices for the sweet fruit.

Dummett was commissioned Captain of the 'Mosquito Roarers'; a loosely constructed local militia of farmers and homesteaders gathered to defend the settlement of New Smyrna against lawbreakers and warring Seminoles. He became a judge in 1833, was the first Tomoka Postmaster, and held other elected positions in the Territorial legislature, later serving as a Representative of St. John's and Mosquito Counties.

1835-1842: Second Seminole War

Chiefs of the many different Florida tribes came to realize fractured resistance was ineffective against Federal troops; they would need a united front to fight. Creeks, Yuchis, Yamassas, Miccosuki, Hitchitis, Oconees, and other lesser tribes joined with the Maroons. Native discontent culminated in the Second Seminole War lasting seven bloody years.

Though the Second Seminole War is historically reported as an Indian war; it was also the largest slave uprising in American history. Negroes given their freedom by Spain in return for fighting with them against the British were labeled Freedmen. Intermarrying with natives and other runaways, they formed a colony deep in central Florida led by runaway slave John Caesar; a rousing orator. Known as Black Seminoles or Maroons; their numbers were estimated at 1000-1600. Caesar proved to be a devastatingly efficient battle tactician; his Maroons augmenting Seminole war parties in the organized onslaught against whites.

December 23, 1835: Maj. Dade leaves Fort Brooke (Tampa) with 117 Troops for Fort King (Ocala)
December 25, 1835: Seminole massacre at New Smyrna

One of those first major attacks was the Christmas massacre against the small settlement of New Smyrna led by the fearsome warrior; Coacoochee. The son of Seminole Chief King Philip and Chief Micanopy's daughter; Coacoochee was known as 'Wildcat' by settlers because of his ferocity in battle. Fighting beside his boyhood friend, Osceola; they were fierce and dreaded warriors.

One can only imagine the panic and terror of New Smyrna's families that Christmas night. With grotesquely painted warriors attacking from the west; mothers and fathers ran, carrying and dragging screaming children to the only means of escape…rowboats, canoes, and rafts moored in the Hillsborough (now Indian) River. Frantically launching, they attempted to cross to regroup at Mount Pleasant; the plantation on the east riverbank of the island owned by Douglas Dummett; head of the local militia. From Mount Pleasant, located approximately between New Smyrna's current North and South Causeways; families that made it across the river fled on horseback and wagons to the north end of the island. Using small boats to reach schooners moored in the deeper water of Moskito Inlet (now Ponce Inlet); the settlers sailed northward escaping up the Halifax River. Seminoles pursued, crossing the river on rafts provided by slaves; looting and attempting to burn Mount Pleasant's manor house near Callalisa Creek; succeeding only in burning a hole in the living room floor. With the settlement a raging inferno, Wildcat and his warriors chased settler families northward to the inlet. There, they plundered and burned the original wooden lighthouse that had just been completed in 1835 on the south side of the inlet, stealing lanterns and mirrored beacon reflectors in the raid. High tides had undermined the foundation of that first lighthouse, rendering it unsafe. It was never operational.

Survivors fleeing carnage in New Smyrna made their way north taking refuge at the John J. Bulow plantation, Bulowville; north of today's Ormond Beach. Crowding within thick walls of Bulow's stockade fortification along with other residents of the Halifax River region; they waited for soldiers to arrive to provide them safe escort to Fort Marion in St. Augustine.

Shortly after the settlers fled New Smyrna that Christmas of 1835, a French schooner capsized between Moskito Inlet and Port Canaveral. About ten sailors survived, swimming to shore. Attempting to hike north on the beach to St. Augustine, the men were stopped by Moskito Inlet at New Smyrna. Unaware of the imminent native threat and unable to cross the inlet until they built a raft, the group camped for the night on high ground along the river on the back side of the island. Cold and wet, they built a campfire. Seeing that beacon, a band of Seminoles crossed the river, attacking and mutilating all the sailors. The location is known as 'Massacre Bluff'.

December 28, 1835: Bartholomew Pons' ride to Fort Marion in St. Augustine

Besieged at Bulowville, the settlers sent their best horseman; New Smyrna's young mail rider Bartholomew Pons, to the fort in St. Augustine to plead for military troop protection. In early morning darkness of December 28, 1835, with flames visible on the skyline marking progress of the advancing Seminoles; Pons galloped north on the 'King's Road', yelling warnings of imminent attacks to isolated dwellers along the way.

The 30-foot wide 'King's Road' was cut through dense foliage and undergrowth during the early British occupation; then restored by the U.S. military in 1833. Beginning at the St. Mary's River, it passed St. Augustine south to New Smyrna ending at the stone wharf. In Bo Poertner's book *Old Town by the Sea*, he quotes Bockelman as naming Pons the "Paul Revere of the (Second) Seminole War".

December 28, 1835: Dade Massacre

One hundred-seventeen soldiers commanded by Major Francis Langhorne Dade were marching one-hundred miles from Fort Brooke (near Tampa) to reinforce Fort King (near Ocala) in response to Seminole attacks along the east coast. They were attacked and slaughtered by Seminoles and Maroons led by Chiefs King Philip and Micanopy. There were three grievously wounded survivors who made their way back to Fort Brooke. The account by nineteen year old Private Ransom Clarke is the only written record of the massacre.

January 17, 1836: Battle of Dunn-Lawton

After almost three weeks at the Bulow plantation with food running low, a decision was made to send a search party of recently arrived troops to the burnt-out Anderson plantation, Dunn-Lawton; hopefully to find hidden food stores and other buried supplies. On January 17, 1836, Major Benjamin Putnam led a small party of soldiers of the St. Augustine Guard augmented by members of Captain Dummett's settler militia on the guerilla mission. The group of about twenty men left Bulowville, floating down the Halifax around midnight. Landing at Thomas Dummett's plantation, Rosetta, on the peninsula bordered by the Halifax and Tomoka Rivers; they tied and hid their rafts in underbrush on the Halifax side. Camping for the night near the Anderson's smoking ruins, the men were discovered near dawn by two braves checking the horses. Their shots alerted an encamped war party on the plantation of approximately one-hundred twenty Seminole warriors. In the ensuing fierce and one-sided battle; four settlers were killed and thirteen badly wounded. All received some injury, including the militia leader, Douglas Dummett; who was shot twice in the neck and stabbed through the left shoulder. Massively outnumbered, Major Putnam ordered a retreat to the boats. Dragging and carrying their wounded to the river, they discovered the tide had receded, beaching the boats. With Seminoles in close pursuit, the men were forced to push and pull the heavy crafts to the water to escape. In the mayhem, two men were left behind. One made it back to Bulowville on his own; it is assumed the other was captured and killed.

Eyewitness James Ormond, a member of the 'Moskito

Roarers', reported that Coacoochee (Wildcat) "led the charge of warriors while mounted on a white or grey horse in full war paint and costume." He was wearing the stolen lighthouse reflectors as a headdress and breastplate.

February 23, 1836 – March 6, 1836: Thirteen Day Siege and Fall of the Alamo

One hundred-forty brave souls and patriot Texians held off a force of four-thousand Mexican soldiers under General Santa Ana for thirteen days before the small Spanish mission near San Antonio was overrun. Army soldiers at the Alamo were commanded by Colonel William Travis while the Texas Volunteers were led by Colonel Jim Bowie. Famed frontiersman, Dave Crocket, was also among the dead. A Mrs. Dickinson, her child and two slaves, one of Travis's and one of Bowie's; survived the onslaught and were allowed to leave. The slaves were spared in honor of the bravery of both Travis and Jim Bowie who died valiantly in his sickbed, reportedly after emptying both pistols and fighting to the death swinging his famous knife. It was reported by Mrs. Dickinson there was a "pile of dead Mexicans" around his bed. It was estimated 1500 Mexican soldiers died during the siege and three attempts to breech the walls before the final battle.

1842- The Second Seminole War raged seven years, ending in 1842, after which most Seminoles were moved to reservations. Some bands refused to leave Florida; instead, retreating into the Everglades, never surrendering to the U.S. government.

*Douglas Dummett fathered four children with his beautiful, green-eyed slave; Namona Leandra Fernandez. Leandra, daughter of a Negro slave and a Seminole woman; lived at Mount Pleasant with their son and three daughters in separate slave quarters built for her behind the manor house. The Volusia County census of 1860 listed the family's ages as: Douglas, 54; Leandra, 45; Louisa, 12; Kate, 10; and Mary, 8; their son Charles, was almost 16. Illegal for Douglas and Leandra to marry because of southern mores' and the rule of law; they were forced to keep their ardent affair and true feelings secret from the settlement. Doting parents; they remained together in love until their deaths.

March 3, 1845: Florida statehood granted

Once the major Seminole threat was gone, the territorial legislature of Florida petitioned Congress in 1845 and was granted statehood, with Florida becoming the 27th state. Population and enterprise then grew in earnest.

After the Seminole Wars ended in 1842 and statehood granted in 1845; hearty settlers returned to the area and New Smyrna again flourished...for a while. Old stone foundations that survived Seminole torches were reused and repurposed. Homes and businesses rose from the ashes; fields were reclaimed, cleared, and crops planted. Babies were born; the community began to thrive once again.

December 23, 1856: Shive family massacre at Oak Hill

The last recorded Seminole attack in the area occurred between New Smyrna and Oak Hill with the massacre of the four members of the Shive family. Bodies of Mr. Shive and their son were found slaughtered and scalped in the yard; the body of their daughter was found among the ruins of their burning home. Mrs. Shive's mutilated body was discovered outside behind a small hill. The gruesome, still smoking scene was discovered by Jane Sheldon's two youngest sons who had been duck hunting in the area. The boys ran to their uncle Arad Sheldon's cabin for help. A posse was assembled from a volunteer company from Mellonsville; tracking the party of nineteen Seminoles for seventy miles until losing their trail in the central region of the state.

April 23, 1860: Charles Dummett's death

This was a day of unimaginable grief for Douglas and Leandra. Illegal for blacks to be schooled in the South, Douglas had sent their son, Charles, to Connecticut for his formal university education at Yale; Douglas's alma mater. After only eight months at Yale, while home for Easter holiday; Charles died from a single shotgun blast. Differing authors' accounts theorize the shooting was from an accidental fall or a hunting accident, either alone or with a friend, citing varied locations and circumstances. But years of extensive research on the Dummetts by author and historian, Marguerite Drennen; credibly makes the logical case that Charles committed suicide. Distraught after the school discovered his mother was a slave, and mortified the confirmation of his birth had become public to his classmates; Charles found himself conflicted in the cruel middle of two worlds. Hot talk of secession and war was in the air with hard and loud lines drawn between sides. Charles returned home to New Smyrna and was dead in a matter of days. The location of the incident, whether at home or in one of his father's orange groves on Merritt Island or Oak Hill has been lost to history. Numerous theories have been espoused...but no definitive written accounts. We do know he was laid to rest on the plantation Mount Pleasant, just shy of sixteen. One has to take into account the confusion in his teenage heart, for if civil war erupted; where would he stand? Would he fight for the South beside his white, plantation-owner father; or would he defend the Northern flag that sought to liberate his mother? Eight months after Charles' untimely death; South Carolina seceded from the Union, shortly followed by Mississippi and then Florida.

January 10, 1861: Florida secedes from the Union

Florida became the third state to secede from the Union becoming the major supplier of beef for the rebel army. Union ships blockaded major ports in an attempt to interrupt food and munitions to the southern troops. With Savannah, Jacksonville, and St. Augustine ports blocked by the North; New Smyrna's Moskito Inlet became a critically important supply route for the Confederacy. Arms, food, and supplies were shipped in from neutral ports in the Caribbean by small fast blockade runners that under cover of night, slipped past more cumbersome, deeper draft Federal gunships. Once inside the inlet, mangroves offered excellent cover.

April 12, 1861: Start of the Civil War

Confederate General Beauregard opened fire on Union held Fort Sumter in South Carolina's Charleston Bay. Major Robert Anderson surrendered the fort. The country was torn by Civil War, and once again New Smyrna faced fiery destruction... this time from Union cannons.

March 12, 1862: Confederate attack on Federal troops in New Smyrna

The *USS Keystone State*, a federal gunboat, anchored outside 'Moskito Inlet' to investigate rumors of blockade runners delivering weapons and ammunition to New Smyrna. Two shallow draft steamers, the *Henry Andrew* and the *Penguin*, were summoned to assist the *Keystone* that was too large to cross the inlet sandbar. Nosing in over the bar, the two smaller boats anchored inside the inlet, launching five small sail longboats with two officers and forty-one men in search of the schooner *Kate;* a blockade runner then loaded with cotton to trade for weaponry in the Caribbean. She was hiding, waiting for a favorable tide and darkness; camouflaged with palm fronds in a maze of mangroves. Federal intelligence reports had not included information two companies of the Third Florida Infantry, commanded by Captain Strain, were hiding in reeds and heavy undergrowth along the old, stone wharf at the end of today's Clinch Street. The Confederate ambush was lethal with eight Union soldiers killed, including the two officers; Lt. Budd and Acting Master Mather, and six others wounded. The rest barely escaped into the mangroves. Union officers were later allowed to recover some of the bodies and property of their dead under a white flag of truce.

July 26, 1863: Union shelling of New Smyrna

The Union retaliated with a vengeance. The sloop *Beauregard* was towed by the U.S. dispatch steamer, the side wheeler *Oleander,* to the wharf in front of the Sheldon Hotel built atop the old fort foundation. The two boats swung broadside bringing their cannons around aimed at the town.

Their relentless artillery fire blasted New Smyrna into oblivion. Settlers, after two decades rebuilding from destructive Seminole Wars, again ran for their lives; this time inland, hiding in thick palmetto hammocks and pine forests. Following annihilation wrought by the 'Army of Northern Aggression'; smaller homes were eventually rebuilt with scavenged materials on what was left of foundations of former sites.

March 23, 1865:   Willie Hardee, Douglas Dummett's nephew (Elizabeth's son), a Confederate soldier, died of a chest wound suffered in the Battle of Bentonville, NC, two weeks before the war ended. He was seventeen.

April 9, 1865:   General Robert E. Lee surrendered his Army of Northern Virginia to General Ulysses S. Grant at the McLean House in Appomattox Court House, Virginia.

April 14, 1865:   President Abraham Lincoln was felled by an assassin's bullet to the back of his head while attending a play at the Ford Theater. That same night Secretary of State Seward was stabbed numerous times in his home but survived the attack.

April 15, 1865:   President Lincoln dies of his wound at 7:20A. Vice President Andrew Johnson is sworn in as the 17th president of the United States.

April 26, 1865:   John Wilkes Booth and co-conspirator David Lee Herold were cornered in a barn on Garrett's farm near Port Royal, Virginia. Herold surrendered when the barn was set afire. Booth refused to surrender and was shot by Union soldier, Boston Corbett.

May 1, 1865: Eight captured conspirators of Lincoln's assassination are ordered to be tried by a military commission.

June 30, 1865: At trial: Edman Spangler sentenced to six years in prison; Dr. Samuel Mudd, Samuel Arnold, and Michael O'Laughlen sentenced to life; Mary Surratt, George Atzerodt, Lewis Powell, and David Lee Herold sentenced to hang.

July 7, 1865: Four assassination conspirators were hanged in front of the Old Arsenal Building in Washington, DC for twenty-five minutes before their bodies were cut down. Innkeeper Mary Surratt became the first woman to be executed by the government.

May 6, 1870: Namona Leandra Fernandez died in Titusville, Florida.

March 27, 1873: Douglas Dummett died in Titusville, Florida.

OLD FORT? *Built in the Spanish style of forts, the New Smyrna bulwark construction method is similar to the Castillo de San Marcos in St. Augustine built in 1672, a prime example of the 'Bastion System' of fortification.

*Scottish doctor Andrew Turnbull built his house atop the stone buttress sometime during his attempt at establishing a colony at New Smyrna in 1768 on his land grant of 60,000 acres to a reported 101,400 acres. Turnbull lived on the plantation for a short time after the colony failed in 1777 after numerous reports of mistreatment of indentured Minorcans were presented to Governor Tonyn. With no one left to work or defend the plantation, natives overran the area destroying the house and fields. After a short stint in prison from charges brought by partners in the colony experiment, Turnbull retired to Charleston, SC with his family. He died in 1792.

*In 1801, Dr. Ambrose Hull received a land grant from Spain for 2600 acres including the site of Old Fort Park. He was in the process of having stone masons build his home atop the bulwark when it was destroyed during the Patriot War of 1812. He called his plantation Mount Olive because of the olive trees planted there by Minorcans from the Turnbull colony.

*In 1830, Thomas Stamps, a South Carolina planter, bought 100 acres of Mount Olive, building his home atop the old stone foundation. It was burned in the Christmas attack by Seminoles in 1835.

*In 1854, John and Jane Sheldon bought 50 acres of the Stamps Plantation. The next major structure atop the stone buttress was the 40 room Sheldon Hotel completed in 1859 and destroyed by Union cannons 26 July, 1863.

*After the Civil War, Jane Sheldon returned building a small rooming house atop the buttress with scavenged materials. Over the years a store and post office were added. The buildings survived about thirty years before being torn down due to dilapidation.

*1920's, federal WPA works made changes to the bulwark during excavation and restoration attempts.

*July 10, 2008, the stone buttress was placed on the National Registry of Historic Places.

*The massive coquina bulwark stands today in Old Fort Park on Riverside Drive in New Smyrna Beach; a silent testament to its long, storied, and mysterious history.

DUMMETT FAMILY FACTS

*Only five of eleven Dummett children of British Marine Officer Thomas Dummett and his wife Mary survived into middle age; Douglas 1806-1873, Mortimer 1810-1888, Anna Maria 1817-1899, Elizabeth 1820-1853, and Sara Jane 1824-1860.

Elizabeth Dummett married Major William Hardee in 1840. He later became a Confederate General. The Hardee marriage bore four children, three daughters and a son who were sent to live with their Aunt Anna in St. Augustine when Elizabeth died in 1853 at the age of thirty-three. The children later went to live with their father when he was transferred to West Point as Commandant of cadets. Their son, Willie, was killed at the Battle of Bentonville, NC two weeks before the end of the war. He was seventeen.

In 1835, prior to the Second Seminole War, Douglas Dummett was commissioned as Captain of Company B, Mounted Cavalry of the 2A Regiment, 2D Brigade, Florida Militia. This Company became known as 'The Moskito Roarers'.

After convalescing from his Battle of Dunlawton injuries, Douglas courted and married Frances Hunter, beautiful daughter of a wealthy St. Augustine family; but discovering his wife had been unfaithful...he returned to New Smyrna leaving her behind. Frances filed for divorce from Savannah, Georgia in March of 1844 after a lengthy separation. There are no known children of their union.

Dummett was a member of the Legislative Council of the Territory of Florida representing St. Johns County from 1843-1845.

Earlier he was the Tomoka Postmaster, elected Judge and Tax collector in New Smyrna, and became a member of the Florida House of Representatives from Mosquito County in 1845.

Anna Dummett converted her parents' large St. Augustine 'Governor's House', built in 1791 during the Spanish Colonial period, into a boardinghouse in 1845. Still in operation and formerly known as the Dummett-Garcia House, it is now operated as the St. Francis Inn Bed and Breakfast, located at 279 St. George Street, St. Augustine, FL. ; www.stfrancisinn.com. The beautifully restored inn features seventeen period themed rooms and suites including 'Anna's Room', the 'Dummett Room', and 'Elizabeth's Suite'; and is listed on the National Register of Historic Places. Busy raising her nieces and nephews at the inn after her sister Elizabeth's death, Anna never married. It was rumored she was a Confederate spy.

Douglas fathered four children with his young slave; Namona Leandra Fernandez. Per the 1860 Volusia County census she was listed as half Negro and half Seminole. She and the children resided in a small house behind the main house of Mount Pleasant. Their children were Charles 1844-1860; Louisa 1848-1888; Kate 1852-1918; and Mary b.1854.

Illegal to educate their children in the South; Charles was sent to Connecticut to attend Yale; his father's Alma mater. Eight months later he died of a shotgun blast while home on Easter break in 1860.

Douglas decreed his son's grave at Mount Pleasant not be disturbed; and the site has been preserved as he wished, though in recent years Charles' remains were quietly transferred to a family plot in Brevard County. The concrete burial crypt sits on a coquina median in the middle of Canova Drive. It is the sole surviving remnant of the plantation, now morphed into a quiet neighborhood south of Flagler Avenue; beachside in New Smyrna. Jasmine shrouded palms stand sentinel among ferns and flowers, while a cracked-marble slab covering the tomb is chiseled with the words: "Sacred to the Memory, Charles Dummett, born Aug. 18, 1844, died Apr. 23, 1860."

Mount Pleasant's manor house was built beachside atop a shell midden on riverfront near Callalisa Creek. Seminoles attempted to burn it during the Christmas 1835 massacre, but the fire extinguished after burning a hole in the living room floor. It stood until the Union shelling of New Smyrna in July 1863.

Illegal for Douglas and Leandra to marry, they lived out their lives in love. Leandra died May 6, 1870, and Douglas on March 27, 1873. The groves property was sold in the late 1860's to the Italian Duke and Duchess (former Jennie Anheuser) of Castlellucia. They built a large octangular home in 1881 locally called the 'Dummett Castle' where after an unhappy marriage, Jennie reportedly hung herself. The property was sold to the Florida Citrus Company in 1892, then in the early 1900's to Judge John Cochran of Martin's Ferry, Ohio who used the castle as a hunting lodge. When the next owner, Eugene Drennen died in 1938, his daughter, author Marguerite Drennen, lived on the property until her death in 1963. Vandals burned the castle in 1965. The Dummett lands are now part of Kennedy Space Center.

Though many facts, battles, timelines, newspaper articles, military letters, and names used in 'WHERE DOLPHINS FLY' are historically correct; this story is a work of love, license, bones, and fiction.

CPSIA information can be obtained
at www.ICGtesting.com
Printed in the USA
BVHW04s2252180518
516621BV00003B/214/P